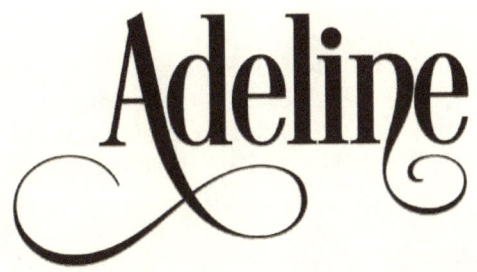

Adeline

LADY ARCHER'S CREED
BOOK THREE

Christina McKnight

Writing with Amanda Mariel

La Loma Elite Publishing

Christina@christinamcknight.com

PRAISE FOR CHRISTINA MCKNIGHT'S NOVELS

THE THIEF STEALS HER EARL

"When I started reading this book I could not put it down...it caused another book-hangover for me. I wanted to see how things would go when the truth of Judith came out and how Simon was going to handle it...loved it."-*Sissy's Book Review*

"Jude and Cart's story is such a delight! So refreshing to see the hero shy, socially awkward and not super wealthy. I love it...This was definitely one of the best books I've read this summer." -*Reviews from a Thrifty Mom*

FORGOTTEN NO MORE

"This author has made me love historical romance again."
-*TwinsieTalk Book Reviews*

HIDDEN NO MORE

"The storyline was really good, the writing was great. So smooth and engaging, I was able to zip right through the story, it flowed so well. I love finding new to me authors and with this wonderfully written story by Ms. McKnight I've found a new historical romance author."-*Bound by Books*

CHRISTMAS EVER MORE

"*Christmas Ever More* was a wonderfully written festive novella full of hope, renewal, love, and new beginnings. If you're a fan of Christina's Lady Forsaken series, this is a must. Even if you aren't caught up, this stands well enough on its own to be a lovely addition to your holiday reading list."-*Literal Addiction*

BOOKS BY CHRISTINA MCKNIGHT

The Undaunted Debutantes Series
The Disappearance of Lady Edith
The Misfortune of Lady Lucianna
The Misadventures of Lady Ophelia

Lady Archer's Creed Series
Theodora
Georgina
Adeline
Josephine

Craven House Series
The Thief Steals Her Earl
The Mistress Enchants Her Marquis

A Lady Forsaken Series
Shunned No More
Forgotten No More
Scorned Ever More
Christmas Ever More
Hidden No More

Standalone Titles
The Siege of Lady Aloria
A Kiss At Christmastide
For The Love Of A Widow
Bedded Under The Christmastide Moon
Bound By The Christmastide Moon

DEDICATION

For Erica

You are the beauty to my inner beast!

ACKNOWLEDGMENTS

There are so many people who support my passion for writing. Here are a few I am blessed to call friend: Marc McGuire, Lauren Stewart, Erica Monroe, Amanda Mariel, Debbie Haston, Angie Stanton, Theresa Baer, Ava Stone, Roxanne Stellmacher, Laura Cummings, Dawn Borbon, Suzi Parker, Jennifer Vella, Brandi Johnson, and Latisha Kahn. Thank you all for accepting me for, well, *me*.

A very special thank you to my editor, Chelle Olson with Literally Addicted to Detail, your skill and professionalism surpass all that I expected. Chelle Olson can be contracted by email at literallyaddictedtodetail@yahoo.com.

Also, a special thank you to historical and developmental editor, Scott Moreland.

And to my proofreader, Anja, thank you for embarking on yet another journey with me.

Cover design and wraparound cover design credit to Sweet 'N Spicy Designs.

Finally, thank you for supporting indie authors.

PROLOGUE

Canterbury, England
February, 1818

MISS ADELINE PRICE, eldest daughter of Viscount Melton, stared at the half-dozen trunks and traveling bags she'd demanded make the journey with her to Canterbury. The coachman had haphazardly tossed them from the mail coach to the frozen, damp dirt at the end of the long drive.

"You cannot think to shove me from the carriage and discard me here." Adeline stomped her boot-clad foot and turned her sharp stare on the driver. Her light brown curls tumbled over her shoulder at her sudden movement. "I will write to my father and have you drawn and quartered the moment you arrive back in London."

"I have work ta do, miss," the driver scuffed. "And I not be paid enough ta deal with the likes of ye spoiled London chits. I don't be find'n me pay as a nursemaid."

"The nerve of—" Her words cut off when the man climbed up to his seat and took the reins, calling to his horses and leaving Adeline in the dust, dirty from the muck kicked up by the departing coach. "Bloody, swag-bellied bull!"

Taking a step closer to her worldly possessions—everything she called hers had been hastily packed and delivered, with her in tow, to the mailing post in London—Adeline sank onto her archaic trunk. The cold evening air slowly wormed its way through the thick wool of her cloak, seeping all the way to her undergarments as a shiver overtook her. She clamped her jaw tight to keep her teeth from chattering.

"A pox upon you, Alistair," she seethed at the empty, rolling hills surrounding her. It was her brother's fault she'd been shipped away from home under the guise of *education*. Adelaide and Amelia, her younger sisters, hadn't been cast out of London for a proper education. No, it was only Adeline who'd been sent away to an all-girls boarding school in the wilds of Kent. "Damnation and hellfire."

Hellfire actually sounded vastly more appealing than perishing due to the cold of night.

Adeline narrowed her glare on the decaying structure nestled between a large grove of birch trees at the far end of the long drive. It seemed an eternity away—and never would Adeline accomplish the task of hauling her trunks the entire distance.

The urge to scream, to stomp her foot and punch something consumed her. If her brother were present, she would throw her handbag at his face; though she was well aware that her young age put her at a severe disadvantage physically.

Bloody, contemptible imp.

At only twelve, Adeline had either said or thought every vile utterance she'd stocked her memory with from years surrounded by four brothers.

She scrutinized the old building, propping her chin on her bent knees, noting the front door opening and two people coming toward her. As they drew closer, it was clear one was a servant dressed in livery garb. The other was a tall woman with her brown hair tied severely at the nape of her neck and outfitted in a black gown a decade older than was fashionable. She appeared to have some authority here.

For the briefest of moments, Adeline contemplated giving up; going along with her brother's plan for her...but then the woman's narrowed eyes traveled from Adeline's head to her filthy gown to her muddied boots as if Adeline were naught but a vagrant, a child not belonging to this fancy, highbrowed school of learning. Adeline stiffened with resolve.

The aching in her body only intensified when she stood to greet the pair. Spending over a day in a mail coach was exhausting, to say the least. However, she refused to admit that she'd been dumped alongside the edge of the road, her possessions unceremoniously thrown from the boot, without even enough coin to secure a more civilized mode of conveyance to Miss Emmeline's School of Education and Decorum for Ladies of Outstanding Quality. Not an inch of Adeline felt *of outstanding quality*, and there was certainly no chance of the pair approaching her being convinced of such from her untidy appearance.

The older woman stopped before Adeline, her stare remaining on her no doubt dirt-streaked face, but giving a tight smile and motioning for the servant to collect the many trunks loitering at the end of the drive.

"You must be Miss Adeline Price." The woman's tone gave no indication whether she was pleased to see Adeline or burdened by her less than proper arrival. "I am Miss Emmeline, headmistress here at the school. Do follow me."

The woman did not wait for Adeline's reply, nor did Adeline verbalize the redundancy of the headmistress' words. The first was much in line with her home in London—no one ever waited for her response. Yet, Adeline holding her tongue was not something she was accustomed to. No matter the occasion, she relished being heard—perhaps there was a valid reason for her exile to Canterbury.

Adeline followed the woman, leaving the servant behind to collect her things.

The wide double doors remained open, and the headmistress led Adeline inside, not pausing to allow Adeline time to remove her cloak but instead continuing down a long hall, torches lighting the way. Adeline's boots echoed loudly as they progressed down the corridor, her cloak and skirts swooshing around her legs as she struggled to keep pace with Miss Emmeline.

Adeline was prepared to demand the woman set a more leisurely pace when she pivoted sharply and entered a large room, gesturing once again for her newest pupil to follow. The room was in severe need of renovations—or possibly a deep scrubbing—and Adeline feared the walls would crumble around her if she ventured inside.

"We do not have all night, Miss Adeline," the headmistress huffed, sinking into the chair behind her desk. "Either have a seat or return to the roadside and await your white knight to come and make everything better."

She was unaware leaving was an option. Glancing over her shoulder and down the hall, she watched the servant lug her first trunk out of the cold and set it none too gently inside the entrance, far too small and cramped to be considered a foyer.

With a deep sigh, Adeline entered the room and stood behind the chair across from Miss Emmeline's large table that served as her desk, its legs crooked and its surface appearing as if one need only set a feather upon it for the table to crash to the ground. It was no wonder she'd never gained the esteemed status as a Mrs, for her cold demeanor would likely scare off any suitor who might fancy her appearance—which Adeline was not reluctant to admit needed far more work than her monotone voice and rigid posture.

"Sit." The headmistress shuffled through a stack of folders, finally settling on one and bringing it in front of her. She opened the file, and Adeline did her best to keep her gaze on the woman as opposed to the papers the headmistress now diligently read. Miss Emmeline's stare moved from the paper to Adeline. No reaction crossed her face when she saw the girl still standing. "Your family writes that you have been experiencing certain, shall we call them issues"—her brow rose—"at home."

Adeline's chin lifted several notches, but she remained silent.

Miss Emmeline chuckled softly before continuing. "I certainly do not foresee you causing a commotion here or becoming a distraction. You see, at my school, we pride ourselves on allowing young ladies to discover who they are, and provide them with the time and resources to help them become the women they long to be." The headmistress took a deep breath after her long-winded and fanciful dribble regarding her school's unrealistic ideals. "Is this something you will embrace, Miss Adeline?"

The only thing Adeline wanted to *embrace* at that moment was her brother's neck for convincing their parents to send her away for a proper education.

Instead of speaking her mind, Adeline gave the headmistress her most innocent and demure smile. It would not do to alert the woman to the sheer amount of commotion and distraction Adeline foresaw herself causing at Miss Emmeline's School of Education and Decorum for Ladies of Outstanding Quality.

"I have been given no other option but to embrace my time here, Headmistress."

The woman's eyes narrowed on Adeline as if she saw right through her innocent grin and coy words. "Very well." She set the papers aside and folded her hands on the table in front of her. "It is time to find out who you will be sharing a room with."

"Sharing a room?" Adeline huffed, folding her arms across her chest. "I think not. I am the daughter of a grand lord, I will not share a room with some vagabond I am not acquainted with."

"I can assure you, this school is responsible for the education of many well-connected young women, ranging from the daughters of successful merchants and shipping men to the offspring of an Italian prince. As the daughter of a viscount, you are no more important or connected than any other ladies under my care and protection."

The rebuff was given without an ounce of anger or shock at Adeline's behavior.

"And, if you think you are the first woman to be sent here under the orders of another, you are wrong." Miss Emmeline relaxed down in her seat, sitting back and resting her head against the back of her straight-backed chair. "Now, to determine your sleeping quarters, you will be called upon to demonstrate your skill in three different departments of learning: academics, art and music, and a physical sport."

"Does the proper setting of a dining table count as a sport?" Adeline challenged.

"No—"

"That is very good because I have servants who are charged with that."

Miss Emmeline pushed from her chair, clearly having reached her boiling point, her patience with Adeline at an end. "You will learn quickly that this school, while instructing our pupils in the arts of decorum and etiquette, places far more emphasis on arithmetic, the sciences, geography, music, and outdoor activities. You will not spend your time learning needlepoint, nor how to properly blush when complimented."

Adeline remained silent as the headmistress pulled the bell cord close to the door and a young woman appeared in the doorway as if she'd been waiting outside to be summoned.

The woman gave Adeline a warm smile and turned to Miss Emmeline. "Is it time to present Miss Adeline?"

"Yes, please gather all the young women, Miss Dires."

With a nod, Miss Dires gave Adeline another quick smile then fled the room, her slippers making nary a sound.

"First, you will present an academic talent, such as recitation of a poem or mathematical equation. Then it will be time for your music or art presentation. You may sing, dance, play an instrument or paint. It is up to you. Lastly, we shall all move outdoors for your sporting presentation. When everything is complete, I will select a room for you to join with other young women whose talents compliment yours."

Adeline's resolve and confidence drained from her at the thought of performing before a gathering of girls she did not know. If it had been Adeline's chore to watch a new student present before the entire school, she'd likely judge the girl harshly.

"I must do as you bid?" she asked.

The headmistress gave her a curt nod. "Or you will not find your evening meal nor a bed."

There was no doubt Alistair would be laughing his arse off at her discomfort; however, he was still surrounded by the familiar at their family's London townhouse, or perhaps her family had traveled back to the Melton country estate. It mattered naught. Adeline was in Canterbury…alone.

It would behoove her to play by the headmistress' rules—at least for the time being.

"Are you ready, Miss Adeline?"

"Yes."

"Is there something you need to retrieve from your trunks for any of your talents?"

Adeline searched for any inkling of what might get her through the next hour or so. An idea sparked as she remembered what she'd stolen from her father's office before leaving London. It was safely stashed in her handbag.

If the woman wanted to see Adeline's talents, far be it from Adeline to deny her the privilege.

Patting her handbag, Adeline smiled at the woman. "I have my academic talent here."

"Let us join the other pupils."

Adeline followed the woman back down the hallway to a door that stood open, revealing a large, high-ceilinged room with torches lining the walls for light as the sun set outside the bank of windows.

Young girls ranging in age from around eleven to those nearly ready for their societal debut sat primly about the room, their heads tilted together in quiet conversation. Several instructors could be seen standing against the walls, keeping close watch on the girls.

Adeline quickly stepped onto the dais at the front of the room when Miss Emmeline waved her forward.

"Ladies," the headmistress' voice boomed loudly, projecting to every corner of the room and bouncing back at Adeline. "It is with great pleasure that I introduce our newest student, Miss Adeline Price."

A round of reserved clapping filled the room when Miss Emmeline gestured toward Adeline as if the congregated girls were too dull to realize the woman spoke of the girl next to her.

Adeline briefly scanned the crowd, her stare lingering on no one for more than a flick of a moment. There was little need to familiarize herself with anyone here—she would be gone soon enough, if not from her horrid attitude than from her family's lack of funds to afford the large expense.

She was startled to find the headmistress gazing at her with sympathy as her hand softly settled on Adeline's shoulder, and she leaned in close to whisper, "No matter how angry you are with your family, this place and these girls are your fresh start. You can be anyone you want to be while at this school. I do hope you embrace this and make a home for yourself here."

Pulling away from the woman's touch, Adeline opened the drawstring on her bag. She couldn't afford the time spent pondering the woman's words, though they were an offer of sorts. A single fact remained, Adeline was here, against her will, and she did not have to like it...ever. Alistair would rue the day he entangled himself in his sister's future. She would not be a mere slip of a twelve-year-old for long. The day would come when he would apologize to her and seek her forgiveness.

Adeline reached into her bag and retrieved the deck of cards she'd secreted away with her in the carriage.

"Please speak loudly and clearly for all to hear, Miss Adeline," the headmistress prodded. "What academic talent will you regale us with?"

It was best Adeline keep her mouth shut and allow her skill to speak for itself, lest Miss Emmeline stop her before Adeline even got started.

Hurrying to the piano set farther back on the dais, along with several other instruments of various kinds, she pulled the bench seat toward the front and knelt behind it, giving the entire crowd a decent view as she removed the band holding the cards together and began shuffling them with expert precision.

The headmistress stepped closer to gain a better view, her brow furrowing; nevertheless, Adeline pushed on.

With one final shuffle of the dog-eared deck, Adeline turned to her audience with a smirk. "Now, it is essential every young woman has the means to procure a decent income, in addition to your pin money." The young girls all nodded in agreement. "There are many ways a woman can supplement her funds, including mending clothes, selling wares, and even becoming a governess or lady's companion. However, it is my understanding that the pupils here at Miss Emmeline's School come from families that would never allow such base actions as earning one's money in such an unsavory manner."

Adeline paused for a moment to allow her words their full impact.

"It is important to remember"—Adeline held up one card, facing the crowd—"each card has a value." She laid the card face up on the bench and flipped the next card. A jack of hearts. "For example—"

"Miss Adeline," the headmistress said, clearing her throat. "Would you mind informing us of your talent before you actually perform it?"

Bollocks.

There was little chance the woman was aware of what Adeline was up to.

"Please speak loudly so all can hear."

"Well, mending clothes and making one's self available as a companion is very time consuming," Adeline stammered before pausing to take a deep breath. "Sometimes, it is not an option for young ladies of a certain nobility. However, that does nothing to decrease a lady's need for a steady source of funds."

"As you've already said, Miss Adeline."

"There is a simpler, less cumbersome way to supplement a lady's pin money."

"And that would entail…"

"Counting cards in a gaming hell, Headmistress."

The woman's narrowed eyes bulged, and her mouth gaped, but she quickly reined in her shock as the other students broke out in laughter and applause.

"Miss Adeline, that is highly inappropriate—"

"But a very noteworthy and useful talent," Adeline cut in. "One that any woman short on funds would find beneficial. And, dare I say, lifesaving."

The young women burst out in another round of riotous merriment as the headmistress clapped her hands loudly and called the room to order.

"Ladies!" she shouted above the din, her voice no longer the unaffected monotone from earlier. "Ladies, quiet yourselves, or you will all be walking the stairs with a large volume of *Robinson Crusoe* on your head until you've managed the climb and descend ten times without it going askew."

Adeline needed to give the older woman credit, for the girls snapped their mouths shut and folded their hands primly in their laps.

"May I assume you hold some musical or artistic talent, Miss Adeline?"

"Certainly," Adeline said with a nod. "I am quite skilled on the curtal."

Miss Emmeline smoothed back her hair before rubbing her cheek. "The what?"

"It is an ancient bassoon, of sorts," Adeline offered. She was well aware that only three such instruments remained in existence, and one was housed at the London Museum. "I would be happy to display my talents if you would point me in the direction of your curtal."

"I am sorry to say we do not have a curtal at this school, perhaps another wind instrument—"

"Will not do at all," Adeline said with a shake of her head. "Mayhap you have a kantele."

Miss Emmeline shook her head.

"A salpinx?"

"We have neither of those instruments."

Adeline did everything in her power to contain her grin of victory. "Then I suppose I will be unable to present any musical skill today."

A sprinkle of laughter sounded in the room. It was nowhere near as loud as when she had announced her skill at counting cards, but still received a stern glare from their headmistress.

"We shall move on to the sporting activity then." The headmistress raised her hands, signaling for the girls to stand as Miss Dires pushed a set of doors wide, allowing a view of the grassy area beyond. "Let us retire outside."

"I—I will not—" Adeline stammered, collecting her cards and slipping them back into her handbag. "I will not perform like some caged animal in a gypsy sideshow."

Adeline widened her stance and crossed her arms. The woman, even with the help of her other instructors, would never force her to carry out any sporting talent.

"No one thinks you a caged animal, Miss Adeline," the headmistress insisted as the other students filed out of the room. "I assure you, this process will assist me in making certain your stay at my school is beneficial and enjoyable to all, not just you."

Adeline lifted her chin, doing her best to stare down her nose at the woman, though she was a good foot and a half taller than she.

"Have it your way," Miss Emmeline said with a sigh. "However, you will room alone for the foreseeable future."

Adeline grinned, satisfied with the commotion she'd caused during her first hour.

"Let me inform you, however, loneliness and solitude are not things young girls are suited to endure long-term. You are new to Canterbury, alone and without the benefit of a friend, your stay here will not be a pleasant one under these conditions."

Adeline's smile faltered at the headmistress' stare. "Is that a threat?"

The older woman shook her head, a pitying look

settling on her face. "No, my dear, it is a promise."

Without another word for Adeline, Miss Emmeline turned to Miss Dires and motioned to her. The young woman scurried over, dipping into a curtsy before Adeline and her employer.

"Do show Miss Adeline to her room." Miss Emmeline didn't so much as spare Adeline another look. "She will stay in the empty room next to mine. She is very tired from her travels and will wait until morning to eat."

"Yes, Headmistress."

In response, Adeline's stomach let out an angry growl.

"I will see you on the morrow, Miss Adeline," the older woman said, her face mirroring the triumphant smile Adeline had worn only a few moments before. "I hope you find your lodgings adequate, if sparse."

She pivoted away from Adeline and Miss Dires, calling for the ladies to join her in the banquet hall for their evening meal.

Adeline had little choice but to follow Miss Dires in the opposite direction out into the hall, her head lowered. She'd gravely underestimated the headmistress. She was not the type of woman to become irritated to the point of anger at Adeline's antics. No, she was the type used to the struggle and conflict raging within her young pupils. If Adeline was to make it through her time away from her family, she needs must either conform to Miss Emmeline's rules or spend the next several years alone.

CHAPTER 1

Canterbury, England
March, 1827

MISS ADELINE PRICE leaned out the carriage window and waved enthusiastically at her two youngest sisters—Arabella and Ainsley—as they stood before Miss Emmeline's School of Education and Decorum for Ladies of Outstanding Quality, their trunks stacked on either side of them with their new frocks, cloaks, and hair ribbons dancing in the light afternoon breeze.

Only recently out of mourning after the death of their father the previous year, the girls were reluctant to leave the family home, but at least they had one another—and at fifteen, Arabella was far older than most young ladies when they arrived in Canterbury. Adeline had not been so lucky when she was cast from the family home after her childish antics and placed on the mail coach headed to the wilds of Kent, after which she was unceremoniously dumped along the main road at the end of the drive leading to Miss Emmeline's School.

This was a new beginning for the pair, a true gift from Alistair, though it pained Adeline to admit it. Sad to see her dear sisters deposited at school, Adeline knew they would return women, ready for whatever society threw in their direction.

She gave one final look at her sisters, their long, light brown locks hanging in identical curls over their shoulders. If she were closer, she'd also note their matching hazel eyes—the same as every Melton sibling...all nine of them. Arabella's new gown hung to the tops of her kid boots while Ainsley, only having recently turned twelve, wore a frock that hit her at mid-calf. There was little doubt the pair was scared and nervous about being away from London, but Adeline was certain the girls would settle in nicely and make friends to last a lifetime—as she'd found in Josie, Georgie, and Theo.

The dust from her departing carriage blocked her sisters from view as a single drop of rain landed on Adeline's nose. A storm was rolling in quickly, and she was glad she'd deposited the girls before the tempest hit full force. She now hurried back toward Rochester where they'd stayed at a small inn the night before.

"I do hope we make it to our lodgings before Maxwell catches his death out there," Adeline's maid, Poppy, sighed. "I have heard the squalls in these parts can bring ruthless winds and merciless rain."

"Maxwell has been driving for nearly five years. I assure you, he is not daunted by a bit of rain and wind." Adeline couldn't help but smile at Poppy, her auburn hair tucked under her cap and a sprinkle of freckles across her nose. She'd met the young girl several months prior when she slipped from her home to meet Josie and Georgie for their morning archery practice in Regent's Park. Poppy had been selling oranges, and Adeline had witnessed a man's cruel threats to her person. She'd come home with Adeline that very day... and had been tasked with assisting all five Melton girls. Where Poppy attained her cultured speaking habits and refined manners, she would not say.

All the same, Adeline, Adelaide, Amelia, Arabella, and Ainsley had been overjoyed to have her in residence.

"Besides, it is a short three-hour jaunt, at most," Adeline reassured the girl. "We may be able to outrun the worst of the storm and be settled in our room long before the unrelenting rains begin."

"If you say so, miss."

"Thankfully, I do say so, Poppy," Adeline replied with a chuckle. "And we both know what I say holds much power."

The girl grinned and turned her gaze to her lap.

Adeline settled in for the long ride back to Rochester, the halfway point between Canterbury and London.

Heavens, but Adeline could not fathom her father allowing her to travel to Canterbury alone on the mail coach all those years ago. She shuddered to think of the malefic things that could have happened to her. She'd been barely twelve and without a proper chaperone. What had the late Viscount Melton been thinking?

However, it took little time to guess exactly what her elderly father had been thinking—ending the war that had raged inside their home for years. Adeline and Alistair had clashed since they were old enough to toddle about the house. Alistair would cut all her hair ribbons, and Adeline would fill his bed with frogs. Her eldest brother would dump a pie from the second-story landing onto her head, and Adeline would retaliate by coating the stairs with soap. Unfortunately, it had been their father, already far past his prime, who'd taken the long fall down the grand staircase, and not Alistair or even Abel, Adeline's younger brother.

Alistair had been the heir apparent, and Adeline merely a girl.

The decision had been simple. She would have made precisely the same choice.

Adeline had to go in order to restore order to the Melton household—if there had ever been true order within their home.

She leaned her head back and closed her eyes, focusing on all that had changed in the last two years. She'd returned to London to make her debut in society. Her dearest friend, Theodora, had wed her brother, Alistair. Georgie had found love with a childhood friend. Her father had died suddenly, though not unexpectedly. And now, two of her four sisters would be embarking on the journey Adeline had taken at Miss Emmeline's School.

A year of mourning and Adeline was no longer the nineteen-year-old, innocent debutante she'd once been. Though she was far from a spinster, she was nearing her twenty-first birthday.

The past year had been difficult, to say the least.

Her mother rarely left her private chambers, and quite often, Adeline and her siblings appeared drowsy as they moved about their townhouse. No one argued, no one ran, and no one caused any commotion whatsoever, an oddity for the Melton horde. Adeline had been so crestfallen at the dour cloud over her family that she'd jumped at the chance to travel to a place she'd once loathed.

Alistair, with Theo at his side, was doing his damnedest to support and care for all of his siblings. It weighed heavily on him, and Adeline felt a measure of sorrow. Not enough to heed his every edict, but at least ample pity to undertake the task of seeing her sisters to Canterbury.

A loud, roaring boom sounded outside, and their carriage was filled with a flash of light.

Snapping to attention, Poppy squealed, her eyes widening.

"The storm is intensifying." True to Adeline's words, a gust of wind rattled the door, sending a cold rush of air through every crack in the carriage walls. She pulled the cloth back to see rain pelting the window and the dark night beyond. The carriage bounced and jolted as they traveled down the rutted country road, tossing Adeline and Poppy to and fro. "I certainly hope Rochester is not overly far."

Adeline was uncertain how long she'd spent pondering the past or how far they'd traveled since departing the school. The tempest had settled upon them far swifter than she'd expected—and with a ferocity she'd never witnessed.

"Prepare ye self, Miss Adeline," Maxwell shouted over the pounding rain as a streak of lightning illuminated the coach once more. "Hold steady!"

The horses neighed into the darkened evening, and the front of the coach dipped, then leapt into the air, and crashed down, sending Adeline and Poppy careening into a heap on the floor between their seats.

"Miss?" Poppy struggled to her knees and then assisted Adeline up. "Are you injured?"

"No, I am not seriously harmed." Her head had bumped the side of the coach, and her knee had scraped along the edge of the seat. Despite that, she was whole. "And you?"

"Only a might bit scared, miss."

The lanterns hanging outside the coach had been extinguished sometime during the last several minutes, casting the interior into near total darkness. The storm raging outside, with its heavy raincloud, blocked any chance of light coming from the moon above.

Maxwell pulled the coach door open as Adeline and Poppy arranged themselves on their respective seats.

"The storm done forced me offa the main road." Maxwell pushed his dripping hair from his forehead as he spoke. "I be think'n we hit a rock and busted somethin'. Though I be need'n ta inspect the damage proper-like."

"How far are we from Rochester?"

"In this storm?" When she nodded, he continued, "I not be know'n for sure, but me best guess would be another two hours, if not longer, miss."

"Were are we, Max?" Poppy asked hesitantly.

"Me best guess is between Goodnestone and Ospringes, but as me be say'n, I canna be sure, Miss Poppy."

"Can we turn back and return to Miss Emmeline's?" Adeline inquired as the rain splattered on the floor from the open carriage door.

"No." Maxwell shook his head, flinging more water about. "The roads be team'n with flood water by now."

"Then what?" she demanded. "We wait here until the storm passes or we float away?"

"Or worse yet, Miss Adeline, we are set upon by highwaymen or,"—Poppy gulped—"wild animals."

"I do not think any highwayman worth his weight in salt would dare journey out in this gale." Adeline paused for a moment, pressing her hand to her forehead as she thought through their predicament. The hour was growing increasingly late, the sun already nestled over the far horizon as the clouds continued to develop overhead. Soon, there would be no light left to guide them. "Maxwell, can you take one of the horses and go for help?"

The wind whipped the carriage door from her driver's hold, slamming it against the side of the coach and allowing more rain and wind inside.

"I not be leave'n ye and Miss Poppy unattended," he shouted over the wailing wind. "Me lord would have me head if'n anythin' happened ta ye."

"Then our best plan would be to fix the bloody carriage and pray we find shelter soon." Simple enough. Neither she nor Poppy were helpless or useless. "Just instruct us how we can best help you repair the damage to the carriage."

The driver forced the door partially closed to keep the worst of the storm from entering the interior. "Not certain there is much ta do, even with ye help, miss."

"Oh, horse brattle," Adeline said. "If there is anything I've learned in the last several years, it is that there is always something that can be done. Now, step aside, and I will have a gander at the damage myself."

The servant stepped back when Adeline turned her severe stare on him.

She hopped from the conveyance before Maxwell could collect the steps. Her feet sank into the muck up to her ankles as the heavy rain soaked through her cloak and chilled her skin.

Her heart plummeted when her gaze settled on the damaged undercarriage.

As if in response, the rain redoubled its efforts in an unrelenting, ferocious manner, and the wind whipped her skirts about her legs.

"Bloody hell."

CHAPTER 2

JASPER BENEDICT, THE Earl of Ailesbury, pulled his heavy woolen cloak tighter around his hulking frame as his carriage leapt and bounded down Spires Road away from his gunpowder plant and toward his home at Faversham Abbey. It had been thoughtful of his servants to notice the growing storm and to send his carriage to bring Jasper home. He'd been so enthralled by the newly presented reports from his production line he hadn't left his office since before midday.

Retrieving the stack of papers from his satchel, Jasper scanned the increase in profits once more. He could scarcely believe the surge of revenue. By this time next month, he'd be able to hire a dozen more villagers, spreading his good fortune amongst the people of Faversham and the surrounding countryside.

He adjusted his position on the padded seat but, as was common, he could not find an angle that did not cause his back to ache unmercifully.

When the war ended, and the need for gunpowder all but disappeared, Jasper had feared for the people living close to Faversham Abbey. Men would be out of work, children would no longer have the luxury of attending school, and families would either starve or move closer to London to find a means to support themselves.

He could not stand by and allow such a fate for the place his family had called home for five generations.

Thunder crashed outside, an outward display of his inner fury at the fate his people had nearly succumbed to all those years ago.

Jasper slid the papers back into his satchel and held tight to the hanging strap above his head to steady himself on the rutted road. The plans to fill in the deep crevices in the earth was likely to happen sooner rather than later, yet it had been hard to justify the expense when the road was only traveled by men going to and from the village to work at the plant. Many of the men walked or rode a horse, and carriages rarely traversed the area, mainly because Jasper was the only nobility for many miles and the townspeople did not travel in fancy carriages but flat-backed wagons when needed. The sturdy wagons used to deliver supplies to the plant and pick up products to be shipped from the port were well-built and accustomed to the harsh terrain.

Another bump sent his knee smashing into the seat across from him, the pain traveling up his thigh.

Bloody hell.

He should have had the roads repaired long ago.

The rain hammered against the top of his carriage as they traveled far too slowly for Jasper's liking. He was tired, aching, and hungry, and hadn't had a drink in what seemed like days. Hours crouched over a desk in a factory where one could barely hear themselves think could drain every ounce of vigor from a man.

Twelve hours away from his home at Faversham Abbey, and there were still hours of work left to do.

Jasper scrubbed at his dirt-streaked face, pulling his hands through his hair. His valet would likely be torn between running for the safety of London and chastising him for staining yet another white linen shirt; all the while holding a pair of shears close to Jasper's unruly, shoulder-length hair. It had been tied back at the base of his neck with a length of baling twine that morning, but at some point, it had slipped away and was forgotten. Perhaps when he'd gone in search of his foreman to command all the villagers return home early due to the coming storm, or when he and his driver went into the gale to batten down the windows and doors to prevent flooding inside the plant.

He cared naught, either way.

No one but his servants would notice his less than proper attire or rakishly long, unbridled hair.

George, his driver, thumped on the side of the carriage. "Carriage ahead, m'lord. Shall we stop and see who it be?"

They slowed as they approached the conveyance, obviously stranded at the edge of the road. The approaching night and storm overhead made it impossible for Jasper to tell if the carriage was damaged or if they were only stopped by the increasing mud underfoot.

"We stop," Jasper yelled as they pulled alongside it to see a man assisting a woman into the safety of the coach. "I do not recognize the conveyance or the driver."

Strangers in this part of Kent? During a tempest? Traveling in such an outdated coach?

The person had either been taken by surprise by the turn in weather or was completely mad.

"You, there!" George pulled the horses to a stop and leapt down from his seat. "What business ye have here?"

Any further conversation was lost in the driving wind and unrelenting rain.

Finally, George knocked on the carriage door, and Jasper reached to open it.

"He says he be travel'n from Canterbury ta London and the storm done forced him offa the main road." His driver glanced over his shoulder at the waiting carriage. "Somethin' broke underneath, and the driver, a maid, and their mistress are stranded."

It was not often that travelers stopped in Faversham on their way to London. The village, though it boasted good, capable people, lacked the draw of entertainment the *beau monde* was accustomed to. There was no playhouse, no fancy dining establishments, nor a tavern. Only honest, hardworking people trying to survive each day.

In Jasper's mind, the area was better for it as there was no place for men to drink late into the night and lose their hard-earned coin at cards.

"I will have a look." Jasper pulled the hood of his cloak up to cover his face and climbed from the coach when his driver stood back.

George's lips pressed into a firm line, and his eyes widened. "Are you sure that be wise, m'lord?"

Jasper held back his growl at the man's question, reminding himself that his servants only sought to look after his best interests. "It is nearing nightfall, and the storm is blocking all light. I will keep my hood raised. Do not fret."

With a simple nod, George led Jasper to the damaged carriage. Beyond the wheels being submerged in several inches of muck, something hung loosely under the coach—likely the brake beam or push bar. There was nothing he or his servant could do to send the group on their way until the coach could at least be pulled back to the cover of the Faversham Abbey stables to be repaired.

"M'lord," George called over the wind. "We need ta be on our way, or we be likely ta get stuck in the mud."

"I agree." Jasper glanced at the carriage window. Two women stared out at him, their noses pressed to the glass. "But we cannot leave them here. The night will grow cold, and the dawn may very well see temperatures close to frost, and that is if the storm passes."

"What do ye think ta do?"

"Sir," Jasper called to the other driver, pulling his hood up to better shield his face. "I'm the Earl of Ailesbury. It appears your carriage cannot be repaired here."

"There be an inn nearby?"

"I am afraid it is a fair distance away," Jasper responded. The man's dejected look pulled at him. "However, my home is not far, and has plenty of room for your mistress, her maid, and you."

The man chewed his bottom lip before glancing toward the carriage. "I will check with Miss Ade—me mistress."

"Do hurry." Another streak of lightning lit the night sky, illuminating the foreboding clouds above. "It is likely the storm will get far worse before it passes."

The man hurried to speak with his mistress.

"Ye think have'n 'em at the Abbey be wise, m'lord?"

"Wiser than leaving them here and finding them injured—or worse, dead—on the morrow."

"Ver'a true."

No matter what Jasper said aloud, the tingling moving through him was similar to the night he'd rushed into his family's burning stables in an attempt to rescue his parents. Everyone in Faversham was aware how that had turned out—for both him and his family.

However, leaving the trio here was no more an option than standing by and allowing the fire to rage around his mother and father.

A spike of pain hit his chest, similar to a lightning bolt hitting a tree. Dredging up the memory was certain to have a lasting effect on him.

The man stepped lightly through the deepening

mud to stand before Jasper as he removed his cap and lowered his head. "Me mistress would meet ye before accept'n ye kindness, m'lord."

Jasper glanced sideways to see George's darkening look. "My master only seeks—"

"It is fine, George." Rain had utterly saturated his outer garment and soaked clean through his trousers to chill his skin. Jasper even sensed his Hessians filling with water as they stood in the pouring rain. "Your name, sir?"

"Max, errr, Maxwell Smithe, m'lord."

"Swell to meet you," Jasper greeted. "Now, please introduce me to your mistress so we can all find safety from the storm with all due haste."

He lowered his head to keep the rain from hitting his face and followed Maxwell.

They halted, and Maxwell opened the door. Jasper peered into the dim interior of the coach to see a woman, her long hair a matted tangle of knots from her time in the storm. She held her cloak wrapped tightly around her as her teeth chattered from the cold.

She stared back at him, her eyes wide, and Jasper feared she could see past his hood. However, he knew that wasn't possible. Even if his hood had slipped slightly, the darkness surely hid his scars.

The woman needed dry clothes and a warm fire— quickly.

"I am the Earl of Ailesbury," he called, his words fighting the noise of the storm at his back. "My home is only a short distance away. You may seek shelter there for the night, and I will have your carriage brought round to my stables in the morning for repairs."

The woman stared back at him wordlessly.

Her almond-shaped, hazel eyes inspected him from his hidden face and down the length of his body. Jasper hadn't felt laid bare before another his entire life. Was she leery enough of him to refuse his offer?

As if on cue, a wolf howled in the near distance, its call echoing above the whine of the storm. Within moments, several others answered.

CHAPTER 3

ADELINE GULPED AT the same moment another round of howling broke through the crashing noise of the storm. She was uncertain what option would leave her the most vulnerable: being washed away by the ever-increasing flood water, set upon by a pack of hungry wolves, or agreeing to accompany the hooded stranger back to his home to wait out the storm. For likely the first time in all her life, Adeline had no urge to act impulsively, no rash compulsion to leap from her carriage and into Lord Ailesbury's inviting coach.

Glancing across the carriage, Poppy appeared as hesitant as she, her fingers clutching the edge of the seat. It was not only Adeline's safety at stake but that of Maxwell and Poppy, as well.

"I will await you in my carriage." The earl nodded to Maxwell before retreating to the cover of his waiting conveyance.

"Miss," Poppy whispered, leaning close as if afraid the man would overhear, but the boom of thunder covered her single word, and the windowpanes in the carriage rattled as the ground shook. "Do you suppose it is safe?"

The storm was no doubt directly above them, and a torrential downpour eminent. She needed to make the decision to remain in their damaged carriage or accept Lord Ailesbury's offer of shelter. Yet, trepidation held her back. She'd never been the Melton sibling to shy away from anything due to personal risk…however…

Adeline nibbled on her lower lip, pondering her situation, and that of her servants.

"The rain be come'n down, miss," Maxwell called, the wind howling through the cracked carriage door.

"Do you think the man safe?" she asked.

"He be have'n a fine coach, nice clothes, and superb horses," her driver replied.

"I did not ask if he is financially endowed." A well-sprung carriage, and the best horses Tattersall's had to offer did not make one *safe*. "I meant, do you think it wise to journey with the earl to his home?"

"I do not think we have much choice," Poppy squeaked.

"Very well," Adeline sighed, collecting her handbag as she prepared to depart her family coach. "Do make certain my belongings—and Poppy's—are brought to Lord Ailesbury's residence."

"Of course, Miss Adeline."

She took the driver's offered hand and stepped back into the rain, surprised to find an unfamiliar servant holding an umbrella to shield her from the worst of the storm.

"Right this way, miss." He waited for Poppy to exit and gestured toward Lord Ailesbury's waiting carriage, the large man already seated inside. "I have coals to warm your feet, and a thick woolen blanket to ward off the chill until we arrive at Faversham Abbey."

Adeline slipped her arm through Poppy's, and they picked their way across the muddy road, attempting to maneuver around the largest puddles.

Finally, they took the two steps into Lord Ailesbury's carriage and seated themselves across from the hulking man. If he'd looked massive outside with his wide shoulders and thick legs, now, he appeared to nearly fill the interior of the carriage. True to the driver's promise, a blanket lay folded between Adeline and Poppy with a metal box of coals under their seat. A single lantern swung on a hook outside the carriage, fighting to remain lit despite the onslaught of wind and rain. It cast a dim glow around the women and on Lord Ailesbury's booted feet, but did not reach any higher on the man, leaving him shrouded in darkness, his hood still raised to shield his face—or so it appeared.

The coach sprang into motion a few moments later, and Adeline waited for the man to speak...or lower his hood...or, at the very least, breathe.

But he made not a sound.

He only sat with his head lowered slightly, making it impossible for Adeline to gain a proper view of his face.

"Thank you for your kindness, my lord," she mumbled, attempting to force him to speak. "It was very gallant of you."

"It is as any gentleman should do," he grunted.

"Yes, but offering us shelter is far more than what is expected."

He pulled the curtain back and stared into the dark night beyond. "It was either that or risk having you perish in the storm."

Adeline scooted in Poppy's direction, hoping for a small peek as he continued to stare at something beyond their carriage, but he allowed the curtain to fall back into place and reached up, adjusting his hood.

"We are arriving now." He pounded on the side of the coach, and they slowed to a stop. "I will let the pair of you out here. My servants will collect your carriage as soon as the storm passes and make the necessary repairs. My housekeeper will see you to your room and have a meal prepared."

Lord Ailesbury crossed one leg over the other and

placed his hands on his lap, relaxing into the plush padding.

Was he dismissing her?

Instantly, she was transported back to her girlhood—being deposited outside Miss Emmeline's without an offer of assistance down the long drive. A sharp retort rushed to the tip of her tongue.

Before she could utter a word, however, the carriage door swung open, and a footman set the steps. No wind or rain swept into the coach.

"Thank you, again, my lord." Adeline stood, her chin notching high as she took the steps down to the cobbled drive, happy to see they'd pulled into a sheltered area that kept the storm at bay. "Come, Poppy."

"Abbington," the driver shouted to the man who had opened the front door. "Please have Mrs. Hutchins prepare a guest chamber for Miss...errr..."

The man's words trailed off as he searched his memory for her name, but Adeline hadn't given it, and neither had Lord Ailesbury or his servant asked.

"Miss Adeline Price," she said with a smile. "But, please, Addington, there is little need to go through all that trouble for me."

"It is our pleasure, Miss Adeline," the servant said. "I am George, me lord's driver. If ye be need'n anythin', do have someone collect me. For now, Abbington and Mrs. Hutchins will take swell care of ye."

"And what of Lord Ailesbury?" He hadn't departed the carriage—and even now, she noted his knees through the open door. "Will he not be accompanying Poppy and me into his home?"

George glanced over his shoulder and back to the waiting women. "He, ah, well...he be have'n work ta see ta in the stables. I be certain he'll join ye for a meal in an hour's time. He likely be make'n certain your servant and horses find dry accommodations."

Peculiar since the earl had told her a meal would be prepared for her. Could it be the man avoided her? And why would the lord of the manor have business to attend to in the stables in the midst of a gale? She tamped down the unease that coursed through her. This was one night...in a strange home...with an unusually mysterious lord. Besides, Adeline would keep Poppy at her side. Certainly, her most trusted maid wouldn't allow anything untoward to occur.

A gust of wind wailed through the covered alcove where she stood, whipping her damp cloak and skirt about her ankles as the cold burrowed through her many layers of clothing. Perhaps it didn't matter what Lord Ailesbury's plan was, only that she and Poppy were delivered to a warm, dry room before the weather gave them the sickness.

She hurried after the butler, Abbington, into the foyer. The warmth hit her square in the face as she crossed the threshold, yet Adeline pulled to a halt, causing Poppy to slam into the back of her when they came face-to-face with a line of perfectly groomed and outfitted servants, each with a welcoming smile and a kind greeting.

A tall, rail-thin woman, her eyes wide with what appeared to be shock—or possibly apprehension—stepped forward from the group of gathered servants. Her lack of cleaning rag or duster, plus her pristine uniform indicated that the older woman held some elevated position among the other staff.

The butler stepped forward, joining Adeline, Poppy, and the older woman. "Mrs. Hutchins is Lord Ailesbury's housekeeper. Mrs. Hutchins, may I introduce Miss Adeline Price. My lord would like her shown to a room and a meal delivered, followed by a hot bath, if she so chooses."

"Of course, Abbington," the woman scuffed. "I know how ta do me job, even if'n it has been a bit."

Adeline glanced over at Poppy, who stood not beside Adeline but a step behind her. They shared a look and a shrug.

"Emily, fetch Miss Adeline her meal and meet us in the lavender room." The entire gathering drew in a deep breath. "And the rest of ye, best be get'n back ta ye chores."

The servants scattered in every direction, and within a moment that only left the housekeeper, Adeline, and Poppy.

"This way, miss." The older woman didn't wait for Adeline to respond but started up the grand staircase, giving her no other option but to follow—and follow quickly. The woman moved fast for her advanced age, her rounded bum shifting from side to side as she climbed the stairs. "Ye room be just down this hall, miss. We be happy ta have ye."

A large set of double doors lay at the end of the hall, but the housekeeper stopped before reaching them and turned to a single wooden door instead. Mrs. Hutchins flipped the latch and pushed the door wide. It was difficult for Adeline to remove her stare from the imposing double doors at the end of the all, despite the housekeeper's attempt to gain her attention once more.

"Ye be comfortable here." She gestured for Adeline to enter. "Ye things be brought straight away, miss."

"Thank you," Adeline mumbled, stepping into the room.

There was not a speck of dust anywhere, yet the furnishings and draperies appeared to be decades old. The sconces on the walls were already lit, and the drapes were pulled back, giving her a view of the storm beyond. Could it be that Lord Ailesbury kept this room ready in case a guest happened upon Faversham Abbey?

"This room is lovely, Mrs. Hutchins."

"I be tell'n the master ye said so." Mrs. Hutchins

rocked back on her heels, a satisfied smile upon her lips and her hands clasped before her. The woman obviously took pride in her household. "Here be ye meal."

Footsteps sounded down the hall, and Emily hurried into the room, placing the silver tray on a low table not far from the roaring hearth.

"Anything else, Mrs. Hutchins?" The young maid kept her eyes on Adeline as she spoke.

"That be all," Mrs. Hutchins said, glancing over at Poppy. "Please show Miss Adeline's maid to the kitchens for her meal."

"Of course." Emily curtseyed to Adeline and waved for Poppy to follow her.

The two young women departed the room, leaving Adeline alone with Mrs. Hutchins.

Adeline wandered to the bank of windows taking up the far wall and glanced out as a streak of lightning lit the sky, causing her to step back in alarm.

"Worst storm these parts be see'n in many a year," Mrs. Hutchins called from the door. "But Faversham Abbey be solid. Don't ye be worry'n 'bout that."

Adeline stepped forward once more, but did not train her sights on the storm overhead but rather what lay below. Lanterns illuminated the stable yard, the doors thrown open wide as she spotted a hooded figure striding toward the house.

Lord Ailesbury. It had to be him, but his hood made it impossible to tell.

Within the blink of an eye, he was gone, and Adeline wondered if he'd been there at all.

"Lord Ailesbury was very kind to offer us shelter."

"He be a kind and generous man, ta be sure." The housekeeper had moved toward the large bed and straightened the coverlet before hurrying over to the low table to remove the cover from Adeline's meal. "We don't be see'n many visitors this far from the main road."

"But you had this room prepared…" Adeline ran her hand down the drapes, noting the frayed edges, even though they smelled freshly laundered. "After being stuck in the storm, I am overjoyed to find a warm room."

The lightning struck once more, followed by a loud burst of thunder. The vast area surrounding Faversham Abbey was lit only for a second, but it was enough to see the towering structure in the far distance.

"What is that?" Adeline glanced over her shoulder to see the housekeeper had paused in her inspection of the room. She turned to look out the window over Adeline's shoulder. "That building in the distance—"

"That be Home Works, the gunpowder plant outside Faversham."

"It is a large building."

"Yes, well, this be the country, but we still be need'n ta put food in our bellies, not that the townsfolk be admit'n ta the kindness Ailesbury be do'n for them."

"Does Lord Ailesbury—"

Mrs. Hutchins turned toward the door, her words cutting off Adeline's question. "Now, ye should eat afore Cook's meal be cold as ice."

"Certainly." Adeline moved from the windows, and Mrs. Hutchins hurried over and untied the cord holding the drapes open. They fell into place over the windows, blocking out the sight of the storm, if not the sound of the wind and rain and thunder. "Thank you again for the dry room and meal."

"I be let'n the staff know ye appreciation, Miss Adeline. Do enjoy ye night. If ye need anythin', just pull the cord by the door. Meself or Emily will come."

And as quickly as she'd shown Adeline to the room, Mrs. Hutchins was gone, closing the door in her wake.

Adeline realized except for Miss Emmeline's

School, her family's country estate, and her London townhouse, she'd never slept anywhere else—especially a place as quiet as Faversham Abbey. Not a sound could be heard as Adeline sat on the lounge and looked around the room. Perhaps she should have requested Poppy remain with her. The room was large, bigger than any at her family's home, and there was plenty of space. The bed was vast enough to sleep Adeline and all her sisters.

When had Adeline ever known the luxury of her own room? Those first few months at Miss Emmeline's School had been the one and only time—until Georgie, then Josie, and finally Theo joined her. Miss Emmeline had been correct: Adeline was not suited for loneliness and solitude, but this was only one night. On the morrow, her carriage would be repaired, and she'd be on her way back to London, and the never-ending noise of her family home.

Her time at Faversham Abbey likely forgotten.

CHAPTER 4

JASPER AND HIS servants, with Miss Adeline's driver in tow, worked to push straw and mud against the edge of the stables to stop it from flooding. He would sacrifice a large portion of hay to feed his livestock if it meant the grain and oats were saved from mold and infestation.

"M'lord," Watson, the Ailesbury stable master, shouted when the winds blew the doors wide once more and thunder threatened from above. "All is as it can be with the added horses. Find ye bed."

"I will secure the latches in the tack room and return to the house," Jasper called.

The frown Watson turned on him signaled the man knew Jasper was stalling.

Which he most certainly was. The woman needed to be securely in her room for the night—without risk of him entering the house to find her wandering the halls. He would have to speak with her, which was not the largest problem facing Jasper…he'd need remove his hood, or appear rather odd for wearing his cloak indoors. He hadn't had need to hide his appearance within his own home in many years; however, the mere thought of exposing himself to the woman made him shiver with fear.

Why had he brought her here in the first place? She was stunningly beautiful—with her honey-colored, light brown tresses and hazel eyes that shone green in the dim light of his carriage. He should have taken her directly to the merchant shop in town. Anderson and his kind wife would have offered the woman and her servants shelter from the storm, leaving Jasper to return home.

He ran his hand along the jamb between the window and the shutter in the back of the room that housed all the Ailesbury horse equipment: saddles, reins, bridles, blankets. The space was secure, no rain penetrating the wooden exterior.

Jasper had no choice but to seek his chambers, and allow the stable servants to find their own slumber.

It had been a long time, since before his uncle's death, that Faversham Abbey had entertained guests, yet his servants kept the entire house so clean and polished one would think a ball were scheduled for that very night. True, his solicitor made the journey from London twice a year, but it had been nearly five months since the man visited to go over the ledgers and accountings for all of Jasper's properties and business ventures. His man of business did not count as a true guest, not like Miss Adeline Price.

Blast it all, but he'd had to ask the woman's driver for her name. His manners were obviously a bit rusty from disuse, but then again, he never had the occasion to socialize beyond his time with his servants and the workers at his plant.

"Sleep well," Jasper called to the stable hands milling about the small fire in the stables' common room before he inched the door open and stepped into the storm. Thankfully, the woman's driver was nowhere in sight and did not witness Jasper raising his hood to cover his scars.

He glanced up at the house as he hurried through

the rain. A light shone from above on the second story.

Something hit him at once…they'd settled Adeline in Jasper's mother's private quarters—the room directly next to his.

He stumbled to a halt as he stared at the window above, the drapes having been closed for the night. Yet, he could still see light around the edges.

As if his gaze commanded it, a hand slipped between the heavy layers of fabric and pulled one side back.

…and there she stood. Her hair fell around her shoulders, but he could not see her expression from the great distance.

Without thinking, Jasper pulled his hood forward, though there was little chance she could see him standing in the darkness between the stables and the house.

She let the drape fall back into place, and Jasper moved toward the house once more, rubbing the rain from his face and brushing at the sleeves of his cloak. Mrs. Hutchins would not be pleased if he tracked water across her clean floors.

Moving soundlessly through the garden and into the kitchen, Jasper allowed the warmth to banish the cold he hadn't realized had set in. His fingers tingled from the drastic change in temperature, and his nose thawed as the savory scents of the kitchen wrapped him in a familiar embrace.

Jasper pushed Miss Adeline Price from his thoughts.

She would be gone soon enough, and everything would be as it had been for years.

"I sent me special duck pie ta the lady, m'lord," Cook called from the open stove where she stirred a huge pot. "It be a rare occasion indeed that even the finickiest a eaters not be fall'n in love with me duck."

Love? Why would Cook think to capture the

woman's love?

"She is a guest for only tonight." Jasper frowned. "We will make certain to be gracious hosts, but that is all."

"Yes, m'lord."

He narrowed his stare on the woman. "What has come over you? Never have you called me 'my lord'."

Cook turned her attention back to the pot she'd been stirring. "Well, we ain't never had a true London lady in the house neither."

"Be that as it may, as I said, she is only a guest—an unexpected one at that—and she will be gone soon."

"If'n ye say so, m'lord."

Jasper only shook his head and continued toward the stairs. He'd been exhausted when he left the plant for the night, and that had been before they stumbled upon Miss Adeline's stranded coach. Currently, he was uncertain how he still stood. A long night of sleep would prepare him for the work he'd need to accomplish when the sun rose. It would be no easy feat to collect Miss Adeline's coach from the mud and bring it to his stables for repairs.

"A word, my lord," Abbington said, as Jasper set his foot on the first stair.

He slowly turned toward his butler. "Yes, Abbington, and please, dispel with the formalities."

The man cleared his throat before continuing. "Jasper." His staff had called him by his given name since his parents' deaths—possibly before. "Mrs. Hutchins and I are overjoyed at Miss Adeline's arrival. We are also confused. It is highly improper to offer her shelter here…without a proper chaperone in residence."

"I do not think there was much choice in the matter." Jasper pushed his hood back and slammed his hands into his trouser pockets. "A storm is raging, and the roads were becoming less and less travelable. It was either bring her here or leave her to her fate. What would you have me do, Abbington?"

"Take her to Anderson's shop." Abbington put increased emphasis on each word.

But Jasper was not a dullard. He'd been well aware of the risks he'd undertaken bringing her to Faversham Abbey; yet, he'd been unable to tame his selfishness. For one night, he would not be alone at his estate, even if he never saw the woman or allowed her to see him, Miss Adeline was still in residence. It had been a long ten years since his aunt died. And his uncle passed only five short years later. Since then, he'd been alone at Faversham Abbey, the twenty bedrooms, four stories, and acres surrounding the manor had never felt as lonesome as they did in recent days.

"Do you assume I did not already think of that?" Jasper sighed, attempting to keep his irritation at bay. He knew his servants were only trying to protect him— and he was overly wary from his day at the plant. "Besides, it was closer to come to the Abbey as opposed to venturing back toward town."

His butler's brows rose in question. "If you say so, my lord."

"I do." Jasper started up the stairs again but paused. "And do not think your wife and I will not have words over her choice of chambers for Miss Adeline."

"I cannot speak to my wife's decisions, as you know, but she has shared with me she is worried about you—all alone here at Faversham." The man fell into silence, knowing the limits to their relationship. No matter what happened in the place they both called home, Jasper was still his master. And he a mere servant. There were boundaries and societal expectations to be upheld.

Even if every day those lines were blurred more and more. "That I understand."

Abbington was no more in control of his wife, Mrs. Hutchins, than Jasper was. Since his parents' deaths—

and later, his aunt and uncle's deaths—the woman had been the only mother figure Jasper knew. In a way, his housekeeper was more familiar with his likes and dislikes than anyone. How was it only at times like this his apparent lack of companionship became overwhelming?

"Do see that Cook prepares adequate food for Miss Adeline to break her fast in the morning. It is a long journey back to London, and I will not have her arriving famished. I think the pheasant Cook was saving for supper tomorrow will do nicely. Please see to it."

"Of course," Abbington said with a chuckle.

Jasper had no urge to ponder why his butler found his demands comical or why he longed to impress Miss Adeline at all. She would return to London, and he would remain in Faversham—where he need not fear the penetrating stares and jeers of strangers.

After the damage caused by the fire that took his parents' lives, Jasper had guarded himself with the assistance of his paternal uncle, Lieutenant Colonel Bartholomew Benedict, and his aunt, Alice. They hired tutors to see to his schooling at Faversham—everything from arithmetic to science to literature. Jasper had even been instructed in the modern styles of dance one would encounter in every London ballroom. Not that he'd ever actually taken to the floor with anyone other than his aunt Alice and Mrs. Hutchins.

He'd fooled himself for years, thinking he secluded himself at his country manor to keep from scaring others with the sight of his scarred face and body, but truly, it was to protect him from the cruel side of human nature. Here, at his home, and even in town, the sight of his scars did not frighten others as it once did. The men at his plant avoided him, but no longer did they shrink in fear of his monstrous appearance.

It was enough to know that someone shared the house with him, besides his servants—who were paid to serve him.

He continued up the stairs and down the hall to his room, not allowing himself to pause outside Miss Adeline's chambers. She would be gone soon enough, and his household would return to normal.

Solitude would once again be his safeguard against the cruel, misunderstanding world.

The Beast of Faversham did not need to hear the words uttered by people who he'd once called friends to know it was what the villagers whispered to one another when he wasn't near.

Yet, could he bear hearing those same words from the tender lips of Miss Adeline Price?

CHAPTER 5

ADELINE SAT IN a straight-backed chair and beheld the table before her as the storm continued to rage outside. With at least eighteen chairs, the long, walnut surface could seat all of her siblings with a chair between each to stop their constant bickering and banter—and alleviate the headache that Alistair claimed to have had since he reached his majority. Not only was the table peculiarly grand, but its top was set as if a gathering of London's social elite would be arriving at any moment to bear witness to Lord Ailesbury's fine feast. Yet, as of the last quarter hour, Adeline had been the only person seated at the table as dish after heavenly smelling dish was set before her.

Not one, not two, not three, but *four* candelabras were stationed at precise intervals down the table, lending the perfect lighting for an evening meal. However, it was now the breakfast hour. Even the cutlery and utensils were fine silver with matching meal rings around the large plate before them. The serving dishes held enough meat, cheese, bread, fruit, and porridge for her family's entire household—servants included. It all seemed overly grand and refined for a mere morning repast.

When she'd entered, she was positioned to the

right of the head seat.

An honored guest.

Adeline knew as much from her time at Miss Emmeline's School. While they focused on academics, decorum and etiquette were also requirements for each pupil.

Still, she wondered who would join her.

Adeline hesitated to touch anything, though she allowed her fingertips to caress the finely cut crystal of the wine goblet set before her. The glass twinkled in the glow of the candles, casting a rainbow of colors on the far wall.

With all the food already set out—and Emily, the servant from the previous evening—continuing to set dish after dish upon the table, there must be others coming.

Yet, the house remained eerily quiet with only the servant's light footsteps in and out of the dining hall to disturb the stillness of Faversham Abbey.

That and the occasional rattle of the windowpanes as the wind and rains continued to unleash their fury on the Kent countryside. Poppy had insisted the storm was near passing, but Emily had not been as confident in declaring the gale was subsiding.

As if the young woman had read Adeline's thoughts, Emily entered the room once again with a large platter of fresh bread, the steam drifting off the evenly sliced portions told her it was still warm from the oven. With a quick smile and a nod, the servant placed the dish before Adeline and hurriedly departed the room once more.

Adeline had not moved to fill her plate, her manners preventing her from doing so until all had arrived to break their fast. Had she arrived unfashionably early?

She'd never been known as one to wake with the sun. Nor had she and Poppy rushed through her morning routine as she donned her last clean gown and had her light brown locks pinned perfectly for her day.

Unease settled around her much like her rain-soaked cloak. In what she felt was another life entirely, Adeline would have been cast in a web of irritation to be left to her own devices in a stranger's home. Instead, she was fairly fatigued with loneliness.

Holding her breath, Adeline listened for any movement from above—or out in the hall—signaling that others would be joining her.

Nothing.

Perfect silence.

Even the noise from the kitchens could not be heard in the dining hall.

Yet, someone must be arriving soon.

Lord Ailesbury—or perhaps his wife.

Adeline straightened in her seat at the thought, her back stiffening. Why had the thought not occurred to her before this moment? Certainly, the earl was wed and likely blessed with several children. While she hadn't gained a clear look at the man, he was of a definite age for a family. Had she intruded on their peaceful existence?

A young, unwed woman traveling from Canterbury back to London, chaperoned only by her lady's maid and driver. It could be that Lady Ailesbury would not risk tarnishing her own family name by associating with such a hoyden as Adeline. Yet, her two youngest sisters had had more of an appropriate escort to school than Adeline had all those years prior. And Adeline was nearing her own majority, an age in which she would be free to make her own decisions without Alistair or her mother's approval.

She glanced around the finely adorned room once more, noting yet again the cleanliness of everything and the fine polish upon the floors and every wooden surface. It did not escape her scrutiny that all the furniture was dated, however. The table and chairs were fashioned from walnut, as opposed to mahogany, a favored wood popular in all of England for the last several decades. Adeline would be surprised if the massive table before her were not designed by Thomas Chippendale himself.

Emily once again entered the room, placing a tray of sliced meat on the table.

Adeline smiled at the servant, gaining enough of a pause from the woman for Adeline to speak before she rushed from the room once more.

"Will Lord Ailesbury and his family be joining me soon?" she ventured to ask.

The servant drew back from the table, keeping her stare focused on the floor in front of her with her hands clasped at her waist. "Ye should eat afore ye meal grows cold, miss."

"It would be impolite to begin before my host arrives—or perhaps his family I have yet to meet." Adeline spoke softly, not wanting to frighten the girl with her inquiries. "I am not so famished that I cannot wait awhile for others to join me."

The woman cleared her throat, glancing over her shoulder at the door she'd entered through. "Ummm, well, miss…"

"Is all as it should be?" Adeline asked, a shiver of foreboding traveling down her back.

"No one be join'n ye."

"But this is an awfully significant amount of food for only me." Adeline laughed. "Lord Ailesbury must be about, at the very least."

Emily hesitantly peeked over her shoulder once more as she slowly backed from the room. "M'lord ate afore first light. And there be no one else in residence."

"No one else in all of Faversham Abbey?"

"Except us servants, no, miss."

"But who will eat all this food?" Adeline gestured

toward the overloaded table, fairly straining under the weight of all the dishes.

"It is for ye, Miss Adeline," Emily mumbled. "M'lord not be know'n what ye favored in the morn. Enjoy ye meal."

Adeline watched in stunned silence as the servant fled the room, her footsteps louder due to her haste.

The scents of the fresh bread and sliced meat mingled with the smell of oats and honey from the porridge. Her stomach let out a loud growl of hunger. If no one were joining her, it would be foolish to let the dishes grow cold. A proper meal before she inquired about the damage done to her carriage was welcome. For all Adeline knew, her conveyance could be repaired and ready to depart within the hour, and it would be nightfall before she arrived in London.

"IS SHE ENJOYING the fare?" Jasper asked when Emily departed the dining hall once more. "The pheasant…was enough prepared? Is there a fruit she prefers more than the berries I collected this morning?"

"M'lord," Emily squealed in surprise, her hand going to her heart. "If'n ye want ta know, go in and speak with her."

"You know I cannot do that," Jasper said in a hushed tone, afraid his voice would carry through the thick, wooden door and into the dining hall beyond. "But I wish to know if she is pleased with her repast."

"She has yet ta touch anythin'."

"Why?" he demanded. "Is she ill from her time in the storm? I will call Doc Hobston to come round."

"No, m'lord." Emily shook her head, a pitying expression overtaking her normally serene face. "She be wait'n for ye—or ye family—to join her."

"What did you tell her?" Jasper shoved his hands

deep into his pockets to keep from grasping the servant and demanding more information. "I should have donned my cloak and hood."

"And that would not have appeared peculiar at all, my lord," Abbington said.

Jasper pivoted to face his butler. "Where did you come from?"

The man only nodded to the door behind Jasper: the butler's pantry.

Jasper sighed, resigned to the fact that not all of his servants lay in wait to listen to his private conversations. Not that Abbington was just another servant. He was one of Jasper's trusted staff, a friend more often than not.

"Can I return to me duties, m'lord?" Emily asked.

Duties? What other duties could the woman think more important than making certain Miss Adeline Price had everything she desired?

"Has the roasted goose been taken in?"

"Ye may go in and check, m'lord." The servant dipped into a curtsey. "I fear I be forget'n all that be served."

With a snort, Jasper turned to Abbington. "Can you summon Mrs. Hutchins, please? I would speak with her about—"

"My lord, Jasper,"—his butler sighed in resignation—"from all I've heard, Miss Adeline is a nice enough young woman. Do join her for her meal."

"I have already eaten." Jasper's excuse was empty, even to his own ears. "Besides, I need to check if her carriage has been brought to the stables as yet."

"I will send word when I hear."

"But I must begin the necessary repairs immediately if she is to depart in time to reach London by nightfall."

"Again, I can send word when Watson and his men—"

A bolt of lightning lit the corridor, followed by the boom of thunder far too close for Jasper's liking. Something slammed in the dining hall, followed by the resounding shatter of glass. A high-pitched scream echoed through the thick door.

His jaw clenched as the sound reverberated in his head, his legs weakening for the span of a mere heartbeat.

Jasper pushed through the double doors as they slammed against the wall behind them. Wind assaulted his face when he scanned the room, searching for what had caused Miss Adeline to shout in terror. It was as if a cyclone had moved through the dining hall—two of the candelabras were blown over, their light extinguished, and another closer to the tall windows had been snuffed. The drapes blew into the room from the open bay windows, shards of glass littered the floor in every direction. Miss Adeline stood, her arms wrapped around herself, her chair overturned behind her.

"Miss Adeline!" Jasper stopped only a few feet into the dining hall.

Abbington shuffled around him into the room, attempting to secure the windows to keep the rain from pouring in, but the latch had been broken.

The woman's back was to him, and she shivered. "Are you injured?"

Jasper should not have raced into action, but instead allowed Abbington to handle the situation. It would have been far wiser to depart and send for a footman to clean up the mess of the shattered window, but still, he stood frozen, his glare on her back as she slowly turned to face him—just as another lightning strike illuminated the room and his marred neck and arm.

His years living with his deformity from the fire should have prepared him for her reaction. He should have been primed for her recoil. He should have anticipated her loud gasp. He should have predicted the look of wide-eyed terror that followed.

However, even after fifteen years of enduring such responses to the scars that covered the side of his face, neck, and down his arm, Jasper was never able to steel himself against the inner pain that coursed through him as others witnessed his outer damage.

To her credit, her shock lasted less than a few seconds before her poise returned and she sighed in relief, glancing toward the now closed windows as Abbington used a cord from the drapes to tie the handles together. Wind and rain still made their way in through the broken pane, but the worst of the storm had been pushed back outside.

Jasper itched to assist Abbington with the mess that had been created.

"Lord Ailesbury?" Miss Adeline asked tentatively.

She hadn't seen his face the previous night. Therefore, she could think him anyone. With his simple white linen shirt and sturdy, brown trousers, Jasper appeared anything but the master of Faversham Abbey. He did not stand on pomp and ceremony in his household. Never did he wear a neckcloth or style his hair in the latest gentlemen's fashion.

He could escape now, repair her carriage, and send Miss Adeline on her way without them crossing paths again.

He *should* flee.

CHAPTER 6

THERE WAS NO mistaking the man for anyone but the Earl of Ailesbury—lord of Faversham Abbey. His size with his broad shoulders and muscular legs spread in an authoritative stance were distinctive and brought to mind the man who'd rescued Adeline from the roadway the previous night. That he was attired in such informal shirt and trousers did not strike her as odd in any way.

It fit him. Perfectly.

And she would recognize him anywhere, no matter if he wore a cloak to hide his scarred countenance or remained in the shadows of the room.

Every inch of her was drawn to him, no matter the apprehension coursing through her at the initial sight of him.

"Lord Ailesbury?" He'd scared her far more when he barged into the dining hall than the commotion from the broken window latch, the shattering of the windowpane, and the subsequent destruction when the wind sent the candelabras falling in every direction.

Thankfully, the wicks had been snuffed in the gust before they lit the fine tablecloth ablaze.

She could not stop her stare from traveling the length of the man. He was all strength with thighs as stout as a tree and a narrow waist that led up to a broad chest heavy with muscles. Even his neck, sinewy and sculpted, spoke of hard labor. If his linen shirt were removed, would the expanse below be rife with ridges and corded power?

"My lord, thank you—"

His jaw clenched, and Adeline's mouth clamped shut.

Finally, she could see his eyes—green, much like the color of new leaves budding in the spring warmth.

What she hadn't expected was the cold, hard stare he leveled on her.

It should be Adeline questioning his decorum as her host. It should be she leveling him with a disdainful glare.

"Have I done aught to anger you, Lord Ailesbury?" Her good sense told her she should be scared, seek out her room until it was time to depart, or at the very least, keep her mouth firmly closed.

Yet, Adeline had never been blessed with any sense of self-preservation.

It wasn't his marred countenance, the scars traveling from the side of his face to his neck and down his exposed arm from under his rolled sleeves that sent a shiver of fright coursing through her. Heavens no, it was the scowl that had settled on his face. No man would have gone to such lengths to save her, bring her to his home and out of the storm, only to show himself as a cruel, abusive man at first light.

His irked expression did not suit him.

Adeline sensed that Lord Ailesbury was no more a man prone to a punishing nature than she was a woman known for her kind disposition.

Sad, but very accurate.

"Have you been injured by the glass, Miss Adeline?" His question cut like a knife, hard and quick, doing nothing to soften his expression. "I can summon

Doc—"

"No, my lord," Adeline rushed. "I am uninjured. I was simply startled by the window bursting open and the candles extinguishing. My heartbeat has settled now, thank you for your concern."

To her utter bewilderment, Lord Ailesbury pivoted and stalked from the room, leaving Adeline staring at his retreating back.

"Do not take offense, miss," Abbington said from his position by the windows. "My lord does not mean any insult, it is only that he is unfamiliar with the art of entertaining."

It was more likely he'd noticed her reaction when she turned and saw his scarred face for the first time. If Adeline could only turn back the clock a quarter of an hour, she would tame her response to his sudden appearance, for she hadn't been frightened or even so much as startled by his wounds. His footsteps quieted as he strode farther from the dining hall, and Adeline suspected if she allowed him to escape, she'd never have the opportunity to make amends for the hurt she caused him.

She did the only thing that proved effective when a man—normally one of her brothers—sought to escape her. Adeline took hold of her skirts, so as not to trip over them, and ran after Lord Ailesbury. She caught up with him in the foyer as a footman helped him into a jacket.

"Where are you going?" she demanded.

"Hunting," he huffed, slamming his hands into gloves and pulling his hood up.

"You cannot venture out in this gale."

"I most assuredly can—and will," he countered. "It is my responsibility to feed everyone at Faversham Abbey, and the storm is likely to pass by the time my horse is readied."

He could feed the entire household—and the

village beyond—if he hadn't been so wasteful with her repast. Adeline kept this to herself. Another thing she knew all too well was that criticizing men on their own follies gained a woman less than nothing. Yet, she would never forgive herself knowing it was she who forced him from his home. If she hadn't reacted as she did, he would not be rushing out into the unrelenting elements under the guise of *hunting*.

There was only one thing Adeline could think to do. "Allow me to collect my cloak and bow from my room, and I shall join you. It is the least I can do after you provided such a grand meal for me."

"You cannot…it is…improper…ludicrous…" he stammered as Adeline turned toward the stairs. "You will not come with me. You will wait here until your carriage is repaired and be on your way back to London."

Adeline flipped around, galled at the man's attempt to order her about as if he were her guardian. "I most certainly can—and *will*—come with you."

"You are not attired properly. The wind and rain will soak through to your skin within moments."

"I thought you said the storm would pass by the time our horses are readied," she threw back at him, unwilling to give up or give in to his excuses.

"*Our* horses?" Lord Ailesbury glanced over her shoulder. "Abbington! See that Miss Adeline finishes her meal and retires to rest before her journey back to London."

"You cannot think to order me ab—"

"This is my home. While you are here, I am responsible for your well-being." Lord Ailesbury's voice thundered around her. She longed to remind him that as master of Faversham Abbey, he did not need to go out in the storm to hunt, but at his narrowed glare, she remained silent. "You will remain in this house until your carriage is ready to depart."

He gave her no further opportunity to debate the issue when he pulled the front door wide and slammed it behind him, once again leaving Adeline and Abbington in his wake.

She expected the servant to absolve his master's rude behavior, but he made no excuses this time.

He knotted his hands behind his back and took in all of Adeline's bluster at the situation as his wounded smile turned to intense scrutiny. "The rain will pass, Miss Adeline."

"Thank you, Abbington." She ducked her head, thinking the man only sought to reassure her she'd be free of Faversham Abbey before long—and out of Lord Ailesbury's way.

"If you will wait in your room, I will have suitable hunting attire brought round, and your bow collected from your possessions in the stables."

Adeline's mouth dropped open, and the butler nodded to cover his conspiratorial smile.

"But…Lord Ailesbury said…" she started before clamping her mouth shut once more. The man had offered to assist her, and she would not dare question his motives. "Thank you, Abbington. Have I ever told you how much my family adores names beginning with the letter *A*?"

"You have not, Miss Adeline," he replied. "But I foresee plenty of time in the future for us to discuss that topic at greater length. You have a hunting expedition to ready for. I will send a maid with a riding habit."

She made no attempt to hide her bewildered stare, but it only had the servant smiling at her. Plenty of time in the foreseeable future? She hardly suspected the storm would prevent her from departing Kent before noonday passed.

Adeline took several steps and wrapped the servant in a tight embrace before hurrying up the stairs to her room. No matter the man's intent, she was thankful for his kindness.

While she'd been below stairs her bed had been made, the drapes tied back, and her belongings repacked and waiting at the foot of the mattress; though Poppy was nowhere to be seen.

Odd. Adeline could not think where the maid had disappeared to. Maybe she'd been summoned below to find her own meal.

Adeline hurriedly undid the buttons at the back of her gown, stripping it away, and sat to await her hunting attire.

She could not risk sending for her maid and thus have her servant recite the danger Adeline could face by accompanying Lord Ailesbury on his hunting excursion. That she'd never used her bow for game, only sport, would not diminish Adeline's resolve. What problems could a moving stag or a flying pheasant present? She was used to plying her skill before audiences in the hundreds, there was little chance she'd allow Lord Ailesbury to distract her focus. She, along with Theo and Georgie, had competed—and won she might add— in several London archery tourneys in the last several years. This could be no different.

Her competitive streak would not diminish because her target was not a stationary, straw-stuffed object. Nor would it wane because her competition was a handsome man with an overbearing streak.

Besides, it would be a new ability Adeline would be pleased to demonstrate for Theo, Georgie, and Josie when next they practiced in Hyde Park.

It was better to beg forgiveness than be denied permission outright.

Another fact Adeline had learned not only at home but also from her many years at Miss Emmeline's School.

CHAPTER 7

JASPER WAITED IN his study for his horse to be readied, pacing from the unlit hearth to his desk and back again, attempting to banish from his mind his less than noble treatment of Miss Adeline. After departing out the front door, he'd slipped back in through the side entrance and hid in his study.

What a damned coward.

He'd brought her to Faversham Abbey when she could have just as easily found refuge in town, only to treat her in a most ungentlemanly manner.

His aunt, Alice, would be appalled at his behavior and would likely return from her grave to haunt him if she were able. But bloody hell...he could not allow Miss Adeline to accompany him out into the storm—and for hunting, no less.

She could be injured. There was a great possibility of her becoming disoriented and lost in the woods.

Or far worse still, her horse could become spooked and throw her.

The land surrounding Faversham Abbey was vast and not easily navigated.

But there was no one to blame but himself. He wasn't so foolish as to not realize that if he hadn't demanded his entire fowl surplus cooked and prepared for her morning meal, they would have plenty of provisions for the next several days. That he'd ventured out in the pelting rain just after daybreak to collect berries from the vines at the edge of his property would likely cause laughter among his servants for months to come.

The truth of the matter was, Jasper had held the advantage with Miss Adeline until a short while ago. He'd taken in her beauty, her poise, and her upturned button nose. He'd watched her walk into his home the night before as if she belonged there. She'd handled his servants with the expert hands of a woman learned in managing a household.

And he'd been forced to hide himself and avoid his servants for fear of revealing the truth.

Blast it all, but it made him feel more than a mere sense of inadequacy. He felt like an outsider in his own home.

He pivoted and started back toward the hearth, glancing out the window as he stalked across the room. True to his word, the storm was clearing, the clouds pushing toward the far horizon, allowing a rare glimpse of the sun during a normally foggy March day.

By now, the blasted woman should be returned to her room as he'd commanded, and Jasper would be free to slip from the house unnoticed. When he was informed that his horse was ready, that was.

He chuckled, thinking of her determination to have her way.

Aunt Alice would have liked the woman immensely, while his uncle would have mumbled about the folly of women raised with a mind of their own. Yet, Jasper's father's younger brother had chosen just such a woman to take as wife. No matter his gruff nature and whispered criticisms, Lieutenant Colonel Bartholomew Benedict was a man who insisted on a woman with spunk and wit. Things his aunt had possessed in spades.

Jasper wondered if his own father, Balthazar Benedict, the fifth Earl of Ailesbury, had the same preference in the fairer sex. Alas, he'd been but a boy of twelve when Lord and Lady Ailesbury died, along with three servants and a half dozen horses, in the fire that had burned the earl's stable to the ground—nearly taking Jasper's life, as well.

Shaking his head, Jasper pushed the old wounds back where they belonged—buried and ignored. There was little to be gained from spiraling into that deep hole of guilt and doubt, or so his aunt had told him for years.

Bloody hell, but he missed the woman…and his uncle. Sad that his time with them here at Faversham held far more memories than those with his blooded parents. His aunt had doted on her nephew since she and his uncle hadn't been blessed with a child of their own. They'd seen to his education, private though it was as they thought it best his tutors come to the Abbey. His uncle had taught him the courage and strength of a soldier, as well as the kindness and compassion needed to help others. Jasper had been instructed in the ways of estate management, including keeping the ledgers, how to resolve disputes between servants and villagers, and household management. The last was due to his aunt's persistence…in case it was many years before Jasper wed.

A knock sounded at the door, bringing him back to the present with a start.

"Enter." He cleared his throat to dispel his gravelly tone.

His aunt and uncle had been gone for many years now. Crying would not bring them back nor give him another day with them.

Abbington entered, his steps sure and his head held high. "Your steed awaits you out front, my lord. The storm has receded, and your bow is at the ready."

"Out front?" Jasper's brow furrowed. He'd never

once had his horse brought round to the front of the house. His path to the best hunting grounds lay behind the manor, toward the gunpowder plant. "Very well. I will depart immediately. Make certain Miss Adeline has all that's needed until her carriage departs."

"Of course, my lord." Abbington gave him a crisp nod before twisting to allow Jasper to pass and proceed him into the foyer.

There was something off with the servant, and Jasper could only think it was the woman's presence in his home. There was little other explanation for his staff's formal attitude and rigid posture. It was as though they sought to impress Miss Adeline.

Ludicrous—and a waste of time and energy, if you asked Jasper.

Miss Adeline Price belonged in London, surrounded by hoity-toity gents and ladies in outrageous garb. She belonged in elaborately decorated ballrooms or ensconced in private opera boxes. She was used to finely furnished townhouses with grand foyers and sparkling chandeliers with hundreds of candles, casting illumination on her below.

Faversham Abbey hadn't seen a proper renovation since before Jasper was born—if not several decades before that. He'd never set foot in a ballroom nor an opera house.

Damnation, he had no recollection of what London looked like except for the drawings and a few paintings his mother had brought with her to Kent after wedding his father.

Though it did not leave him with melancholy or wanting a stay in the grand city.

He and Miss Adeline came from two different worlds, and Jasper needed no further proof of that than his stumbling upon her stranded alongside the roadway.

Jasper pulled up short when he entered the foyer.

He rubbed at his eyes, blinked several times, and

even tilted his head to the left a smidgen.

There was no way he did not imagine the vision before him. Perhaps he was ill and hadn't taken a moment to realize it, or his thoughts of Miss Adeline had conjured the dreamscape before him.

Certainly, one of the two explained Miss Adeline Price's appearance at the bottom of the staircase, garbed in a riding habit of the deepest scarlet he'd ever seen with a bow slung over her shoulder.

Jasper would recognize the habit anywhere, though it had been over twelve years since he'd seen it.

"It fits admirably, does it not Lord Ailesbury?" The woman had the nerve to spin around, her heavy skirts staying about her ankles and her bow remaining high on her shoulder.

"Who gave you that habit?" He would enact swift justice on the servant who dared disobey his command.

"Poppy brought it to me," she said with a shrug. "It is well made with a master's skill at stitching."

A squeak sounded from above, and Jasper narrowed his stare on the landing in time to see Emily—and Adeline's maid, Poppy—scatter out of view. So, his servants were in cahoots with hers.

Interesting.

"I am happy you approve," he growled.

Miss Adeline froze, glancing down the front of her as her face paled.

"I will change immed—"

"Do not bother, Miss Adeline," he drawled. "It is not your fault the habit was delivered for your use. You could not have known the significance. However, my servants are well aware."

Jasper had no need to glance upward again because Emily's gasp had been all he needed to hear. The servants had been warned—if not directly—that their meddling was unwarranted and unwanted.

At least, he was confident there were a few loyal

Ailesbury servants not plotting against him. The woman would see soon enough it mattered naught that her attire was suitable and her bow at the ready, if she were unable to keep up when he mounted his steed, she would have no recourse but to remain at the Abbey.

With a satisfied smile, Jasper turned toward the front door as Abbington pulled it wide—revealing not one, but *two* bloody horses held by none other than his stable master, Watson.

Jasper clenched his jaw to keep from demanding to know why a second horse had been prepared when he'd made his wishes very clear to all involved. The notion of instructing the whole lot of them to pack their possessions and depart Faversham for good would be highly satisfying.

"Which horse shall I ride?" she asked, hurrying past him to coo to each beast in turn as she placed quick kisses to their muzzles.

Bloody hell if that damned riding habit did not cling to her curves as if the blasted thing had been tailored especially for her.

ADELINE GLANCED SIDEWAYS at Lord Ailesbury, rigid atop his mount as they cantered across the open meadow behind the Faversham stables in the direction of the wooded area beyond. While the storm clouds had receded to the horizon, an entirely different bank of clouds had settled upon the earl. He'd barely uttered a word after he assisted her onto her horse—a grey mare with an even step and solid stature—but she refused to allow his outright refusal to look at her to dampen her spirits.

This was her first hunt.

No matter that she'd been an unwelcome addition to the hunting party.

Adeline was determined to enjoy herself.

Certainly, she knew she'd one day be invited to take part in a house party that boasted a spirited stage hunt, but she'd never dreamed of hunting with the purpose of feeding an entire household. It was a daunting thought. What if they returned with nothing? Would several servants go without a meal? What if she did something wrong and scared away...bollocks but Adeline wasn't even aware what exactly they'd be taking aim at.

Fowl? Poultry? Or perhaps something far larger?

She'd never shot her bow from a horse before, especially a moving horse. And what if her target also moved?

If Theo were present, she'd quickly assess all information and instruct Adeline on the most successful course of action in such a situation. But her friends were in London, and Adeline was stranded in the wilds of Kent with a most fierce lord.

She should be, at the very least, a bit wary of the stranger and his servants. Yet, Adeline had the odd sense she'd been at Faversham for years, not less than a day. Strange, especially knowing she'd never particularly favored country life, and the Abbey was far more remote and removed from society than even her family's country estate.

Relaxing in her sidesaddle, she spurred her horse into a full gallop and took off across the meadow toward the strand of trees she assumed was their destination. It only took a moment for Ailesbury to match her pace...and race past her.

The man did not know her well if he thought she'd allow him to best her.

With a more pronounced kick, Adeline laid close to her mare's neck as the beast jumped into an outright run. The wind pulled at her carefully coiffed hair, sending pins scattering to the earth in her wake. Adeline shook her head, sending her curls tumbling down her back as the breeze caught them, creating a trail of locks behind her. She'd never before felt so free…and alive. Never had she been allowed to ride a horse in such a brazen manner. Leaning closer to her mare's neck, she cooed to the beast, imparting words of gratitude and prodding the animal ever on. She shook her head back and forth against the horse's neck, sending the last of her delicately placed hairpins cascading in the wind as the cold numbed her nose and her eyes watered. She cared naught; instead, she embraced what once would have been a discomfort.

Almost too quickly, they each pulled up on the reins and slowed their horses to a canter as they approached the trees.

She risked a glance over her shoulder and spotted Faversham Abbey in the far distance, tendrils of smoke drifting skyward from at least seven chimneys. The manor appeared larger from across the meadow, if that were possible. She wondered if a servant looking out the tall windows, perhaps on the third or fourth floor, could spot them across the grassy expanse separating them from the Abbey. Adeline doubted it, but what a grand view the servant would have.

Turning back, Lord Ailesbury had dismounted his horse and slung his quiver and bow over his right shoulder before stepping toward her to assist her to the ground.

Adeline shook her head and waved him off as she jumped down, landing with a slight bounce and a smile. Once again, the habit moved seamlessly with her as she reached up to untie the cord holding her own bow and quiver to the horse's side. There was obviously a story behind the garment, though no one had seen fit to inform her of it. Was it possible that Lord Ailesbury had once been wed, and the habit had belonged to his wife? That would explain his dour mood upon seeing her and during their ride across the meadow.

The cut and fabric of the garment were much like the rest of Lord Ailesbury's home: in excellent condition for such a dated piece. The material was far stiffer and sturdier than was popular among the *ton* in recent years. In fact, it appeared new and hardly worn, if anyone had donned the riding habit at all. The color, a scarlet so deep it mirrored the hue of freshly spilt blood, suited her complexion and hair color splendidly. The hem reached just below her ankle and grazed the floor when she'd walked through the foyer earlier. Both Poppy and Emily had gone on and on about how well the garment hugged her frame.

Maybe she'd ask Lord Ailesbury if she could keep the garment when she left Faversham Abbey. Certainly, Alistair would send the coin to pay for it, if the earl did not demand payment in excess of the habit's worth. There was time, when they returned to the Abbey, to inquire on the matter.

"We leave the horses here." With both sets of reins in hand, he pulled the pair toward the nearest tree and tied them loosely to a low-hanging branch, giving the beasts ample line to graze at the base of the tree—or sample any low-hanging fruit from above. A pear tree, if she was not mistaken.

Relief eased the tension caused by Adeline's assumption that they'd be hunting from atop a horse. The ground was preferable, a steady surface was key to a superb stance and accurate aim. Another lesson Theo had drilled into her head from nearly her second day at Miss Emmeline's School.

"I do not doubt your competency with a bow; however, taking aim at a moving target requires much practice." He did not spare her even a glance as he spoke—or more accurately, lectured her—about the finer points of bow hunting. "Our bounty today is turkeys."

"A question, my lord?" When he halted, but did

not turn to face her, she asked, "Why does a servant—your gamesman—not fulfill the hunting requirements for Faversham Abbey?"

Even her father had kept a gamesman at their estate. He'd been very accomplished at the position and had seen fit to send fowl and other meats to London for Lord Melton and his children to enjoy.

"I am the only gamesman at Faversham." His words were clipped, spoken through clenched teeth. "Follow closely. Do not stray from my side. Do not make any commotion. And whatever you do, do not become lost. I will not take on the responsibility of notifying your family of your demise."

"That seems rather morbid and uncalled for, Lord Ailesbury," Adeline huffed. "I resent the implication that I am incapable of caring for myself while on the hunt."

"You were certainly *incapable* of taking care of yourself on a proper roadway..." he mumbled, his words trailing off but stating all he'd meant to impart. "Regardless of the situation at hand, I have a responsibility to my people to provide sustenance, and I cannot allow anyone to jeopardize my ability to feed those who depend on me."

She pursed her lips and inspected the man's back as he moved farther into the trees ahead of her. If she'd had a proper floor beneath her, she'd have stomped her foot at Lord Ailesbury's wicked rebuff. The earl acted as if his pantries were not stocked with vegetables, fruits, nuts, cheeses, and bread aplenty. Judging from the repast set before her that very morning, no one under Ailesbury's care was in jeopardy of starving—at least not in the foreseeable future.

However, even if they found no turkeys this day, Adeline was reluctant to give the man any further cause to lay the blame at her feet.

"This way, Miss Adeline," he hissed, motioning to

the path he'd chosen into the underbrush, both of them keeping their bows slung on their shoulders. "We must hurry in case the storm decides to shift course and return with a vengeance."

She carefully followed his progress deeper into the wooded area, lifting her feet high and mimicking his movements. The trees overhead were eerily silent except for the remnants of the wind that still lingered from the storm. Eventually, Adeline had need to use both hands to hold her skirts high to avoid them snagging or ripping on the thickening undergrowth. This was made all the more difficult as the canopy overhead blocked more and more of the sparse light attempting to penetrate the foliage.

From the angle in which she trailed him, she gained a clear view of the scars that covered the lower half of his cheek and down his neck, leaving his ear unmarred. They were unlike anything she'd seen before, and she could not pinpoint what could have caused them. Had he been born with them, or injured at some point? And how much of his body did they cover?

In the dining hall, his sleeves had been rolled to his elbows, and the scars had shown there, as well.

Suddenly, Adeline collided with Lord Ailesbury's back, his solid warmth pressed to her front. She nearly fell to the ground before he reached out and steadied her, a frown marring his face at her distracted stumble. Far too quickly, he released her, and the spike of longing that followed was foreign to Adeline.

He pointed to an area not far off where a group of large birds—turkeys?—ambled about, obviously unaware of the hunters stalking them. They were huge, enormous in height for a fowl and wide in girth. She'd eaten turkey on many occasions, the Christmastide season being one of them, but never had she thought the creatures so colossal.

From his smirk, Adeline knew her shocked

expression gave her away.

But, how were they to transport one massive turkey, let alone several, back to Faversham Abbey with only their horses for assistance?

"They are massive," she whispered close to his ear. "One alone would be enough to feed my entire family."

Lord Ailesbury's chest puffed in pride. "Faversham is praised far and wide for our quality turkeys and pheasants. Will you take the first shot, or shall I?"

It was a challenge. Ailesbury was, in a way, calling her bluff. In that moment, Adeline had a choice. She could pass the first shot back to him, or retrieve an arrow from her quiver and load her bow. The large birds were grazing, much as livestock did in a pasture or meadow. If Lord Ailesbury took first shot, the group would likely be on the move, and Adeline's chances of taking one down and bringing food back to the Abbey would be significantly decreased. Again, Theo would be able to calculate the exact decrease and variances in both scenarios, but there was no time to dwell on that.

Removing an arrow from her quiver, she set her stance, loaded her bow, and took aim.

As they'd journeyed deeper into the woods, the wind had died down and could barely be felt, but the dim light would certainly affect her alignment.

The turkeys were as large, if not bigger in size than the targets she and her friends used in Hyde Park and during tournaments. Her aim could be slightly off and still hit its mark. The bullseye was not as important…or was it?

"Is there a specific place it is best to aim for?" she asked.

"I think it wise to concentrate on hitting one before we speak of aim." His shoulders lifted and fell several times as if he chuckled to himself over Adeline's concerns.

The man did not believe her an expert

markswoman.

"The heart it is." She would show the fool that underestimating a woman, especially Adeline, was something many had lived to regret.

She drew a deep breath to quiet the thrashing in her head, aimed, and released her arrow.

It soared through the air in a straight line, veering slightly but correcting itself to drive deep into where Adeline assumed the bird's heart lay. Her aim had been so accurate and her bow so silent, that none of the other turkeys seemed to notice their fallen comrade.

Triumph soared through her as she held her fist high and gave it a solid shake.

In quick order, Lord Ailesbury released one arrow and then another…felling two more large birds.

Adeline stared wide-eyed at the man. How dare he ignore her skill—worse, overshadow her accomplishment with his speed. She lifted her bow.

CHAPTER 8

JASPER GLANCED AT the horizon, noting the growing layers of storm clouds that would, with all certainty, travel in their direction shortly. They'd be caught in the coming gale if they did not hurry back. With two turkeys tied securely to his pommel and one on the back of Miss Adeline's mare, they were ready to depart the wooded area a short ride from Faversham Abbey.

The plan had been for him to take down a turkey before Miss Adeline did aught to frighten the finicky birds away. To Jasper's continuing befuddlement, the woman had executed a brilliant shot and taken down the first bird. Not to be outdone, he'd shot in rapid succession to take down two more. Not that his estate required three turkeys, but his pride would not allow him to...

He shut his mind down before that train of thought took over. He was not an envious or jealous man. He was not easily prodded into competitions of strength or skill. Especially where a woman was concerned. He'd held his first bow at age six, and he hadn't expected Miss Adeline's skill to compare to his in any way—though that was unfair of him. Nonetheless, she'd surprised him with her aim.

More accurately, she'd baffled him completely. He kept his eyes trained on the area before him to keep his reaction hidden. The last thing Jasper needed to do was show the woman he was impressed by her skill.

At some point in their short association, he'd viewed her as helpless and in need of protection. That had been a misguided notion on his part.

"Very well done, Miss Adeline."

The woman did not so much as bless him with a glance at his words of praise.

He'd need remember to keep any and all acclaim to himself in the future—not that the pair of them had a future.

Standing close to her mount, Miss Adeline attempted to tame her wild hair that had been pulled free of its pins by the wind as they raced across the meadow, but with nothing to secure it, her task was nearly impossible. Jasper didn't remember his aunt—or his mother—having so much hair. It cascaded over Adeline's shoulders and down her back, with plenty left over to fall across her face in wild abandon.

They should return to the Abbey with all due haste. With all likelihood, her carriage was repaired and awaiting her departure.

However, something kept him from rushing home.

Jasper untied a length of cord from his quiver and handed it to her. "This may help."

Miss Adeline stared at the cord he held out to her, her brow furrowed as she continued to struggle with her light brown curls. Finally, she accepted his offer and made quick work of knotting the cord at the base of her neck, giving it a tug to make certain it would hold.

The silence between them seemed to stretch on until Jasper found himself shifting from foot to foot, tugging at his ear, and sweeping his own loose hair from his face. Anything to banish the uncomfortable quiet.

"Did you learn your skill with a bow from your

father?" he asked. Why had he asked about her sire—or anything of a personal nature at all? It would open the way of conversation to his own family, and that was something Jasper had no intention of speaking about. "Ummm, I mean to say..."

His words trailed off when her face lit with a smile.

It was obvious to Jasper now that Miss Adeline had been awaiting his praise.

"Heavens, no," she said, running her hands down her skirts. "My father, the Lord keep his soul, was well into his advanced years when I was born. And while my eldest brother is adequate with a bow, he cannot claim prowess over me."

"I am sorry to hear that your father is not still unto this earth." Again with the unwise topic of family, but Jasper would not be a gentleman if he allowed her words to go on without comment. "However, if you did not learn from your father or eldest brother, perhaps another relation?"

"Abel has no interest in sports. If Alfred and Adrian fancied themselves accomplished with a bow, I would not have been present to witness it." She shrugged, leaning down to retrieve her bow before looking at her mount. The turkey was secured where her bow had been on the ride here.

He wanted to question her more on her skill with a bow; however, it was none of his business.

"You see, I was sent away to an all girl's school at twelve. My youngest brothers were only eight and five at the time; they were not allowed outdoors with the rest of us." She paused, some inner debate clouding her face. "I was actually returning to London after escorting my younger sisters, Arabella and Ainsley, to Miss Emmeline's School of Education and Decorum for Ladies of Outstanding Quality in Canterbury when the storm hit. Do you know the school?"

"No, but my, my, that is certainly a mouthful," he

said with a chuckle.

Her shoulders fell as if disappointed with his answer. "I suspected you might know the place as it is only a short distance from Faversham."

"I do not travel often." *Or at all.*

"Well, to answer your original question, I learned my skill at archery while I was away at school. I and my bosom friends—Theo, Josie, and Georgie—practiced day and night, as there was not much else to occupy the long years." Miss Adeline stiffened as a loud boom of thunder sounded in the distance. "I think it is time we return to the Abbey."

"I think that wise." He took her bow and quiver, along with his, and tied them to the back of his saddle before assisting her onto her horse. "You must miss your friends now that you've left the schoolroom."

She looked down at him from her sidesaddle and laughed. "Oh, my friends are never far, and London is a veritable treasure trove of archery tournaments. I've competed in several since my return to town; came close to winning a few, too. However, since my father passed and my brother became Viscount Melton, I have had to assist my mother with caring for the young ones."

Jasper calculated the years in his head as he turned and mounted his own horse. Miss Adeline could not be more than nineteen, possibly twenty. Her return from school was likely around her seventeenth birthday, or at least his own education told him that debutantes were normally presented to society around that age. Her father must have died quite recently.

"Our time of mourning ended only several weeks back, and my brother, as our guardian, thought it best that Arabella and Ainsley attend school as I did." She sighed, slouching in her saddle. "It will give my mother a bit of solitude, even though finding the funds for schooling will be difficult."

For once, Jasper did not curse a woman's tendency

for chatter. If she spoke of her own family, that kept her mind occupied on matters other than *his* family.

"You have a rather large family." It wasn't a question. He spurred his steed into an even trot, allowing Miss Adeline to ride alongside him. "How many siblings have you?"

He glanced at her just as she shook her head and flipped her tied hair back over her shoulder, her brownish gold eyes sparkling with mischief as she began reciting. "Alistair, Abel, me, Adelaide, Amelia, Arabella, Alfred, Adrian, and Ainsley." She paused and used her free hand to tick off the numbers in her head. "Yes, that is all nine. I must say, sometimes I forget one of us."

"Nine children?" he said aghast. "Your family could coordinate an entire group of cricket players!"

A single raindrop hit his cheek, but Jasper merely brushed it away. It had been many years since he conversed with someone who knew naught about him and Jasper was unfamiliar with them. The shocking thing was that he was actually enjoying their back and forth.

"Heaven knows my father would have paraded us about in matching attire if he'd thought of it." She glanced up at the darkening sky, lifting her elegant chin and exposing her swan-like neck to his view. "Alas, it is more likely he would have banded us together to raise our voices in a soft harmony, that is if any of us possessed an ounce of talent. What about you, my lord, any brothers or sisters?"

He swallowed hard, turning his focus to the Abbey in the distance. "I am afraid not."

"Well, that is likely for the best," she mumbled. "A horde of siblings can try any person's patience, even a serene woman such as myself."

At that, Jasper could not fight his chuckle, though he was hard-pressed to decide if it was due to her comment or the notion of Miss Adeline ever masking herself in serenity.

They fell into a companionable silence as they continued toward Faverhsam, the storm pressing at their backs as the wind increased by the minute. Yet, Jasper was hesitant to speed up their pace. Soon enough, Miss Adeline would depart his estate in her newly repaired carriage, leaving Jasper alone once more.

It was something that had never caused him a moment's thought or a night's lost sleep. Jasper was more than accustomed to living alone with only his servants and the few townspeople who did not run in the opposite direction when he approached as companions. His duties at the gunpowder plant and managing his estate kept him busy most days, without time to dwell on his singular lifestyle. Would things have been different if his parents had lived and the opportunity to journey to London was available?

Soon enough, they arrived back in the stable yard, the sight of her dismantled carriage greeting them.

Watson, George, and Miss Adeline's driver were all crouched next to the conveyance discussing something in hushed tones as Watson pointed at the undercarriage.

Dismounting, Jasper threw the reins to his waiting stable boy, though he did not move fast enough to Miss Adeline to assist her before she slipped to the ground on her own with a grin. He was uncertain what he'd thought London misses to be like, but the woman before him was not as he'd expected.

Exploring the reasoning behind *why* this made him smile was not high on his list of priorities.

His servants turned toward him, their expressions darkening as they exchanged a look between them.

Jasper made an attempt to wipe the grin from his face. "Have you discovered the damage and what is needed to repair it?"

Watson motioned for him to have a look under the conveyance. As he lowered to his haunches next to the trio, Miss Adeline leaned far over, attempting to gain her own view of the undercarriage.

"It appears the brake push bar has been worn clean through and—"

"Cause'n the reach bars ta dislodge," Watson finished for him, wiping the sweat from his brow. "Gonna be a might difficult ta repair. Gonna have ta see the blacksmith in town ta retrieve the parts."

Jasper pushed back to his feet. "Of course, of course," he sighed, somewhat relieved Miss Adeline would not be departing Faversham only to enter yet another storm. She was safer here. For even if her carriage were mended, there was a high probability it would become damaged again in muddied conditions. "I will begin dismantling the coach further while you seek out the blacksmith."

A spattering of heavy drops hit the side of the lifted carriage as the storm bore down on the stable yard.

"It be best ta roll the thing inta the stable for cover," Maxwell, Miss Adeline's servant, suggested. "The tempest be return'n—and it looks ta be mad as a frog in Lord Melton's travel'n trunk."

Miss Adeline burst into laughter at her servant's remark, as Watson and George looked at him to see if he understood the irony of Maxwell's words. When Jasper only shrugged, they turned back to their work.

"I suppose I will retire to the house to freshen up."

"That would be wise," Jasper replied. "We shall endeavor to have the carriage repaired by noonday and have you on your way then—if the storm allows it."

"And the turkeys?" she asked.

Bloody hell, he'd all but forgotten about the birds tied to their saddles. "I will send word to Cook, and she will have them brought in."

Adeline's stare flitted about the gathering of men before settling once more on Jasper. "Then I suppose I am no longer needed."

"It was fine having you on the hunt, Miss Adeline," he said with a curt bow. "I will bring you word shortly regarding the status of the repairs. Oh, and I will have your equipment returned to your room."

"Thank you, Lord Ailesbury." She dipped her chin, still stalling her departure to the Abbey when another thunderous boom echoed. Leaping in fright, she turned and hurried to the main house.

Her departure left three sets of eyes following her progress. There would have been a fourth, but Jasper noted Maxwell attending to the woman's bow and quiver.

"*Fine having you on the hunt?*" Watson mimicked Jasper's refined accent.

George slapped his open hand to his mouth to hide his own smirk.

Jasper had expected as much from his servants. "The pair of you were not there to witness it, but Miss Adeline is an expert markswoman. If I told you her skill could, on any given day, best my own, would you believe me?"

"Are ye certain it not be her fine English beauty ye be more taken with, *m'lord?*" Watson asked. "Because, she be one a the prettiest flowers we be see'n in these parts."

Jasper's stomach hardened, and he took a deep breath to stifle his need to rebuff the man's accusations or, at the very least, demand that he not speak of Miss Adeline in such a scandalous manner.

Instead, he calmed his flash of anger. "Miss Adeline Price is the epitome of a proper London lady. She is above reproach, and will remain as such for the duration of her stay at Faversham Abbey. Make no mistake, the punishment will be swift and severe if I hear word of anything spoken to the contrary where Miss Adeline is concerned."

Both George and Watson took a step back at Jasper's curt words.

"Yes, m'lord," George muttered, keeping his stare on Jasper's Hessians.

"Of course, m'lord." Watson waved George back toward the damaged carriage as the rain went from a light falling to a consistent drizzle. "We be get'n ta our duties now. I will hurry ta town as soon as the carriage be outta the storm."

With the woman disappearing into the house, Jasper turned to assist his men—giving his mind something to concentrate on besides the English beauty waiting inside his home. The fact was, she would be departing as soon as Jasper and his men finished with their task. What was said between them—all she'd shared about her family and friends—and what was not said—anything about his past—would mean nothing to either of them. She would return to London and society, and Jasper would remain in Kent. She would wed a noble lord, and he would care for the people who called Faversham home. Their lives could not be more different from each other.

Jasper ignored the emptiness that resurfaced in his being for the first time in years.

All four men began pushing the carriage toward the open stable doors where a place had been cleared to work. The hay and equipment normally taking up the common area of the stable had been pushed toward the horse stalls to accommodate another conveyance beyond his own coach. The stable boy had led Jasper and Miss Adeline's horses into the long corridor to the left, preparing to remove their saddles and brush the beasts as was required after each mount was removed from their stall. The kitchen staff must have collected the turkeys; though Jasper hadn't noticed when.

On the surface, it was a day like any other at Faversham Abbey.

His servants completed their tasks and chores as they always did with their master at their sides. Each man, woman, and child at his estate carried the burden of making certain all was taken care of, and Jasper was no exception. It gave him a sense of fulfillment he would certainly be despondent and empty without—as he'd been immediately after his parents' deaths and before his aunt and uncle had been summoned to care for the young lordling.

Jasper would never return to that helpless, lost, and broken child.

If it took working until he fell into his bed exhausted without any energy to go on each day, then that was what he was prepared to do.

"M'lord!" Watson rushed back into the stables. Jasper had been so preoccupied, he hadn't realized the man had departed for the blacksmith's shop in town. "Jasper! Come look!"

Jasper, along with several other stable hands, ran from the building into the rain.

In the distance, a lone rider on horseback rode at a breakneck speed across the meadow he and Miss Adeline had crossed less than an hour prior. The man arrived in the stable yard within minutes, his mount frothing at the mouth from the hard trek—his rider in no better condition.

Jasper recognized the man as one of the villagers in a position of leadership at the gunpowder plant, yet, Jasper had been very specific that operations at Home Works be shut down for the duration of the storm. The flooding made it nearly impossible for most workers to make the journey to the plant on foot, and it was precarious on horseback. Why ever was the man coming from the direction of the plant and not the village?

The man leapt from his horse, and a stable boy rushed forward to take the reins when the man doubled over, struggling to gasp for breath. "M'lord...Lord

Ail…Lord Ailesbury," the villager stammered.

"Slow it down, Landers." George stepped forward and patted the man's back. "What have ye ta say?"

"It be—" Landers took a deep gulp of air, inhaling through his mouth and exhaling through his nose as he stood straight to face Jasper. "It be Grovedale, m'lord. He be trapped at the plant."

"At the plant?" Jasper demanded, his words laced with both anger and fear. Anger that someone had openly disobeyed his orders, and fear because Jasper knew that Grovedale and his servant, Emily, had wed the year before. "Tell me what happened."

But Jasper was already running for his own steed and had mounted before Landers said another word.

Ripping the reins from the post they were tied to as the groom had begun tending the horses, Jasper kicked the beast into action and charged from the stables toward the plant. He kept his attention on the uneven ground of the meadow as he allowed his horse his head, the gelding knew the way to the plant as well as Jasper himself.

Never once did he glance over his shoulder to see if his servants followed.

From the fright on Landers' face, there was no time to think…only time for action.

CHAPTER 9

ADELINE ENTERED THE Faversham kitchen, happy to see Emily's familiar face as she and two other servants carried in the morning's spoils. It was a room normally dominated by servants and off-limits to the master's family—at least in her family homes—however, Adeline was a guest, and she was uncertain what to do to occupy her time until Lord Ailesbury summoned her to depart. In other cases, she would have sought a restorative walk about the property, but the intensity of the storm was increasing once more, and she had little urge to wander the Abbey alone. Besides, while snooping around Lord Ailesbury's home would have, at one time, felt like an adventure, since gaining a certain understanding of the man, she saw it as more of an invasion of his privacy than anything else.

And so, she strolled through the foyer, down a corridor, and toward the only sounds she could hear.

Of course, the kitchen was the liveliest room in any home.

Which was certainly why her parents had specifically forbidden all of her siblings from partaking in any rousing activity to be had within the room.

Adeline *was not* forbidden to enter the kitchen at Faversham Abbey.

"Good day, miss," Emily called, lifting a large bird onto a table at the back of the room. "Ye and the master sure did spear three plump turkeys. It be true ye took down the first?"

Adeline laughed, walking to where the servants struggled to lift the second bird. "Gossip certainly travels fast at Faversham."

All three women turned open-eyed stares on her. Even Cook, who hadn't paused in her stirring of a large pot to greet Adeline, pivoted to face the commotion at the back of her kitchen.

"No, miss," Emily rushed, hurrying over to Adeline. "No one be gossip'n—"

Adeline smiled at the women, who one by one allowed their terrified expressions to overtake their faces and their gazes to drop to the floor. "I certainly did not mean to insult anyone here or insinuate that you spoke out of turn." She grasped Emily's hands, and the servant stiffened at the contact. "Besides, I am a firm believer that gossip is never all negative. In fact, if it were not for the wagging tongues of London, my dear friend, Theodora, would not have admitted her love for my brother, scoundrel that he is."

"I only overhead m'lord speak'n ta the stable master of ye skill with a bow."

"He mentioned me?" It took four sets of eyes narrowing in her direction before Adeline realized she'd spoken the thought aloud. For one of the first times in her life, a deep blush overtook her. "I meant my skill. Yes, my skill. Lord Ailesbury was certainly dubious to have me accompany him."

"Aw, well," Cook chimed in. "Ye certainly showed him ye worth, yes ye did. It do the lad well ta be put in his place, if only e'er once in a while."

Emily, along with the two other maids, broke out in a fit of giggles. Adeline was helpless to stop herself from joining in.

"It was rather satisfying to see the astonishment on Lord Ailesbury's stuffy face when I took down that turkey." They all laughed once more. An odd bout of homesickness struck Adeline—not so much for her family but for her closest friends. It was usually Josie, Georgie, and Theo who commonly brought Adeline's laughter. Though, as of last year, Theo had become family when she wed Adeline's eldest brother.

Adeline glanced through the open kitchen door, past the meager gardens, and to the stable yard beyond in time to see Lord Ailesbury run back into the structure and flee on his horse in the direction they'd ridden earlier.

The hairs at her nape stood on end. She need not be close to know something was amiss.

Shouts could be heard as one of the servants called for horses—for him and another man—as Maxwell ran toward the kitchen, where Adeline stood. All stares in the room focused on the commotion in the yard, the activity in no way lessened by the storm.

When Maxwell skidded through the door and into the room, he glanced about, but for whom or what, Adeline could not tell.

"Maxwell." Adeline rushed forward as the man's shallow breaths turned ragged. "Where is Lord Ailesbury headed in such a hurry?"

"A man, Grovedale…he is trapped at the plant."

"Grovedale?" Emily shrieked, her head shaking from side to side. "Ye be certain that be the name?"

"Yes, ma'am," Maxwell confirmed. "The stable master sent me ta get Abbington. He needs ta summon a physician to the plant. Now!"

At some point, Mrs. Hutchins had entered the kitchens, witnessing the spectacle. "I'll find my husband," she called, turning and rushing from the room.

"But where is Lord Ailesbury going?" Adeline

demanded, giving Maxwell a solid shake.

"He and the others be go'n ta lift the wall from the man."

Then Maxwell pulled from her grasp and hurried to follow Mrs. Hutchins in her search for the Faversham butler.

Emily wailed, falling into Cook's waiting arms as the portly woman patted the maid's back. She cooed her reassurances that all would be fine. Lord Ailesbury would save her husband; she was certain of it.

It gave Adeline enough time to slip out the door and run toward the stables. With any luck, her mare would still be saddled, and she'd be on her way long before anyone noticed she was gone. Luck was on her side when she pushed through the downpour of rain into the stables. Everyone was in motion, stable hands and servants saddling every available horse for the journey to the plant. She knew the place they spoke of as it was not far beyond the wooded area she and the earl had hunted in. It was the large building she'd seen from her bedchamber window when the lightning struck, illuminating the intimidating facade in the distance, as Mrs. Hutchins had informed her.

Her mare stood, tied to a post, to the left of her damaged carriage.

Glancing around, Adeline searched for a box or stepping stone to help her up into the sidesaddle without requiring assistance from one of the servants. Any of them would likely demand she remain at the Abbey, and she could not risk that.

Adeline could be of use at the plant, especially since the servants were still rushing about, readying horses. If she were there quickly enough, her assistance could prove useful. Her mare was saddled and prepared to depart immediately.

A small wooden box stood along the far wall behind where the mare was tied. Adeline rushed over and peeked inside.

Oats and grains for the livestock, but it was only a third of the way full.

She braced herself and pushed the box, nearly falling to her knees when the thing slid across the hard-packed dirt with ease. Once in place, she leapt onto it and into her saddle. The mare skidded sideways, unprepared for her weight, and Adeline was able to untie the reins. She pulled the horse around and followed the same path Lord Ailesbury had taken out of the stables and then she turned sharply. Kicking her horse into a run, Adeline reached the meadow, but Ailesbury was already out of sight. The gunpowder plant lay to the north of the woods, only a short ride away, yet the drowning rain and unrelenting gusts pounded her face. The wind wildly caught her hair as the cord Lord Ailesbury had given her loosened and disappeared in her wake.

The storm thundered overhead, and the rain began to soak clear through her thick riding habit, yet Adeline pushed on, finally arriving at a road. She rubbed the rain from her eyes, certain the area was familiar. It was the road her carriage had been stranded on. The large structure, not far from that point, would have been hidden by the darkness the night before.

As she grew ever closer, the building appeared abandoned—a relic of past times when the war demanded production of gunpowder and explosives at an alarming rate. Adeline knew of the plant only because Miss Emmeline's father had gained employment at Home Works while the British fought valiantly to vanquish Napoleon. Now, the structure appeared aged and weathered, half shielded by a grove of trees.

Adeline nestled her face against the mare's neck, shielding herself from the worst of the storm as the road curved, leading her into a large area of open ground. A gathering of people, clustered about a small outbuilding attached to the main plant, had Adeline pulling her horse to a stop.

Her pulse drummed in her head as she slid to the muddy ground.

No one noticed her arrival as she ran toward the crowd, pushing her way to the front. The sheer number of people gathered made her think the entire village had come. The able-bodied men, with Lord Ailesbury in their midst, attempted to lift a large piece of wood. Even from her vantage point, Adeline noted that the heavy wall would not budge, no matter how much the group strained.

Adeline glanced to the people surrounding her, their torches held high, all fighting to remain lit, and marveled at the community's dedication. In her experience, it was peculiar for a man to even so much as pause to help another in trouble, let alone an entire village braving a tempest with ferocious winds and penetrating, ice-cold rain to do so. Everyone stood in muted silence as the men struggled to get to the man trapped beneath the fallen wood free.

Every grunt from the men, the soft crying of a child in the crowd, and the uneasy neighing of her horse echoed in her head as Adeline stood motionless. She'd been senseless to think she could help Ailesbury in any way. Her chest tightened in pain as a man slipped, his feet sinking into the mud as his side of the wooden wall fell.

"I canna believe the Beast of Faversham allowed such a thing ta happen—and ta Grovedale. It is a fair shame, it is," an elderly woman hissed to another woman next to Adeline. "If that not be grave enough, the man stalks the plant, push'n the men ta work e'er harder."

"Ye cannot be blame'n the Beast for this. He could not know what was ta happen." The woman pulled the crying toddler into her arms as they fell back into silence while they watched the rescue efforts.

The Beast of Faversham?

They could not be speaking of Lord Ailesbury. Sure, his body was marred, but that did not mean his soul was corrupted, as well. The earl was present…just as all the villagers were, putting forth his best effort to extract Grovedale from beneath the wood that trapped him.

"Must be awfully terrify'n for the lord," another whispered on Adeline's other side, but she did not remove her stare from the men before her. "The tragedy of lose'n his ma and pa in that fire, and now another—"

"It not be the same at all, Louisa," a man argued. "That fire kilt not only his sires but his servants and horses, too. The Beast be blessed ta have escaped with his life, scars or no."

Adeline focused on Lord Ailesbury, his voice rising above the din of the storm, calling for the men to work together. He'd removed his coat at some point, and the muscles of his broad shoulders flexed against the thin linen shirt he wore, wet and sticking to his back. The tendons in his neck strained as the group lifted again. His raw, unrestrained strength was utterly captivating.

With a collective grunt, the men heaved again, but only Lord Ailesbury's side moved, revealing a two-foot gap.

"Rathers!" Ailesbury shouted through gritted teeth. "Pull him free."

A young man, certainly a year or two younger than Adeline, crawled through the mud and slipped his hand under the wood. When Rathers yelled, two men stepped forward and pulled the young man back by his feet.

"Hurry." Ailesbury strained to hold the wooden wall up, his knuckles turning white and his eyes closed tightly as he concentrated. He could drop the wall and forever trap the man beneath. Adeline had never felt an ounce of the terror that surged through her in that moment.

Very likely, she'd never forget it.

A cheer erupted when the trapped man slid out behind Rathers, their hands clasped tightly.

Lord Ailesbury had saved the day!

The men dropped the wall, the wood letting out a groan as it settled into the muck created by the rain.

Adeline had been so intent on the scene before her, she hadn't realized her entire body trembled from the cold.

Men knelt around the injured man, but the earl remained separate from the crowd, pushing forward to congratulate the villagers who'd helped rescue Grovedale. Oddly, no one went to thank Lord Ailesbury, or so much as even looked in his direction to ask about his condition. The vast width and thickness of the wooden wall told Adeline it was heavy, indeed. If it weren't for the earl, Grovedale might have perished in the mud beneath.

Finally, Ailesbury turned toward the villagers but made no move to join them.

A little boy shrank back and began to cry when he saw the earl watching the group as they huddled around Grovedale. The boy's mother pulled the lad close and shushed him.

Several townsfolk cast nervous glances in the earl's direction before turning away, as if afraid to be caught gawking.

But then, a young girl escaped a woman's hold and rushed to Ailesbury—casting her thin arms about his legs. Adeline was too removed to note the girl's words but her beaming smile was enough.

Ailesbury responding frown also spoke volumes as the woman hurried over to collect the child, careful to keep her eyes trained on the ground and never meeting Lord Ailesbury's intense stare.

The realization struck Adeline then: the villagers

were terrified of Lord Ailesbury.

But, why?

Adeline had no time to consider the question because the earl scanned the crowd, his glare stopping on her.

In that moment, she wondered if it wouldn't have been wiser for her to fear Lord Ailesbury, as well—perhaps just a bit.

He cast a fearsome picture as he skirted the villagers and stomped in her direction, his narrowed glare keeping her rooted to where she stood.

CHAPTER 10

JASPER DIDN'T NOTICE the milling crowd who shrank away as he stalked toward the woman. He didn't pay any mind to the driving, bone-chilling rain that assaulted his face. He didn't so much as flinch when another thunderous boom shook the ground beneath his waterlogged Hessians.

In fact, the only thing Jasper saw was red.

Anger. Fury. All-out rage!

The hue that threatened to completely take over his vision was similar in shade to the color of Miss Adeline's riding habit…his *mother's* riding habit, the garment she'd worn on the morning of the day she passed in the stable fire—along with his father, their steward, and several other servants. Yet, in that moment, the habit was soaked clean through, darkening the material to a near onyx hue. Jasper had a difficult time comprehending the sheer weight of the gown as it hung on Miss Adeline.

Nevertheless, he held no compassion for her current circumstances: wet, cold, and shivering.

The bloody woman still held her head high, not an ounce of panic as he stalked toward her. People he'd known his entire life scattered when he walked toward them, even with a smile on his face; however, Miss

Adeline stood her ground…and *smiled* at him!

It was unfathomable she'd remained alive long enough to stumble upon Faversham Abbey. She had no notion of the danger she'd put herself in being at the plant, in this storm, surrounded by the villagers.

Or perchance it was Jasper who did not seek to subject her to the idle chatter of Faversham proper.

Either way, the closer he got to her, the more his irritation spiked, and the quicker the villagers dispersed until only a handful remained.

"What are you doing out here in the storm?" he barked over the sound of the growing tempest, now fully upon them. "You will catch your death."

She ignored his question; instead, she stepped forward and clasped his forearms. "You were magnificent, Lord Ailesbury," she commended, a new light filling her hazel eyes until they fairly glowed in the darkness. "The man, Emily's husband, certainly would have been crushed without your help."

"I asked what you are doing here." He paused, sucking in a deep breath, only to have it exhale in a rush. "It is not safe."

"Not safe?" A haze of confusion clouded her stare. "You worry about my safety, my lord. What of yours? You are the one who rushed into a collapsed building to single-handedly lift an entire wall off a trapped man with no regard for your own well-being."

"I did not single-handedly—" His words cut short when her brow rose as if challenging him to deny his own bravery, or dispute the outcome of this night had he not come immediately. "It matters naught who helped and who didn't, this is my plant. I am responsible for everyone who dedicates their time to its success."

"Come now." She shook her head, rain dripping down her face, plastering her long locks to her cheeks and neck. "That was about far more than mere responsibility."

Would he admit the overwhelming need to save Grovedale, his deep-rooted need to make certain the tragedy that'd taken his own parents did not happen to one of his servants? He'd been a young boy, but their death had altered his life in ways a child couldn't understand. But to lose a spouse? Jasper shuddered to think of the heartbreak Emily, his dedicated maid at the Abbey, would have endured had Grovedale not been rescued. Nor would he dwell on the repercussions within the village as a whole if more locals died because of Jasper and his family name.

Hell, Jasper had never forgiven himself for his lack of strength during that stable fire, but now he was a man. A man who'd worked tirelessly for years to build his strength so as not to ever fail another again.

No one under his protection would perish if Jasper had anything to say about it. Including the foolish woman before him, her body now wracked with shivers from the cold rain and heavy winds.

"We should return to the Abbey, immediately." Jasper didn't wait for her to answer, nor give any thought to the villagers departing without so much as a kind look in his direction. Had Miss Adeline noticed the group's outright fear of him? "I will collect my horse and assist you up onto yours. Remain here, I will return in a moment."

At his hard stare, she nodded.

Turning, Jasper made his way toward the side of the building where he'd tethered his steed, making certain to keep his distance from the remaining villagers. There was no need to draw attention to their strained relationship if Miss Adeline hadn't already taken note of the peculiar way the townsfolk avoided the Beast of Faversham.

"M'lord?" a thin voice called at his back.

Jasper's first instinct was to keep moving, collect

his horse, and be gone from the plant—Miss Adeline safely at his side. He had no interest in a confrontation with a villager regarding anything that'd happened that day. He only longed to return to the Abbey, be out of the cold, don dry clothes, and serve himself a tumbler of Scotch.

And so, Jasper lowered his head and continued toward his horse.

"Lord Ailesbury!" the man persisted.

Jasper slowed and turned toward the vaguely familiar voice. Grovedale walked—or rather hobbled—to keep up with Jasper's pace. Jasper stopped when he saw the man's struggles. He was injured and in need of a physician…and several days' rest.

"Grovedale. You should find your way home. I can have the cart and horses readied for your trip if needed." Jasper attempted to keep his stare focused on the man's face and not his clutched arm and lame leg—nor the blood slowly seeping through the man's trousers. "I will send the physician posthaste. And your wife, as soon I return to the Abbey."

"I—" The man's eyes clouded, though if they were true tears or only the runoff from the rain dripping down his face, Jasper was uncertain. "Thank ye, m'lord, for save'n me. I be eternally in your debt."

Grovedale lowered his head and placed his good arm across his chest, his hand clenched in a tight fist.

"No, it is I who owes you," Jasper countered. "I should have had those walls checked years—"

"No, m'lord." Grovedale vigorously shook his head. "It be me. I shouldn't have been work'n at all. Ye shut the plant down for a reason."

"Be that as it may, I am still responsible for your injuries. I will make certain the physician is at your disposal, and Emily has a fortnight off. And you can take as much leave as needed until you are recovered."

"But we can't be do'n that. We'll starve, m'lord."

Jasper slashed his hand through the air, halting the man's protest. "Everything will be taken care of, Grovedale. Rest, and keep Emily close. That is what I demand of you right now."

"Yes, m'lord." Grovedale bowed, taking a step back, bowing once more. His face contorted in pain the entire time. "Ye be too kind, m'lord."

"It is what any lord should do for his people," he countered. "Now, be off. Watson has arrived with the cart."

The servant turned slowly and hobbled back toward the waiting villagers, all avoiding Jasper, their backs to him as they greeted Watson and prepared to load Grovedale.

He'd told himself for years it was better this way. He was Lord Ailesbury. He was the master of Faversham Abbey. He was the owner of Home Works. There was no requirement that these people be his friends, or he theirs. Though that had never stopped the terrified, lonely little boy inside him from longing to return the relationship between his family and the people of Faversham to what it had once been—before the fire, the many deaths, and Jasper's disfigurement.

The rain had lessened at some point during his conversation with Grovedale, the winds even relenting slightly as the clouds parted overhead.

That did not decrease his need to see Miss Adeline home…err, to the Abbey, before she fell ill from the cold.

Jasper untethered his mount and turned to retrace his steps through the gathering mud to where she waited, except she wasn't where he'd left her. Instead, she was a few paces from where he and Grovedale had been speaking a moment before, only her triumphant smile at his bravery had disappeared. Her hand was now pressed to her chest, fingers splayed as her mouth hung open.

Shock? Amazement? Adoration?

He hadn't the slightest notion what expression she tried to convey—or, far worse, what she'd overheard during his conversation with Grovedale.

JASPER DISMOUNTED AT the front door of the Abbey, only pausing for a moment to see that a footman assisted Miss Adeline from her mare before he strode toward the house. He was a sopping, muddy, filthy mess, and she was little better. As they rode back in silence, chills had set in, making it increasingly difficult for him to keep his hold on the reins.

He could only imagine the struggle for her to remain in her sidesaddle, burdened with the weight of her saturated gown and the icy bite of the wind in her face.

The most outrageous occurrence rocked Jasper to his core.

He was angry—or *still* angry.

He hadn't felt such raw, powerful fury in many years. He'd truly only been overcome by this level of emotion twice: directly following his parents' deaths, and then again when his aunt had succumbed. Aunt Alice had been like a mother to him, and she'd been taken far too early for a woman as caring and alive as she.

On those two occasions, Jasper had been well aware what caused his shift in mood.

But, as he stalked into the foyer, he could not reconcile what had upset him so on this occasion.

Was his ire at Emily for offering the bloody riding habit for Adeline to wear?

Was he angry at Abbington's part in locating the woman's bow and quiver among her stowed belongings?

Did he resent his stable master's betrayal for having a horse saddled for her to ride?

Or, more pointedly, did his annoyance lay solely with himself for bringing the woman to Faversham Abbey in the first place?

Jasper wasn't certain how he'd expected his servants to react to their surprise guest, but catering to her every whim, even defying his orders, was not it at all.

Faversham was not a safe place for the likes of Miss Adeline, especially when the woman was hell-bent on finding trouble at every turn.

He growled as Abbington wrapped a blanket about his quaking shoulders at the same time his wife, Mrs. Hutchins, did the same for Adeline.

When had Jasper started thinking of the woman as simply Adeline?

She was still a stranger to him—and he to her.

"See that *Miss* Adeline is taken to her chambers immediately, and have dry, clean clothes brought for her." He addressed Abbington and his housekeeper, who no doubt watched his every move. "We cannot have her returning to London and her family ill."

Or have her stranded for a longer period of time at Faversham Abbey while she convalesced.

His feet sloshed in his Hessians as he stomped into the library, slamming the door behind him. The echo dared any of his most loyal servants to betray him again—or to so much as stray a single step from his commands.

Bloody damnation.

The woman was nothing but a distraction, a dangerous disruption to his orderly life.

Jasper poured himself a healthy tumbler of Scotch, emptied the glass in one swallow, and poured another before moving before the hearth. After only a moment of pacing, he tossed the blanket Abbington had wrapped around his shoulders to the lounge followed by his wet jacket. His shirt and trousers were also soaked through, but blessedly, the spirits had halted the worst of his shivers.

The energy he'd exerted while extricating Grovedale was enough to keep the worst of the cold at bay, and his clenched jaw stopped his teeth from chattering. Miss Adeline hadn't had the same adrenaline rush to keep her chills under control.

If anyone deserved to catch the ague, it was Jasper.

He'd brought the trouble into his normally peaceful and well-maintained home. It was his own fault that memories, longings, and guilt from his past assaulted him at every turn since the woman arrived. It had been years since he explored his unending guilt over his parents' deaths or allowed the all-consuming anger to take hold of him in such a way.

The carriage needed to be repaired with all due haste.

As soon as Watson returned from seeing Grovedale home, he would demand the servant work all evening—and into the night—to make certain Miss Adeline was on her way back to London at first light.

Jasper took a healthy swallow from his tumbler, welcoming the sting as it traveled down his throat and warmed his stomach further.

It was imperative that he suppress his anger and keep the beast that threatened to overtake him at bay. It would not be at Jasper's hand that the villager's suspicions were confirmed. He may appear the beast outwardly but he'd worked every day of his life to make certain that inside he was kind, compassionate, and ever the noble gentleman and lord.

One day, he had faith, his ugly mask would fall and his people would see the man beneath.

Today had not been that day, no matter the good Jasper did.

Tomorrow…tomorrow he would send Miss Adeline on her way, repair the damage to the gunpowder plant, announce his plans for expansion, and move to hire additional villagers at both his estate and Home Works.

Adeline would be gone, though forgotten was an entirely different matter.

Even in his current mood, Jasper could picture how she'd looked as she watched him earlier after Emily's husband had been pulled from the debris. There wasn't even a need to close his eyes. No, she was there, before him, as he stared into the open flames of the hearth.

Her hair had been tousled and tangled in wild abandon…something Jasper had gotten used to seeing. Gone were the perfectly curled and pinned tresses he'd witnessed in the dining hall that morning. Vanished was her assured nature after donning the scarlet riding habit as he'd admired her at the bottom of the stairs before their hunt. Her eyes had been alight with what? Fright, terror, pride, amazement, and…something bordering on affection? He must have been mistaken, catching a glimpse of her and infusing his own inner feelings onto her.

Truthfully, Jasper had been possessed by a sense of fright and terror when he agreed to allow her to hunt with him. That had swiftly changed to pride and amazement when she took down the first turkey with her superior skill at archery.

But affection?

It was an utterly foreign emotion to Jasper.

Certainly, he cared for his servants. He'd outright loved his aunt and uncle, and must have held the same feelings for his blooded parents, even though he'd been too young to truly understand the bond that existed between a boy and his family.

No, there had been no look of affection or

adoration.

It simply could not exist between the pair of them. Adeline belonged in London, and Jasper at Faversham Abbey.

It had been an act of selfishness that he'd brought her to the Abbey to begin with, but by no means could be *keep* her at Faversham.

Never should their paths cross again once she departed on the morrow.

CHAPTER 11

ADELINE STOOD INSIDE the library with her back pressed against the door, watching Lord Ailesbury pace back and forth before the fire as he downed yet another glass of what she could only imagine were spirits. He'd been so consumed with his musings, that he hadn't heard her slip into the room and close the door behind her.

The light from the hearth cast a shadow across the entire room as he pivoted once more and followed the same path he had several times earlier. His profile was to her, and Adeline took the time she had to explore the harsh line of his jaw, the aristocratic set of his nose, and his long, cocoa-brown hair. His garb was not that of an earl, but everything about the lord screamed wealth, power, and control. His stride was sure and solid. The sun-kissed, golden glow of his skin spoke to his many hours—and days—working out amongst his people…those same people who'd just as quickly turned their backs on him.

As he reached the far side of the room, he turned once more, his chin lowering, and his empty glass clutched tightly to his chest. This was the side of him that was at odds with everything she knew of the man thus far. Yes, his scars were not who he was, but from this angle, Ailesbury appeared alone, helpless, and adrift. His posture was not as rigid, his shoulder dipped slightly. His footfalls were not as precisely pronounced. He almost appeared fragile, as an infant did shortly after birth until they grew strong enough to hold their own head high and ultimately walk on their own.

Not an infant, but a bird with a clipped wing.

This man before her—his drive to help those around him, his need to care for all who called Faversham home, his reclusive nature—longed to soar. Something held him back, though, and it was not his injuries.

No, it had nothing to do with his outward self.

Suddenly, Lord Ailesbury paused, letting out a quiet sigh before closing his eyes and turning his stare to the ceiling above. His hand fell from his chest, the tumbler sliding from his grasp to the rug-covered floor before it rolled under the edge of the lounge, forgotten.

Adeline held herself back from going to him and wrapping her arms around him, doing all within her power to right the situation…every wrong done to him…anything that could bring him to the low point he was in at that moment.

Yet, she didn't move. She was an unwelcome guest in his home. No matter how wonderfully his servants treated her, Adeline suspected the earl only wanted her gone. Returned to London and her family. He would desire her nowhere near where she could bear witness to what transpired within Faversham Abbey.

She should flee, return to her chambers, and discard the wet riding habit for a clean, dry gown, putting as much distance between her and Lord Ailesbury as the large estate would allow. It was seemingly what he wanted and, surprisingly, Adeline realized she desperately wanted to please the man before her, even if that meant never seeing him again. He'd bidden her go to her room and change, yet she'd disobeyed him. It was the old Adeline resurfacing.

The young, impulsive, headstrong girl who'd arrived in Canterbury at twelve, and the same woman who'd departed the place nearly seven years later.

This was not the woman who'd been forced to stand back and watch as her best friend and brother found a love Adeline suspected would always be denied her. It was the broken woman who'd been made to sit back and watch as her father passed away, forever cast in the light of a stranger to his eldest daughter. Now, she was the woman who'd been charged with delivering her youngest sisters to boarding school because her mother barely found strength to leave her private chambers following the death of her mate and husband.

Only a day at Faversham Abbey, and Adeline had reverted to the selfish child she'd once been before loss and a brief glimpse of love had entered her life. Yes, she'd been an outsider, watching Theo and Alistair as they embarked on their journey to wedded bliss, but it had opened her eyes.

At Faversham, Adeline was faced with a man who'd seen true horror and devastation. She did not know the extent of his hardships, but what she'd overheard at the plant had been enough to allow her to see the folly of her recent actions.

A fire had taken Lord Ailesbury's parents and left him marred, forever burdened with the lasting scars of what had transpired. She sensed she knew him better than before, but also, not at all. Even his given name was still a mystery to her. Why did he keep himself secluded here at the Abbey, and what had happened after his parents' deaths? Surely, he must have been taken care of by someone other than servants, possibly sent away to school as she'd been—though for utterly opposite reasons.

She'd spoken of her father's death during their hunting excursion, yet he'd kept his own past close, refusing to speak about it with her. They were strangers, two people forced into one another's lives due to the storm. He hadn't sought her out, selected her because of some connection between them, nor had he given any impression that he'd been happy to welcome her as a guest into his home.

The fact was, she'd been forced upon him. And as a gentleman, Lord Ailesbury had taken the honorable path: offered her safe, dry lodging, ample food, and the promise of a repaired coach.

Adeline pulled the blanket more securely around her shoulders as her teeth threatened to chatter again. If only she could move closer to the hearth, gain a bit of the warmth offered by the roaring fire; however, she sensed Lord Ailesbury was in far greater need of the heat than she.

A loud crack of thunder rattled the windowpanes, and Ailesbury's eyes snapped open, their olive-green hue turning as vibrant as the lightning streak outside as they flashed in her direction.

"Lord Ailesbury—" Her fingers tightened their hold until her knuckles ached.

His glare narrowed on her as his shoulders straightened once more and he shifted to face her. His chin lifted at the same time his hands landed on his hips, and he frowned. For a brief second, Adeline could have sworn another battle raged in his eyes, as if the earl debated his next move until, ultimately, he held firmly to his anger.

He did not blink, did not shift his glare away from her or relax his posture as they stared at one another.

And Adeline held her breath, fearing if she made so much as the smallest movement, the spell freezing them both to their spots would evaporate, and Lord Ailesbury would demand she leave his library.

With agonizing slowness, his cold stare left hers and traveled down her body, the riding habit clinging to

Adeline's every curve. Leisurely, he took in the sight of her, his chilly glare melting as he once again stared her straight in the eyes.

He dared her to move.

He taunted her to speak.

He challenged her to so much as take the deep breath her aching lungs demanded.

The silence between them was louder than any tempest.

Lord Ailesbury held her stare, wordlessly demanding she turn and depart the room or face the consequences of her lack of action.

Yet, Adeline would not back down. She would not cower in fear and run for safety. She knew enough about the man before her to know he would never cause her injury or harm. There was nothing for Adeline to fear in the earl's presence.

Nothing about the man scared her, least of all his physical scars.

They did not influence her opinion of him in any way.

What did change everything was what she'd learned about his past.

Adeline hadn't any idea why she purposefully disobeyed his command and followed him into the library, silently closing them both in together…alone.

But at that precise moment, with the fire crackling in the hearth behind him and the storm subsiding outside, Adeline had no doubts why she'd come to this room—to this man.

They had lived a thousand lifetimes together in the last day.

She'd born witness to his commitment to his servants, his people, and his land.

He'd rescued her from the storm along that deserted road. He'd rushed to her aid when the windowpane shattered in the dining hall. He'd watched with a measure of pride as she'd shown him her skill with a bow. And she'd stood by with her own sense of pride as he saved Grovedale from certain death. She'd also had to stand by and watch the villagers treat him as if he were an outsider, a pariah, a man who did not belong on his own land.

And for what?

She'd wanted to demand answers of them all. She'd longed to rail against the injustice of it all. If the earl hadn't spotted her and quickly brought her back to the Abbey, Adeline might have confronted the lot of them—and given them the sharp reprimand and scolding they so richly deserved.

The blanket slipped from her shoulders, cascading down her body to pool at her feet, and Adeline stepped toward him.

One step.

Two steps.

Three.

Short, unhurried paces made difficult by the immense weight of the riding habit she wore.

How had she not noticed the nearly crippling heaviness of the garment before now?

Four steps.

Lord Ailesbury's stare shifted from cold and narrowed to widened confusion as he matched her step for step.

However, as she moved closer, he moved *away* until his shoulders pressed into the mantel above the hearth.

…as if he were *terrified* of her.

CHAPTER 12

AS IF BY some grand scheme concocted by a deity Jasper had no belief in—and likely one that cared not a whit for him—Miss Adeline Price not only stood before him but proceeded to walk his way. His entire body stiffened when the blades at his shoulders came into contact with the rough wood of the hearth mantel.

The blanket his housekeeper had set about the woman's shoulders lay forgotten by the door.

Adeline strode toward him, all confidence with a sensual sway to her hips.

Did she always saunter thusly?

Jasper wracked his memory in an attempt to determine how he hadn't noticed the woman's allure before this moment.

Certainly, he had not been completely unaware of Adeline's beauty.

However, finding a woman beautiful and longing to strip every inch of clothing from her body were indubitably different things. Only a moment before, he'd been questioning the look he'd seen in her eyes outside the plant—convinced he'd misread everything he'd seen.

Jasper hadn't misread anything. All the confirmation he needed was right before him in

Adeline's stance, mirroring his from a moment before. Uplifted chin, penetrating glare, and purposeful air. Those were his mechanisms...his tricks...to send her fleeing the room in fear of what the Beast of Faversham would do next.

The foolish woman had used his intimidating position against him, driving *Jasper* back in fear.

But what did he fear, precisely?

What *didn't* he fear, was a far more appropriate question.

He feared his need to have Adeline at Faversham Abbey, even when she was but a stranger who'd been stranded alongside the road. He feared his intense reactions to her—both anger and lust—and the control he felt slipping with each breath. And what he feared most of all...watching the woman depart Faversham, which would happen at first light. It had to happen. There was no other choice for either of them.

The sooner, the better...for all concerned.

The last thing Jasper wanted was the woman overhearing something she had no business knowing. Or asking questions on subjects he had no answers for.

She stalked toward him, the shadow cast by his body and the fire shrouding her in mystery though her eyes held none. Suddenly, she was the hunter and he the prey. Why did that suit him so?

Halting several paces from him, Adeline bent at the waist and slid her hand under the lounge. When she straightened once more, a smirk upon her plump lips, she held his forgotten tumbler. For the life of him, Jasper could not remember setting the thing down, let alone it having rolled under the lounge.

She set the glass on the low table before the chaise and returned her stare to his as she continued toward him.

Belatedly, Jasper realized his folly in not escaping when she'd been preoccupied retrieving the glass.

"May I ask you a question, Lord Ailesbury?" Her voice was so soft it could barely be heard over the crackling fire at his back.

"Jasper," he mumbled.

"Pardon?" Her brow furrowed, and her pace slowed.

"My name, it is Jasper." It had only been with Adeline's arrival that his servants took to calling him anything but his given name.

"Jasper." The single word dripped like honey from her lips, the corner of her mouth notching up. "Jasper," she repeated, her hooded, hazel eyes scanning him from head to toe as he had with her after realizing he wasn't alone in the room.

No one in his employ spoke his name with such reverence.

At that moment, he thought he would answer her any question—travel the earth ten times over, journey to the sun, and die of thirst in the Sahara, if only to find the information she longed to know.

"Tell me what happened to your family," she whispered. "The villagers…they spoke of unimaginable things."

A jolt of pain so powerful he nearly fell to his knees spiked his chest, and his breath left him in a rush. It was something he and his servants lived every day knowing, yet never spoke of. It was the cloud that had descended on all of Faversham all those years ago, one that had never lifted, never cleared, never faded. They'd all gotten so used to the darkness and their beast, that no one sought the light any longer. At least not since Jasper's aunt had died. She'd been the only spot of sunshine in all of Faversham, never allowing her shine to dim no matter the mourning that continued around her.

"Please, tell me what happened to your parents." Adeline moved toward him again but stopped when

Jasper flinched. "Who raised you? Why are you here, in this huge home, all by yourself?"

Why had he thought the woman would come and go, letting him escape being forced to face all these question—the heart of his past? Though Jasper was certain his heart had stopped beating when he was unable to save his parents, their servants, and the horses from the fire that had consumed the Faversham stable.

He didn't want to discuss this, especially with Adeline. It was a burden he never would have wished to place on her shoulders, for it was his and his alone. Yet, her concerned stare drew the words from him.

"My mother and father perished in a fire that claimed the lives of several Faversham servants along with a half-dozen horses." When she remained silent, and whatever vice had held tight to his chest a moment before began to lessen, allowing him to breathe, he continued. "My paternal uncle and his wife came to the Abbey and saw to my upbringing."

Not a hint of pity or judgment shadowed her face. "Your scars..." With each word she spoke, Adeline kept her eyes on his. "They are from the fire."

No question, meaning no denial was needed on his part. "Yes."

"How old were you?"

"Twelve." Jasper swallowed to keep the sob within him, not daring to say another word, lest his voice tremble as much as his body did.

He'd spoken enough, shared more than he planned, but he would comment no more on the subject.

Jasper would not confess that it was all his fault: the fire, the deaths, and the continuing distrust of the villagers. If he hadn't had a habit of staying up late, reading by candlelight in the rafters, his parents would never have come looking for him in the stables. Yet, that night it hadn't been his candle to set the blaze, nor had he been in the stables when the fire commences. Though, from the reaction of the servants, Jasper might as well have been completely to blame.

"I'm so sorry for your loss." She took the final step toward him and reached out to take his hand. Her skin was soft, and warm, despite her still damp clothing. She must have removed her gloves when they returned. Jasper hadn't noticed. What he did know was that her delicate caress was not meant for him. In no realm of possibility had Jasper done enough to deserve the innocent, pure touch of an unblemished lady. "I cannot imagine—"

He cleared his throat, shrugging away her hold on his hand. "Let us not imagine it at all."

He turned toward the hearth, his forehead only inches from the mantel, but the warmth was welcome. The look of injury certain to overtake her at his refusal to speak further on the subject was not something Jasper wanted to see, let alone attempt to withstand.

Something about Adeline had Jasper silently vowing to not let her down. He didn't want to disappoint her, but he had no choice but to turn away from her. It was for her own good, even if she didn't understand.

"Your aunt and uncle are kind people?"

"Were," he corrected. "And yes, they were the kindest, most caring relatives an orphaned child could ever hope for. They made certain I wasn't alone and saw to my education."

"What University did you attend?"

That she'd latched on to the change in topic both surprised and unsettled him, bringing him around to face her. "My educational needs were attended to here at the Abbey."

Adeline retreated as a spark of unease filled her eyes at his harsh tone. A measure of guilt coiled around his chest. It was not her fault that the mere thought of his past filled him with an overpowering need to escape, to flee, to…hide.

"They passed away years ago—my aunt when I was seventeen, and my uncle when I was twenty-two." He pushed through the pain, needing to repair the damage he'd done a moment before. "They prepared me well for my responsibilities as the lord and master of Faversham Abbey. I have everything I need, and seek to provide well for those who depend on the Ailesbury Earldom."

It was Adeline who turned away next, pacing to the lounge. She seemed to debate something in her head before deciding there was no harm and lowering herself to sit. She crossed her ankles and slid them under her as she folded her hands in her lap. It was all a dramatic show, the stilted conversation grounding to a halt as she arranged her skirts and refolded her hands.

Too late, Jasper realized the woman was making herself comfortable as if she expected the candid conversation to continue, and her time at Faversham was little more than an afternoon social call. Adeline seemed to forget that she still wore her borrowed wet habit and that her hair hung loosely down her back and over her shoulders.

"What of your responsibilities in parliament?" she asked.

It was difficult for a man to assume such duties when all his time was spoken for in Kent. "I have yet to accept my seat as there are many things that keep me otherwise engaged here in the country." She seemed to allow his words to sink in. "I have always meant to one day travel to London. However, the—"

"You've never been to London?" she asked.

The truth of the matter was far more shocking than she knew. "Since my parents' deaths, I have not traveled more than an hour's ride from Faversham Abbey."

Her mouth fell open, and her shoulders tensed.

"What of holiday trips?" He shook his head. "Meetings with advisors, vendors, and clients for Home Works?" Again, he gave his head a firm shake.

"My father's solicitor, Barclay, visits Faversham twice a year. He handles outside investors and the export of gunpowder from the plant."

"Have you never been to a proper London ball? The opera or playhouse?"

"No, I fear I am a mere country squire who has no knowledge of town life."

"May I ask why?" She stared up at him from her seat on the lounge, but her eyes held no pity, only interest.

"At first, it was to keep me from the prying eyes of those who would gossip and speak disparagingly about me until my burns healed. However, with time came the scars, the villagers' gossip, and my aunt's never-ending need to protect the boy she loved as a son."

"And so you rarely left Faversham."

"And so, I *never* left Faversham Abbey or Ailesbury land until after my aunt's death."

"Not so far as even the village?"

He shook his head. "No, though I tried once. I'd heard from Mrs. Hutchins that the merchant in town was hosting a grand Christmastide gathering at his home. I hid in the stables until my Aunt Alice and Uncle Bartholomew had retired and took to their room. I slipped from my hiding spot and ran toward the village, or at least the direction I assumed the village lay in, but I was met by nothing but never-ending fields, rolling meadows, and eventually, a creek. I was cold, exhausted, and hungry by the time I finally found my bed at daybreak."

Jasper snapped his mouth shut before admitting he'd cried himself to sleep—and then lied to his aunt about how he'd caught the cold that plagued him for an entire fortnight.

"I know now that even on that wild, reckless night, I never left Ailesbury land."

"I am certain they only sought to protect you," she murmured.

"Of that, I have no doubt." Especially after learning the villagers had taken to calling him the Beast of Faversham.

A light knock sounded at the door.

"Come in," Jasper commanded.

"Watson, my lord," Abbington announced, stepping aside to allow the Faversham stable master into the room before departing.

"Watson." Jasper clasped his hands behind his back, relishing the warmth on his bare palms. "I hope Grovedale arrived home safely."

"Yes, m'lord," Watson said, glancing at Adeline and quickly back to Jasper, uncertain if he should acknowledge the woman's presence—alone—in the library with his master. "And the physician quickly after. The man be mostly unscathed, just sore."

"Very good." It was the best news Jasper had heard all day.

"But I be here about Miss Adeline's coach." He risked another glance to where Adeline remained seated and quiet. "Good eve, Miss Adeline."

Adeline smiled, and Watson blushed.

"Good evening to you, too, Watson." Jasper marveled at her decorum as she nodded a greeting to his servant. If there had been tea, she would have poured the bloody man a steaming cup. "Many thanks for seeing the man home. I hope Emily arrived at her husband's side, as well."

"Of course," Watson stammered.

"You were saying, Watson?" Jasper asked, aiming to recapture the man's attention. But when Watson looked back at his master, Jasper was certain Watson had forgotten what he'd come to tell him. "The coach?"

It was the only prodding needed as Watson nodded vigorously and refocused on Jasper. "Yes, me apologies. Miss Adeline's coach canna be repaired—" At Jasper's scowl, Watson collected himself and rearranged his thoughts. "What I mean ta say, is it be much longer ta fix it, and even then, it be likely the coach would break down again afore reach'n London."

"Oh, no," Adeline protested, jumping to her feet. "I must return, or my brother will think something awful has happened to me."

For the first time since her arrival, the thought struck Jasper that the proper thing to do would have been to send a servant to London, even with the storm, with word of Adeline's safety and the repairs needed for the carriage. Instead, he'd thought only of making certain she found refuge at the Abbey, without thought of her family's concern.

ADELINE WELCOMED THE servant's intrusion, yet she did not relish the news he'd brought. Her carriage was beyond repair, or at least it could not be mended at Faversham Abbey. Watson's news should have filled her with a sense of helplessness. Instead, she only thought of more time with Lord Ailesbury—Jasper. Eventually, it would be necessary for her to find her way back to London and her family, but a few more days' respite was certainly not all bad.

After the storm had passed and the roads dried, she would buy passage on the mail coach, much like she'd done to come to Canterbury that first time. Certainly, Alistair could not object to her making the journey alone with only her drive and maid, though she hoped Jasper would allow her to borrow the funds for the fare.

To think he'd lost both his parents at the same age Adeline had been cast from her family's home and sent to a school where she hadn't known a soul. At least her family had been alive and whole. The same was not true for Jasper.

"She and her maid will take my traveling coach," the earl announced, brushing his hands together as if all had been resolved and the remedy was best for everyone.

Yet, his proclamation meant she'd likely be packed up and shoved off toward home at first light. God, Adeline glanced about the room until her gaze settled on a small clock on the table by the windows. Seven o'clock…in the evening.

A meal would likely be served shortly, and then she'd be sent to her chambers for the night, that is if Jasper didn't demand she dine there alone as she was still outfitted in the damp, borrowed riding habit. She'd paused briefly before sitting on the lounge, worried the water from her skirts would damage the fabric of the furniture, but ultimately, she'd decided her skirting was not saturated enough to cause lasting injury.

"Wonderful, m'lord," Watson replied with a curt bow to Ailesbury and then Adeline, where she still stood.

"Wait," Adeline said, stepping away from the lounge. "If you have not traveled beyond the village, how can you be certain your carriage will not suffer the same fate as mine?"

Watson chuckled, and Jasper frowned as she looked between the two men.

The servant spoke first, "Because, m'lord maintains his carriages hisself. He not be overlook'n anythin', I can say that for certain."

"He does?" Adeline asked, turning back to Jasper. "That is very interesting. I was aware you owned the plant but—"

"Oh, he be do'n far more than that, miss," Watson said in a conspiratorial tone, leaning in close to Adeline.

"My master looks after the livestock, the crops, and all the repairs—both here and in the village."

Yet, Adeline had witnessed the villagers turning away from him after he'd risked his own safety to save Grovedale.

"Watson." The warning in Jasper's tone was similar to when he'd caught her at the plant. "As I was saying, ready the carriage for Miss Adeline and her maid. Maxwell can ride up top with George to London. They will leave at first light and arrive with the noonday sun."

The smile fell from Adeline's face, and her spirits dipped. She would see no further reprieve, gain no more time with Jasper.

"And, as Miss Adeline has voiced concern, I think it best I accompany them to town and the safety of her brother's townhouse." The man did not so much as smile at his news, his mouth drawing into a straight, serious line.

"You do not have to do that," Adeline countered. "I am certain we shall make the journey without incident."

She would never insist he make the trip to London with her; never expect him to leave his home, his duties, his people to make certain she arrived safely. The prospect of hours nestled in the closed carriage, no one but Jasper and Poppy for company, should excite her after thinking she'd be departing Faversham and would never see the man again. Yet, the idea of Jasper in London terrified her.

He'd lived a sheltered existence at the Abbey. Something he was accustomed to.

Things were not the same in London. People gossiped in parlors, in ballrooms, at the opera, at the playhouse, in the parks, in the gardens...and most never even bothered to lift their fan to hide it.

"It would assuage my gentleman's honor to know you made the journey safely," Jasper said as he moved to the sideboard and poured a clear liquid into another polished, glass tumbler. "We shall leave at daybreak, and I shall return not long after nightfall."

The words were spoken low, as if he were reassuring himself that the decision to accompany her was not the grand mistake Adeline feared it would be.

Lord Ailesbury punctuated the decision by throwing his head back and swallowing the liquid he'd poured from the sideboard.

His resolve instilled a measure of confidence in Adeline at Jasper's plan.

Abbington stepped into the room once more as Watson bowed and made his departure.

"Dinner, my lord," the man announced.

"I will take my meal in my room, Abbington." Jasper set his glass back on the table. "Please see that Miss Adeline eats her fill. I am certain she is ravenous after our long, eventful day."

He stepped before her, made to take her hand, but paused when he seemed to remember her fingers were bare. Instead, he issued a quick bow and turned to leave the room.

"Until the morrow, Miss Adeline," he called as he crossed the threshold.

She gave Abbington a weak smile as he gestured for her to proceed him from the room, following in Lord Ailesbury's wake.

Adeline was most certainly, positively, undoubtedly starving—but not for any food to be had at Faversham Abbey. Her cheeks heated at the thought, and she ducked her head as she passed the butler to hide her flaming face.

CHAPTER 13

ADELINE STRETCHED HER arms above her head and arched her back with a low groan, careful not to knock into Poppy, who slumbered on the seat next to her. The maid had been like a hawk the entire journey to London, completely at odds with her less than attentive demeanor while at Faversham Abbey.

And what a comfortable jaunt it had been. Jasper's traveling coach was as he'd proclaimed, well-maintained and lavish, with an even, smooth ride to match—so far superior to her own family's carriage she might as well have been riding in a market cart before. Now, she had the sense she traveled like a queen—or at least a princess. As they'd rolled through the small towns on their way from Kent to London, people had stopped to gawk and wave as they passed. Young children dropped whatever they held and ran alongside, shouting their hellos.

If Alistair were in possession of such a fine conveyance, Adeline would endeavor to spend more time traveling…to Somerset, Essex, Bath, Dover, and, oh, certainly a trip to Kent. She would visit her sisters at Miss Emmeline's School each and every month, without fail.

Images of the man sitting across from her invaded

her sweet fantasy. Would she long to stop at Faversham Abbey, as well?

She glanced to where he sat across from her, his scowl focused out the window as they entered London proper. When he met her in the foyer at the Abbey, prepared to depart, she'd been taken aback by what she saw. Gone was his casual appearance as he'd oiled and tied back his dark hair with a shiny black ribbon, his boots were polished until they shone, his coat and neckcloth—while outdated by society standards—were clean, pressed, and well-tailored. His trousers were not as form-fitting as was commonplace among the London *ton*, but they accentuated his muscular thighs. The height of his collar and the tie of his cravat hid the worst of his scars, but still Adeline could see them below his ear and at his cheek.

To her chagrin, Jasper—err, Lord Ailesbury—could walk into any Bond Street shop or stroll the rows at Hyde Park, and no one would think anything of it. His aristocratic nose, hard jawline, and reserved arrogance were the makings of a most sought after lord.

Bond Street and Hyde Park were one thing...the Melton horde was another. With eight siblings, Adeline could never accurately predict what they would say or do. Thankfully, Arabella and Ainsley were in Canterbury, and Adeline's mother hardly left her rooms. But that still left all four of her brothers, Alistair, Abel, Alfred, and Adrian, and her two sisters, Adelaide and Amelia. Plus, Theodora... Adeline could not forget her dearest friend-turned-family-member. Part of her argued she should inform Jasper what was to come once they arrived at her family's home. Although another part of her—a far more insistent part—suspected that if he knew, he'd likely push her from the moving carriage as it rolled past her family townhouse and hurry back to the Abbey as quickly as he could.

She refused to dwell on why she cared so much

about her family's opinion of the earl.

He'd merely rescued her from the storm, provided shelter and food until it passed, attempted to repair their family coach, and now returned her to the loving embrace of her kin.

Simple. Uncomplicated. And unquestionably noble of Lord Ailesbury.

Unfortunately, in Adeline's mind, nothing about Jasper was simple or uncomplicated—though she never doubted his noble intent.

Certainly, it was her actions and thoughts that were not quite so pure.

Her skin grew warm every time she thought of him rescuing Grovedale from harm.

A tingle shot through her each time she pictured him in his library, pacing before the fire, with the light making his shirt all but transparent. His corded muscles, his broad shoulders, his powerful stride…then it had all broken down when he'd dropped his tumbler and allowed his head to fall backwards as his eyes closed.

It had been meant to be a private moment. Had he been reflecting on the past? Relieved about the present? Or dreading the future?

Adeline did not know, nor had she asked. What she was certain of, was that she could have stood there, her back pressed against the closed door, and watched him in his private musings all night—and possibly into the next day.

As they traversed the congested London streets on their way to her family home, Adeline noted a transformation in the man sitting across from her. He no longer looked bored nor irritated. His pensive scowl gradually altered to a look of utter disbelief—he was enthralled with the scene outside his coach. They rolled down the wide street, taking their place in the slow-moving line of coaches and horsemen, no one paying them any mind. It was far different than the fascinated looks they'd received as they traveled through the remote countryside.

Adeline glanced out her window, attempting to see the London streets from Jasper's eyes as if she were seeing it all for the first time.

Women promenaded down the walk on the arms of finely dressed gentlemen, with their servants following, their arms heavy with their masters' Bond Street purchases. A shopkeeper swept the wooden walk outside his shop and waved to a man on horseback. A cart, loaded precariously with fruits and vegetables for the market, careened to the left to avoid a man who stepped into the street without first looking. The sharp shrillness of a child's scream drew Adeline's attention to a mother and son, standing outside Samson's Ices, the babe pulling and straining toward the shop and the delights within.

"My aunt, Alice, said my parents would bring me to London with them when I was a babe," Jasper said, sitting back in his seat and turning toward her. His unexpected words startled her—he'd been silent most of the trip, even dozing for a while. "However, I remember nothing about the city or our time here."

His stare turned hooded, and Adeline wondered if his thoughts had traveled to his deceased parents or his aunt, whom he spoke of with such reverence and kindness it was as if she were the only mother he knew. Yet, he hadn't been a babe when his parents died— twelve is young adulthood. Adeline had traveled to Canterbury all on her own by mail coach at the same age.

"London can be overwhelming and stiflingly grand if one is not versed in city life, my lord." She added the *my lord* in preparation for the time to come. She needed to keep in mind that Jasper was only the man who'd stumbled upon her unusable carriage and offered assistance, he was nothing more to her. He could be nothing more. "I have found that one either falls in love with the hustle and bustle of London, or they depart and return only when forced."

His brow drew low as he allowed that to sink in. When he remained silent, and her maid, Poppy, began to stir, Adeline sat back against the velvet cushion.

All too soon, the carriage shifted, indicating they'd turned off the main street and onto the lane that led to her family townhouse. There was no time left to warn him about her peculiar family, nor her overbearing eldest brother. There was no time to make apologies for anything that might spring from her siblings' mouths.

There was no time to even so much as tamp down her nerves because the traveling coach swayed once more as it turned into the rounded drive of the Melton Townhouse and drew to a stop.

CHAPTER 14

Jasper took a deep breath, begging his heart to cease its racing and the unease that coursed through him to vanish. He would only see that Adeline made it inside safely, her belongings unloaded and returned to her home, and then he would be on his way back to Faversham Abbey. Simple, uncomplicated—certainly the courteous thing to do in such a situation.

Or, at least that's what he'd chanted to himself the previous night as he'd tossed and turned, dwelling on the fact that come morning light, he'd be trapped in an enclosed coach with the woman who either reduced him to a fumbling mess or incited his anger every time they shared the same space. The chant had not disappeared during their long day of travel, either; it had only been reduced to a silent plea that rattled around inside of him, causing his head to pound.

Glancing out the window once more, his coach pulled to a stop outside a modest townhouse, as the door sprang open and several footmen ran forth. His driver, George, hadn't even disembarked his perch before he was greeted by a man in cream and blue garb. The sheer number of servants exiting the house, all dressed in the same attire, had Jasper praying that departing his carriage would be unnecessary. Certainly, coming confrontation unnecessary.

"I will remain with the carriage, m'lord," his servant said with a gentle tone. "Miss Adeline be a nice miss. I be sure her family be likewise."

Very well, Jasper thought.

There was no need to turn tail and run. Even George had faith in him.

He moved from his place by the carriage and held out his arm. Adeline responded by placing her hand in the crook of his elbow. All he could think about as he stared at her hand on his arm was the feeling of her bare hand from the night before—and how he'd pulled away far too quickly.

All Jasper had need to do, was explain to Adeline's guardian the irreparable damage that had been done to his carriage. Yes, the mechanics of it were simple enough to explain. Also, his presence in London was understandable. What gentleman of worth would send a woman off in a carriage alone when the risk of injury— or even possibly death—was great?

His carriage could have been set upon by highwaymen.

The coach might have thrown a wheel, or one of the horses suffered a lame leg.

Miss Adeline could have fallen ill during her travels due to her time in the storm at Faversham.

They were all valid concerns.

Jasper repeated these rationalizations in his head over and over as they started toward the front door.

"Do strive to become less tense, my lord," Adeline whispered with a smirk.

At her words, his shoulders only stiffened more. It had been many, many, *many* years since he'd put himself in a position to meet strangers. While his aunt had seen to new tutors on a regular basis, they were well-informed by the time they arrived at Faversham Abbey of Jasper's condition—his scars, as it were—and they never appeared affected or taken aback by his injuries. Even the villagers had grown accustomed to his appearance and rarely shied away from him. Though never did they seek him out or endeavor to gain his notice.

But strangers?

Not only those he did not know, but also people who meant a great deal to Adeline…

That should be of no consequence to Jasper; however, for some reason, it was a heavy burden to carry.

What if they thought him a beast due to his visible scars? What if they determined he'd caused harm to Adeline? Or worse yet, what if they recoiled in fear and threw him from their house without a word, leaving him with no choice but to return to the safety of Faversham Abbey?

That was exactly what he'd hoped for only moments before.

Lifting his chin, Jasper stared straight ahead as they crossed the threshold into her home.

He'd dealt with the jeers of the village children, he'd overcome the shame when villagers avoided him, and he'd even been able to look past Adeline's first reaction to his scarred appearance. Certainly, her family's opinion of him was of no consequence.

"Good day, Donovan," Adeline greeted the man who'd instructed the footman outside.

"Lovely to have you home, Miss Adeline," he replied with a curt bow before closing the door in their wake.

"Always lovely to be under my brother's roof," she retorted.

When the man's solemn expression hinted at amusement, Jasper sensed there was a private jest between the pair he was unaware of.

"Donovan, may I introduce Lord Ailesbury." She

glanced up at Jasper through lowered lids before turning back to the man. "Lord Ailesbury, this is the Melton butler, Donovan. He takes great care to keep all of us under control so as not to anger my dear brother."

At that, the man did openly smile, bringing his hand to his mouth with a cough to cover the chuckle that nearly escaped him.

"Lord Ailesbury." The butler nodded in greeting. "I cannot speak to keeping Miss Adeline—or her siblings—out of trouble, but there has not been a Melton child lost on my watch."

Both Adeline and the butler laughed softly before Jasper noticed her posture straighten and her eyes scan the foyer—the empty entryway.

Peculiar, seeing as how Jasper expected to find her brother waiting for them, especially with Adeline having been delayed over a day at Faversham. Was the family not worried about her whereabouts?

Adeline released Jasper's arm and set her hand on her hip as her toe began tapping on the polished floor.

"Out with you!" she commanded after a moment, and Jasper turned his attention to the area surrounding him.

Besides him, Adeline, and the butler, there was no one else nearby.

Jasper inhaled deeply and held his breath as he listened.

Nothing.

Not a sound could be heard in all the household, which struck Jasper as odd with so many family members in residence. It would be nearly impossible to quiet his own home to this extent, and it was only him and a handful of servants.

"Do not make it necessary for me to find you." Her stern tone had Jasper on edge as she tapped her foot several more times and let out an exasperated huff.

He'd not known her long, but he suspected her

irritation was a ruse.

Finally, her frown turned to a smile as three identical heads of light brown hair popped around the jamb of an open door. Three sets of widened hazel eyes showing themselves.

Jasper would be a fool not to notice the resemblance as the trio stepped fully into the foyer.

Adeline's siblings—or, at least three of them.

"Lord Ailesbury," she said, a spot of merriment in her tone. "May I introduce Mr. Alfred Price, Mr. Adrian Price, and Miss Amelia Price? As you can see, my father had a fondness for names starting with *A*."

Calling them *children* seemed off as two were nearly out of the schoolroom by Jasper's estimation. Even the youngest was not far behind.

"It is an honor to make your acquaintance." Jasper bowed to Miss Amelia first, and then before both boys. "Your sister has shared much about you."

Three identical brows arched in question, and the group focused once more on their sister.

"She didn't tell you about Adrian's tendency for sweets, did she?" the eldest boy, Alfred, asked. His intense scrutiny said that Jasper's answer held much importance.

"Of course, she would never share such a private matter," Jasper confided.

"What about Amelia's habit of taking jaunts about the house in her sleep?" He elbowed his sister in the side with a chuckle.

"I do not—" The girl at his side shrieked as her face blossomed with embarrassment, a mirror image of her older sister, though her hair was shorter and her complexion paler.

"A gentleman would never speak of such a thing, and neither would a proper lady," he chastised the boy, yet kept his tone light. "And your sister, Miss Adeline, is undoubtedly a proper lady."

"Where is Alistair?" Adeline cut in, stopping the banter before someone's feelings were injured.

Jasper hadn't any notion what it was like to have siblings—younger or older—but he could sense how teasing could easily get out of hand.

The trio looked between one another, their faces draining of the joy they'd had at seeing their sister safely home.

It was the youngest boy who spoke, the older two siblings avoiding Adeline's stare. "Alistair and Theodora are waiting for you in the study. Brother is awfully cross that you dallied on your way home. I dare say you—"

Adrian's voice stopped as Adeline pushed past him and started out of the foyer and down an empty hallway.

Jasper only paused a moment before hurrying to catch up with her. If her brother were vexed at Adeline's tardiness, it was his fault. He'd been the one to send his sister out into the England countryside in a decrepit carriage. If the man did not see that and still needed someone to cast the blame on, Jasper would take it. He'd been waylaid by the storm and unable to repair Adeline's carriage.

Either way, Adeline was not to blame for any of this, and Jasper would be damned if he'd allow her to be punished for something not in her control.

CHAPTER 15

ADELINE DID NOT slow for Donovan—or Jasper. But she knew both followed as she stormed toward her brother's study—the butler because it was his duty to announce her arrival, which would not happen. And Jasper because she'd become very familiar with the heaviness of his footfalls. Though his pursuit did not slow her down either.

Pushing the door open, Adeline sent it slamming against the wall, eliciting a shriek from Theo as she jumped from her seat on the lounge, dropping the book she'd been reading to the floor at her feet. Adeline's anger subsided slightly when her friend—and now sister-in-law—smiled and rushed to her.

Their embrace was as it always was: genuine.

Much like everything about the woman before her.

Theo pulled away, bringing Adeline farther into the room.

"I am overjoyed to see you are safe," Theo gushed, clutching Adeline's hand. "I was ever so worried, but I see there was naught to fret over as you are home and in one piece. Isn't that right, Alistair?"

Adeline gave her friend's hand a tight squeeze, signaling that Adeline was truly fine and was prepared to handle whatever mood Alistair was in before stepping away to face her brother.

Alistair glared at her, his lips flattened and his hands folded on the desk he sat behind. His posture and stare were meant to intimidate her; however, Adeline had done nothing wrong. In fact, she'd been put in jeopardy because of him.

"You are a day late arriving home, Adeline," he said, staring down his nose at her, which she could only assume was made difficult by his seated position. "I gave you leave to spend one night at Miss Emmeline's School, but that would have seen you home yesterday. Where have you been?"

Adeline crossed her arms over her chest and matched his glare with her own, but she refused to give any explanation as to her whereabouts after leaving Arabella and Ainsley at Miss Emmeline's School.

"Theodora—with the help of Lady Josie and Lady Georgina—have worked tirelessly in preparation for your twenty-first birthday celebration tomorrow eve. They have been worried sick that something dreadful happened to you." Alistair sighed, and the fight drained from him. Could it be that he wasn't angry with her, only concerned over her safety? "But that is neither here nor there. You are home"—he took in her appearance from head to toe—"and you seem to be in as much the same condition as when you left."

Same condition as when she left?

Certainly not. So much had changed. She'd met Jasper, hunted for true game, witnessed the rescue of a man in peril, and survived a six-hour journey in the confines of a coach with the Beast of Faversham.

Conditions had changed greatly in the last several days.

Finally, the news sank in. Birthday celebration? "My birthday is not for another fortnight." She glanced at her brother as he sat back in his chair and then she looked to Theo, who could barely contain her smile.

"If she had planned it for the actual day of your birth, you would have expected it, and the surprise would have been ruined."

"One could say the surprise has been ruined anyways," she mumbled.

"Be that as it may," Alistair countered. "Theo and your friends—though for the life of me I cannot comprehend why they all are so dedicated to you—have been planning this celebration for months, and I will not allow anything to go awry."

Adeline wanted to inquire if that was because it was *her* special day, or if because Alistair would do all in his power to keep from letting his wife down.

Odd that even if it were due to his commitment to Theo, it did not cause any irritation to bubble up within Adeline. A year prior, her brother's attention and dedication to anyone besides her would have caused Adeline great hurt. At some point, that had changed. It may have been when she truly realized the love Alistair held for Theo, or it could have been the passing of her father. She was uncertain which, but it was a welcome change.

An unburdening of sorts.

"Come, sit, and I will tell you all about what we have planned for—" Theo's words cut off as she focused on something—or someone—over Adeline's shoulder.

Alistair's stare also went to the threshold of the room.

Jasper… Adeline had nearly forgotten he'd followed her down the hall.

Her brother slowly leaned forward and pushed to his feet, his stare now narrowed on the door behind Adeline.

"Alistair, allow me to introduce Lord Ailesbury," Adeline said loudly in an attempt to remove some of the attention from Jasper and return it to her. "Lord

Ailesbury, this is my brother, Lord Melton—or plain Alistair, as we call him."

"Lord Melton will do," Alistair growled.

Adeline had the urge to step in front of Jasper, blocking him from view. It was a ludicrous notion as he was easily two times her size.

"Lord Melton." Jasper stepped into the room with obvious disregard for his own safety. "I am sorry to announce that it is my fault Miss Adeline was delayed in her return to London."

Alistair frowned.

Adeline never should have been so foolish as to allow Jasper to escort her in from the coach.

"Dear brother." She turned on her most charming smile. "There was a grand tempest in Kent, and my carriage broke down. Maxwell attempted to repair it, but the wind and rain made it impossible to see what the problem was."

"I was traveling home and stumbled upon Miss Adeline's carriage. I offered her and her servants shelter from the storm at my home, Faversham Abbey," Jasper continued, moving farther into the room. "I'd hoped to have the conveyance repaired and get your sister safely on her way home with all due haste; unfortunately, the damage to the carriage exceeded my original estimation."

Alistair looked between her and Jasper before glancing at his wife for direction.

That was a new occurrence. It was rare that her brother paused to think before scolding and punishing Adeline for whatever he perceived she'd done.

"When our carriage could not be mended, Lord Ailesbury offered the use of his traveling coach," Adeline continued. "It was very kind of him."

"It was my duty as a gentleman," Jasper said from behind her.

Adeline kept her stare trained on her brother,

trying to assess his reaction to Lord Ailesbury's presence. He eyed the earl for a moment longer before nodding as the tension left him.

Alistair had come to some decision. Whether it was in regards to Ailesbury's presence or Adeline's explanation of everything that had occurred over the last several days, she was uncertain.

"Lord Ailesbury must attend the dinner party and ball tomorrow evening," Theo announced, clapping her hands. "Yes, there is more than enough room for one more. And everyone will be enthralled with the tales of Adeline's rescue from the storm."

The urge to insist that she would have been able to care for herself if Jasper hadn't stumbled upon her was on the tip of her tongue. She'd been in little jeopardy of perishing during the storm. Certainly, she, with Maxwell's help, would have been able to find themselves shelter to wait out the wind and rain. All the same, she had no need to downplay Jasper's gallant arrival and assistance, though it had hardly been necessary.

"That is very kind of you, Lady Melton; however, I must return home."

Theo's lower lip pushed out in a pout, something Adeline had never witnessed the woman do. In fact, it was more the type of tactic Adeline would use to gain what she wanted. Why would Theo endeavor to keep Jasper in town?

Alistair cleared his throat, obviously taking some unspoken cue from Theo. "Yes, I insist; you must remain in London for the celebration. It is the least we can do to repay you for returning Adeline safely to us."

"As I said, I had no intention of remaining in London, and therefore have not come prepared with proper attire, especially the kind befitting a ball."

"But, you must stay," Theo pressed.

Adeline shouldn't insist he stay, she was well aware

of his past and his lack of interest in town life. It was completely possible Jasper had never attended a ball before. He had said as much. But that did not stop her from longing for him to remain in London and close to her.

"There are fine tailors on Bond Street," Adeline urged. "They can have an entire wardrobe prepared for you by tomorrow night."

"Unfortunately, I can attest to that fact and my sister's firsthand knowledge of such matters. If it is a proper coat and trousers you lack, they can be commissioned without much fuss." Her brother scrubbed his face, likely remembering Adeline's selfish trip to Bond Street after their return to London for her first Season. She'd had nine gowns commissioned without her brother's approval. Little had she known the financial consequences of her petty actions, and all to try and punish her brother for keeping such a close watch on her. "And, if need be, I can have a room prepared for you here. We are a bit cramped. However, with Arabella and Ainsley away at school, a room can be readied."

"Of course," Theo nodded, her brown curls bouncing about her shoulders. "I will send for the housekeeper immediately."

Jasper held up his hand to halt her, and Adeline feared he'd decline their offer in favor of journeying back to the country where he was more comfortable. She should encourage him to return to Faversham—his people needed him at the Abbey and at Home Works. Any reason she had for wishing him to remain in London was not for his benefit but solely for her own pleasure.

"I have my own townhouse on St. James. I was planning to make a stop there before departing London." Jasper turned toward Adeline, and she knew his resistance was quickly slipping away. He had never mentioned a property in town; though it was not surprising as most of society maintained a residence in London even if it went largely unused. "I can remain in London for two nights, at least, in order to attend the party. I was unaware your day of birth was close, Miss Adeline. I would be honored to attend your celebration."

"We are grateful to have you, Lord Ailesbury," Theo all but crowed, her smile so wide it was a wonder her face did not crack under the strain. "I will retrieve the tailor's card for you at once."

Theo glanced about the room as if having forgotten they were in the study, before spotting her lap desk and hurrying over. Everyone in the room watched in silence as she lifted the top and riffled through the contents before returning with a card in hand.

"Only last week, we had my husband and his younger brother fitted for their celebration finery." She held the card out to Lord Ailesbury. If she noticed the scars on his neck, Theo was polite enough not to let her eyes linger on them. "If you prefer, the tailor will gladly journey to your townhouse for fittings."

Adeline watched in muted silence as Theo took over as hostess, her rightful duty as Viscountess Melton. At some point over the last year, Adeline's dear friend had changed until she was barely recognizable as the shy, quiet girl she'd once been.

Yet, the same was true of Adeline, wasn't it?

Those around her might not notice, but she certainly did.

"The dinner and ball will be held here on the morrow. Eight o'clock sharp," Adeline heard Theo say. "My husband and I are pleased you will attend."

"The pleasure is all mine, I assure you," Jasper contended. "Now, I will take my leave."

"Thank you for seeing my sister home safely." Alistair moved to the front of his desk as Jasper nodded and turned to depart.

"I will see you out, my lord." Adeline was not about to give the man time to say his farewells to her, as well. She purposefully faced away from Theo and her brother, not wanting to see their reactions nor show them hers. "I must needs make certain all my things have been removed to the house."

CHAPTER 16

JASPER HAD LITTLE other option but to match Miss Adeline's stride as they walked side by side back toward the foyer. He'd thought to give his farewells and slip from the house without further commotion; however, given what he knew of Adeline thus far, she was not one to make things simple…in any way.

"Are you truly going to come to the celebration tomorrow night?"

Her question was the exact same as the one bouncing about in his head.

A question he hadn't the answer for yet; nonetheless, he heard himself reply, "It would be impolite to turn down Lord and Lady Melton's invitation, would it not?"

"Perhaps," she sighed, setting her hand on his arm in an attempt to slow his pace. "However, I understand you are needed in Kent. Please, do not stay in London on my account. There are repairs to be made at the plant, Grovedale to check on, your estate to maintain—"

He halted suddenly, Adeline wobbling to a stop next to him. "If you are unhappy with my acceptance of your brother's invitation, I will give my regrets and depart." The last place Jasper wanted to be was somewhere he wasn't wanted. And never would he willingly force himself to dress like a London dandy and attend a ball where he knew nearly no one and was unaware of the social protocols involved. He'd never attended a dinner party, let alone a soirée for such a grand occasion. The possibility that he might embarrass Adeline and her family was not at all easy to ignore.

Adeline's eyes widened. "I am the opposite of unhappy at your acceptance, it is only that I do not wish to cause you unease. You were very open about your lack of interest in town life, and I would never force you into a situation not of your choosing."

"Very noble of you, Adeline," he said, realizing his mistake quickly and glancing about to make certain no one had overheard him call her by her given name. "You should know, however, I am not one to accept an invitation if I am not willing to fulfill the obligation."

"That is exactly it," she grumbled, also keeping her voice low. "I do not seek to be an *obligation* to you. Mayhap I was during my time at Faversham Abbey, but now I am home and no longer your responsibility."

Jasper blew out a raspy breath. "Do consolidate your thoughts, Miss Adeline. Either you wish my attendance at your celebration, or you do not. Which is it?"

"Of course, I want you there," she huffed.

"Then it is settled," Jasper said with a curt nod. "I will contact your brother's tailor as soon as I arrive at my townhouse, and I will see you at dusk tomorrow evening."

It seemed an eternity away, hours that would be spent in an unfamiliar house, in a strange city, and surrounded by unknown servants. He'd had no plan to visit his London residence. If he remembered correctly, his man of business in London kept a staff of five in the townhome at all times to maintain the property and keep vandals at bay. It certainly was not because they expected their master could arrive unannounced at any time.

He'd be lucky if a suitable room could be found for him.

For a brief moment, he pondered returning to Lord Melton's study and accepting his offer of lodging. But doing that would keep Jasper in very close proximity to Adeline, and that was something he must avoid. Keeping his hands off her for the entire carriage ride had been made possible only because Adeline's maid had kept a vigilant watch over the pair.

He needs must remember who he was, and who she was. Where he belonged: Faversham. And where she belonged: London.

There was no more proof needed than their few moments outside after disembarking the coach. She'd stepped right up to command the servants in their duties and speak with those seeking her ear. He'd been happy to watch from the shadows.

Night and day, they were.

She shone brightest in the sun, while he was mostly hidden amidst the shadows.

Though, Adeline was different. She hadn't pushed him into the darkness and demand he exist there as the villagers did. It appeared she desired him at her side.

An awkward silence stretched between them, both lost in their own thoughts yet continuing to stare at one another.

Finally, it was Adeline who spoke. "Will you meet me at Regent's Park tomorrow morning? Ten o'clock? That is my usual practice hour. I will be there with my bow. I know you are adept at hunting, but I'd relish the opportunity to see how you fair with a true target."

How could he deny her anything? Her hazel stare locked with his, and everything and everyone disappeared as she inched closer to him. He should instruct her to remain a respectable distance away as they were no longer at the Abbey. His trusted, loyal servants were not herein.

George waited by his coach, but other than him, Jasper knew not a soul but Adeline.

A sudden realization had him stumbling back a step. He trusted her.

He wasn't remaining in London because of her brother's invitation. He'd decided to stay in London for *her*. Part of him suspected he'd made the decision long before leaving Faversham Abbey that morning.

"Yes, I will meet you," he conceded. Or at least he hoped she thought he agreed with reluctance. Because the alternative would be that he was willing to throw society's rules out the window to have another day, possibly two, with Adeline. "How will I find you? I suspect the park is large."

Her smile, coy but enchanting nonetheless, told him she'd known all along he would accept. Though his reasoning had little to do with competition and targets and everything to do with her. In the short time they'd been in London, Jasper had noticed a different side to her, a side she'd either kept hidden in Kent or, more likely, a part she hadn't had need to express there.

Good or bad.

Jasper hadn't decided.

"I am certain you will not miss me," she replied with a soft laugh as a maid departed a room down the hall, and Jasper took a step away from Adeline. "I will bring a bow for your use."

"That is appreciated, for I doubt I can throw an arrow and hit the target." He leaned in close as the maid turned a corner and moved out of sight. "Fare thee well, Adeline."

"And you, Jasper."

He turned, strode toward the foyer, and departed the Melton townhouse with a grin that had been absent when he entered not long before. His coach waited in the drive, George in his place with the reins.

"Kebberstone Townhouse," Jasper shouted, climbing into the coach.

"Kebberstone?" He ignored the surprise in George's tone. "Right away, m'lord."

Jasper had little doubt his servant knew the way well. He'd served his father for several years before his sire's death and had even made the journey to London to collect Jasper's solicitor when the need arose.

Settling back against the seat, Jasper turned his stare to the fabric-covered ceiling of the coach as it moved evenly back onto the lane and headed toward his townhouse on St. James, the magnitude of his rash—though conscious—decision settling heavily upon his shoulders.

Returning to a townhouse that had been all but deserted since his parents' deaths, commissioning a proper wardrobe for his stay, and attending his first London ball. A few days prior, Jasper would have never thought to find himself away from the Abbey, let alone making the journey to town.

And it was as if Lord and Lady Melton hadn't so much as noticed his scars—nor questioned Adeline's arrival home in the company of a stranger. And how had Adeline not told him her birthday was only a few days off? Not that he'd have done anything with the information. For, certainly, it would be scandalous for him to buy her a gift: flowers, new hair ribbons, a necklace. That was not a stranger's place.

Perhaps a note of congratulations would be appropriate, for he would have been in Faversham, and she in London.

He could not deny how drastically their situation had altered since that very morning.

"M'lord?"

Jasper opened his eyes and glanced in the direction of George's voice to find him standing in the open doorway of the coach. Jasper's mind had wandered so far he hadn't noticed the conveyance had pulled to a stop, nor George climbing down from his post, or the opening of the door and the light that flooded the interior.

"We have arrived, m'lord."

"As I can see." He departed the carriage and glanced up at the three-story townhouse before him. If he'd been here in his youth, he had no recollection of it. "Do you think the servants will be shocked?"

"I won't be say'n that, but happy they certainly be."

Happy? To meet a lord they'd never served? To remain all but forgotten in London as Jasper continued on at Faversham?

No, he could not fathom them being happy about getting called into action with no warning by an absent master.

"Let us get on with this," Jasper mumbled. "I have agreed to attend Miss Adeline's birthday celebration, and it is imperative I am ready before tomorrow eve."

Before he reached the set of double doors, they swung open.

Jasper narrowed his eyes, praying they would adjust quickly to the dim interior of the home, to see who stood within.

"Lord Ailesbury? Is that you?" a voice called out. "Well, I'll be a holly sprig in July."

A familiar voice. A comforting voice. A voice that even after all these years, Jasper could never forget.

"Conover?" Jasper's chest tightened, afraid he'd mistaken a distant memory for the present. "It cannot be."

"It is, my lord, it surely is." His father's valet stepped over the threshold of Kebberstone Townhouse, and Jasper wrapped the man in a tight embrace.

"I had no idea you were in London." Jasper had wondered for years what had happened to his father's most trusted servant. "I must admit, I am overjoyed to see you."

"And you, my lord," Conover bowed. "You have grown into a fine man, if you don't mind me saying so."

"I don't mind at all," Jasper said with a chuckle. "And your wife, is she within?"

The man nodded, his jowls jumping up and down. "She is, she is. She took over the housekeeping here at Kebberstone. And Mrs. Bays moved with us, too."

At the mention of Mrs. Bays, his old nursemaid, his stomach rolled, and unease filled him. Her husband, who'd served as the steward in Faversham, died in the fire—because Jasper had been too weak to save him. Unable to save anyone.

He'd always wondered what had happened to the woman. He'd been too young to question her disappearance then, but as he aged, Jasper had assumed she returned to her family—perhaps even remarried and had children.

"We are pleased you are here, my lord."

Jasper clasped the man on his shoulder as they turned to enter the house. "You might not say that after you hear what is needed and with all due haste."

"Oh, I assure you, nothing will lessen our excitement to be of service to you, Lord Ailesbury."

A line of servants stood at attention in the foyer, though Jasper was unsure when they'd been summoned or how they all arrived so quickly. He smiled to Mrs. Bays and Conover's wife and nodded to several others who were vaguely familiar to him from his youth.

"Delilah, have a room readied for Lord Ailesbury. The master's room," Conover commanded. "My lord, can I presume you still enjoy duck soup and apple pie?"

He hadn't seen the servant in nearly fifteen years, and the man had never been responsible for Jasper, yet he remembered his favored childhood meals.

"Yes, you presume correctly."

"I will have Cook prepare both." Conover beamed. "Is there aught else I can do for you, my lord? A bath, perchance? Or…a drink. Yes, I can have whatever liquor you favor brought to…the study, the library, or your chambers—immediately."

Jasper chuckled, a weight lifting from his shoulders. "Neither is necessary. I am in need of a tailor, though. I have been invited to a ball tomorrow night, and I have need of proper attire."

Conover tapped his chin in thought. "Well, I can summon—"

"I have been given the name and directions for a tailor favored by Lord and Lady Melton if that helps," Jasper offered. "I know this is short notice, but I will also need other assorted shirts and trousers, for I have little idea how long I will stay in London."

"Very good, my lord." The servant clapped his hands, and the line of staff dispensed, all except Delilah, the butler's wife. "I will send for the man straight away."

"Thank you, Conover." Jasper followed Delilah as she headed toward the stairs.

"My lord?" Conover called.

Jasper halted and faced the servant.

"We are ever so happy you are here."

"As am I, Conover, as am I." He continued after Delilah—up the stairs, down a hallway, left turn, and down another corridor to stand before another set of double doors. This pair did not open to reveal a friendly face from his past.

"We kept the room nice, as well as the entire house, my lord." Delilah paused, her hand on the latch as if debating her next move. "It is just as your parents left it. We were not given any other instructions."

When Jasper nodded, the housekeeper opened the door, and he faced a nearly full-size portrait of his parents. In the pose, his father stood behind where his mother was positioned in a chair, with a tiny boy seated on the floor beside her.

The child didn't look familiar at all, though he knew the boy to be him at about age four; however, the man and woman were exactly as Jasper remembered, though his father's jawline and nose were a bit more severe than he recalled. His mother's neck more swanlike than his memories held, and her hair far darker than Jasper's was now.

Other than those trivial discrepancies, they were as Jasper envisioned them. The couple he'd nearly perished trying to save from the fire. The parents who'd called him farther and farther into the fire where they'd been trapped under a fallen rafter as the blaze consumed the stable.

Jasper knew, with certainty, he never would have been able to save them. He'd been too young and small, the rafter too heavy for him to lift without assistance, and the fire's flames far too hot for anyone to sustain enough breath to pull the couple free.

Why did he remember the sound of their voices urging him forward, farther into the burning building? It was the nightmare that woke him night after night for more years than Jasper wanted to count. He'd prayed it was a false memory—a boy's guilt materializing in his dreams—but he clearly recalled his father shouting at him to save them, that if Jasper only hurried, they would all three be rescued.

But Jasper had not been strong enough, had not had the strength to make it far into the stables before his lungs filled with black smoke and his mind grew hazy and slow. His body had followed suit, and he'd lost consciousness only ten feet into the stables. A servant had pulled him from the fire as the flames licked at his neck, arm, and leg—scorching his skin.

He should have been abed, as should his parents, but instead they were searching the house and stables for Jasper. He'd selected the hidden room under the main stairs that night for his reading hour. He hadn't been the cause of the fire, yet that did nothing to diminish his guilt at the outcome of it all. It was not his candle that started the first but he was the reason his family perished—they would not have been anywhere close to the stables if Jasper hadn't been found on many a night sleeping in the rafters.

"Can I have a meal brought up, my lord?"

When Jasper brought his stare to the housekeeper, he noted that she kept her eyes trained on the floor at her feet, as if attempting to give Jasper a moment of privacy, yet suspecting he also needed someone there to pull him from the past to his present.

He cleared his throat and blinked several times to dispel the tears that'd clouded his vision. "I think I shall await word from the tailor in the study."

If his voice cracked as he spoke, she did not react to it.

"Very well, Lord Ailesbury." She pulled the door shut and gestured with her arm back toward the stairs. "I will show you the way."

He held back, allowing her to lead the way. It gave him several more moments to compose himself. Never had he thought the mere image of his parents would bring back so many long-buried memories—or emotions he didn't remember having.

Perhaps sending his regrets to Lord and Lady Melton and returning to Faversham Abbey would be the best choice for Jasper.

With any hope, Adeline would not even notice his absence. And with time, Jasper would bury the memory of her, just as he had his parents.

CHAPTER 17

"WHAT IN THE bloody hell is going on?" Alistair demanded the moment Adeline slipped back into the room. "Who is that man, and what was he doing accompanying you back to London?"

"Jasper—Lord Ailesbury—was only doing what any man of worth would do when a lady is in peril."

Her brother snorted and dropped back into his chair.

"My love—"

"Do not *my love* me, Theo," Alistair barked. "I cannot have you taking her side on this. You are not fourteen-year-old girls at boarding school any longer. This could very well ruin her reputation."

Theo flinched at Alistair's harsh tone, and her brother immediately shrank back in his chair. If there was one constant in her life since her father's passing, it was Theo's and Alistair's love and dedication to one another. At first, it had galled her to see them so close, her brother taking over a place in Theo's life that had been Adeline's for so many years.

"There is no harm done as yet," Theo sighed, easing into her chair before Alistair's desk. "No one saw her arrive in his company, and if they did, Poppy was with her."

Alistair scrubbed at his face and gave Theo a weak smile before glancing up at Adeline. For the first time, she noted his exhaustion: the dark circles under his eyes, the hard lines of his face, and his pale skin. How long had it been since he'd found the time to venture outside the house?

However, Adeline could not let her brother loose without having her own say regarding the matter at hand. "It is your fault I was stranded in Kent, dear brother."

"How do you support that claim?" He steepled his fingers on the desk, and his glare hardened.

She'd thought long and hard on the journey back to London about how she'd handle Alistair. "If you had not sent Arabella, Ainsley, and me off in that decrepit coach, I would not have found myself marooned along the side of the road without means to fix the thing." She took a deep breath and continued before Theo and Alistair could cut in. "It was a blessing that Jasper happened upon us during the storm, or it could have been my cold, dead body returned to you, as I would have surely perished in the tempest."

Alistair shook his head with a chuckle.

"What?" Adeline demanded, her blood fairly boiling at his disregard for her safety.

"There is little need to sensationalize this matter, dear sister, and I insist you cease your theatrics."

"You think I am overreacting?" she seethed, glancing to Theo for help. However, her friend seemed intent on inspecting the stitching on her pleated skirts.

Alistair raised his hands, palms up, and shrugged.

It was his way of making her answer her own question.

Adeline huffed. She would stomp her foot and demand her brother see reason, yet she assumed he'd see that reaction as childish and it would only serve to reinforce his earlier statement.

It would be in her best interest to calm herself, especially if she thought to meet Jasper at Regent's Park on the morrow.

She sank into the chair next to Theo and faced her brother across the desk. It was strikingly apparent they were related, as it was with all the Melton children. Their hazel eyes and light brown hair were distinctive to their family.

"Tell me more about this birthday celebration you've planned, Theo," Adeline conceded, deciding to steer clear of any further argument regarding Jasper and Adeline's time in the country at his estate.

Her friend immediately turned a bright smile in Adeline's direction. "I cannot say it is I who is responsible for the planning of the party, only the organization of it. It was Josie and Georgie who came to me with the idea."

"How did you convince Felton and Alistair?" Adeline was well aware that Felton, Georgie's new husband, was still working tirelessly to make certain he could support his wife in the fashion she was accustomed to. Any funds spent on Adeline's birthday celebration could very well jeopardize his future business plans.

"Oh, Alistair was easy to convince, and Felton falls in line with whatever Georgie desires." Adeline laughed along with Theo. If there were a second in command of their foursome, it would be Georgie. Adeline sometimes wondered if her dear friend had been the first to arrive at Miss Emmeline's School, if things would have been different in their friendship. "Not that my own wishes do not hold significant weight with my own husband."

Theo winked, and Adeline laughed once more.

How far her shy, reserved, academic friend had come since her return to London nearly two years prior. As far as sisters went, Adeline was thankful Alistair had chosen this woman to join their family.

"What have you planned for the celebration?" Adeline was shocked to realize she'd all but forgotten her twenty-first birthday was upon her. She could remember it being solidly on her mind when she departed London on her way to Kent, but—perhaps because of Jasper?—the special day had escaped her mind. "And who has received invitations?"

"Everyone in bloody town has been invited—and the Lord help us all—but they have all accepted," Alistair mumbled. "Lord Ailesbury being the last."

Alistair gave both Adeline and Theo a stern look as if to dare either woman to invite another soul to the party.

"If you are worried about the number of guests, why extend the offer to Jasper?" Adeline asked.

"If my dear wife—and her friends—seeks to send us all to the poorhouse, who am I to argue?"

"What your brother means to say is, we noticed how you spoke of Lord Ailesbury and his kindness to you, and thought it only fitting an invitation be extended."

"Yet, Alistair worries over my reputation—and that of our family."

Adeline glared at Alistair, but he'd returned his attention to an open ledger on his desktop.

"It is not your reputation that worries me, Adeline," Theo said softly. "Actually, it was your gracious words about Lord Ailesbury."

"The man saved me from certain death. Of course, I would not speak harshly of him."

Alistair snorted once again, keeping his eyes trained on his desk.

"You must agree it is a rare occasion indeed when you speak to a person's merits." With her words, Theo looked away from Adeline.

"What do you mean by that?"

"You are not known as a…shall we say, agreeable

or kind lady, Adeline," Alistair bit out. "This Lord Ailesbury being the exception."

Adeline's stomach hardened, and a sense of betrayal lanced through her. "How can you say that?"

"You spread word at Miss Emmeline's School that Headmistress preferred the company of animals to people."

"That was five years ago," Adeline countered, crossing her arms.

"And what about insisting Amelia would only find a suitor if she painted her face like a harlot and wore clothing to match?" Alistair grumbled.

Adeline suppressed her smile. "Well, the girl is quite contrary and whines more than the stable master's new lot of puppies when they desire their mother's tit to feed."

"Perhaps it is you who should be worried about gaining the notice of potential suitors," Alistair said, returning his stare to her. "Amelia has yet to be presented to society, while you have been…"

"I have been what?" she demanded when he allowed his words to trail off.

"In mourning this past year," Theo finished for her husband.

"Let me reassure you, Lord Ailesbury—Jasper—is a kind man. I was well cared for while at Faversham Abbey, as Poppy and Maxwell can verify." Why did she feel the need to offer such support in Jasper's favor? Nothing untoward had occurred during her stay in Kent—not that Adeline hadn't daydreamed of very inappropriate things; though that was something she would not speak of with her brother present. Maybe one day in the distant future, she, Theo, Josie, and Georgie would all chat about it in hushed tones as Adeline regaled them with tales from the Abbey. "Besides, I dare say you could learn a lesson or two from the earl."

"Be that as it may," Alistair said through clenched

teeth. "As your guardian and the head of this family, I have a duty to keep the reputation of all under this roof above gossip and speculation—or risk seeing us all ruined."

"Adeline, please understand the immense burden placed on your brother this past year—and even before that," Theo said, coming to her husband's defense once more. "With your mother in a persistent state of mourning, his responsibilities to Abel, Amelia, Adelaide, Arabella, Ainsley, Alfred, Adrian—and you—have been fairly crushing."

"And I do not have the time to contend with your childish escapades and flights of fancy." Alistair slammed the ledger closed and turned to return it to its place on the shelf to his left.

"Then it is advantageous for everyone concerned that I will reach the age of majority in a fortnight and will no longer be in need of a guardian," Adeline snapped, her brother's back immediately stiffening at her callous remark. "At that point, I will endeavor to remove at least some burden from you, dear brother."

"You cannot mean that—"

"Oh, but I do, Alistair," Adeline responded, pushing from her chair.

"Thankfully, I am still within my rights, for at least the next fortnight, to send you to your chambers."

"I would like to see you try."

"Come now, the pair of you are acting as if you loathe one another," Theo cut in.

Adeline held her brother's narrowed glare for a moment longer but sighed and turned to Theo. "I do not, nor have I ever, loathed my brother. However, his high-handed nature has resurfaced of late, and I find it trying on my nerves."

"Trying on your nerves?" Alistair boomed.

"Stop!" Theo commanded, jabbing her finger at her husband and then toward Adeline. "The pair of you are so similar you fail to see you both have need to be in control." Adeline blinked several times and refocused on Theo, shocked at the woman's outburst. "However, allow me to tell you both something. Until Adeline's birthday celebration is over—and it is deemed a success—*I* am in control. Josie, Georgie, and I have worked ourselves to the very bone putting together this grand event, and I will not have the likes of either of you ruining it. Do I make myself clear?"

Theo's brow pulled low as she turned her glare on both Adeline and Alistair.

They both nodded in unison.

"Very good," Theo said, the tension draining from her shoulders. "Now, Adeline, if you will kindly accompany me to the drawing room, I will show you what we have planned for your special day."

Her friend did not wait for Adeline to answer but marched from the room, leaving the door open, as if fully expecting Adeline to follow.

Which she did, with all due haste.

CHAPTER 18

JASPER WALKED THROUGH yet another tall patch of grass. The dew and moisture from the early morning drizzle clung to his new Hessians and threatened to sully his freshly tailored trousers as he explored the far reaches of Regent's Park for Adeline. He'd questioned his servants the previous night, and departed in the required time to arrive at the park with a bit of time to spare. Thankfully, he had because he'd been searching every grassy meadow and grove of trees in the blasted park for nearly a half hour.

Bloody hell.

His foot caught on a clump of roots, splattering dirt up his pant leg and knocking him off balance.

Jasper quickly gained his footing and stomped around another cluster of trees.

Why had he agreed to meet Adeline at all?

Though he'd made the decision and would uphold his promise, it hadn't been necessary to request an appropriate shirt, trousers, and jacket for the outing—yet, request them he had. The tailor recommended by Lord Melton had been all too happy to assist his new client in preparing for his first ball in London—and rushing several other garments, as well. Jasper was little more than a debutante praying her new gowns arrived before her grand entrance into society.

Nodding to two gentlemen on horseback, Jasper spotted the trail the man had come from and a clearing beyond. Certainly, he was close to reaching the far end of the park by now—and the ache in his feet from his stiff boots would make the return trek unpleasant, to say the least.

He should have requested a horse for the trip instead of his coach.

Or, at least insist that his driver, George, accompany him into the park. Though he knew the risks of leaving his coach and horses unattended.

From Lord Melton's attitude the previous day, Jasper could not believe the man would allow his sister time in the park unchaperoned. However, the viscount had sent her to the country without benefit of a well-maintained carriage. Adeline's elder brother was not capable of anything in Jasper's mind.

He felt his temperature rise at the thought of the man's reckless disregard for Adeline's safety. She was a proper lady, after all, and to send her to Kent without a second thought was irresponsible and highly careless.

Jasper would speak with the man about holding Adeline in higher esteem. Either that or find a proper mate for her and allow *that* man to care for her properly.

If Jasper were to wed a woman like Adeline—

He shook his head to dispel the preposterous thought.

He would never wed Adeline…or any woman like her.

If his short time in London had taught him anything, it was that Jasper did not belong in her world. She was used to catering servants, fancy clothes, days spent shopping, and nights spent at the opera or in a crowded ballroom.

Jasper was more attuned to days at the plant, laboring over business, and nights spent finding his bed shortly after sunset and falling into fitful bouts of sleep—alone.

She was the beauty in every room.

He was the darkness that clung to the shadows.

There was little more Jasper deserved than to be shut away at Faversham Abbey.

Female laughter floated on the breeze, reaching Jasper as he arrived at a large expanse of meadow. Across the rolling lawn, he spied four women, Adeline among them.

His initial response was to turn around and flee. Hurry back to his carriage as quickly as possible, and send his regards to Adeline about missing her at the park.

Unfortunately, his mind did not convey the urgency to his legs, and Adeline spotted him before he could leave. She waved and began in his direction, her bow slung over her shoulder. As she grew closer, he noted the back of her skirts had been pulled through her legs and tucked in to a makeshift belt at her waist, making it appear as if she wore wide-legged pants.

Behind her, three women paused and stared in his direction.

These must be the women she'd spoken of while at Faversham, her schoolmates from Canterbury. He did recognize the dark-haired woman from the previous day, Lady Melton.

"Lord Ailesbury," Adeline called as she grew closer. "Welcome!"

"Miss Adeline," he bowed as she stopped before him. "It is an honor to see you again."

She linked her arm through his and pulled him toward her waiting friends. "Do relax, Jasper. No one can hear us. I am glad you came, and I apologize for my brother's impolite behavior yesterday."

"Well, I am certain he was worried about you."

"As a man watches over his prized livestock," she

said with a laugh.

Not a thing about her comment struck Jasper as comical.

As they arrived at the gathering of women, he saw that each wore their skirts as Adeline did, and there were quivers filled with arrows leaning against a nearby tree. Two targets were set up at a distance, and from his vantage point, Jasper could see that the women must have been practicing for some time already because the bullseyes and inner rings of each target were shot clean through in several spots.

No footmen or chaperones lingered within sight.

The foursome was all but alone in the park.

Lady Melton sent a smile his way, and Jasper nodded in greeting. Another dark-haired woman kept her stare trained on the ground as she slipped behind Lady Melton. The fourth woman, blond-haired with an upturned nose, inspected him from head to toe and back again. With a sniff, she seemed to accept what she saw.

"Lord Ailesbury," Adeline said, her tone bouncing with merriment. "Allow me to introduce my dear sister by marriage, Lady Theodora Melton, whom you met yesterday. And the Ladies Georgina and Josephine." She indicated each woman in turn. "Ladies, please welcome Lord Ailesbury to our morning archery practice."

"It is lovely to see you again, my lord," Lady Melton said, inclining her head.

"We have heard much about you," the blond woman, Lady Georgina, all but purred.

"I certainly hope they were all positive things," he replied.

The woman who cowered behind Lady Melton squeaked, and her eyes lifted, showing her wide stare.

Jasper cleared his throat, nervous that he'd made an unfavorable first impression. "It is a pleasure to meet you all. Adeline—errr, Miss Adeline—spoke highly of you all during her time at Faversham Abbey."

At his side, Adeline's stare dipped to the ground, and her cheeks blossomed with heat.

Had he caused her embarrassment?

"Adeline spoke of your skill with a bow, though, I must confess, hunting is not the same as target practice or competing before large crowds of spectators." It was Lady Melton who spoke.

"My lady—"

"Please, call me Theo," she said. "It is preferable among friends."

With a bit of shock, Jasper realized this doubled his number of friends in London. "Theo, I can assure you, finding myself the center of attention is not so far out of a normal occurrence for me." It had been the way of things every time he departed the Abbey and journeyed to the plant or into town. London was to be no different. He reached up and adjusted the collar of his jacket where it did an admirable job of hiding his scars. "While I have never plied my talents to target practice, I can assure you my people have never suffered a single day of hunger."

"Hunting?" Lady Josephine clutched her neck as the color drained from her face. "I could never bring myself to harm a poor, defenseless animal."

"If it meant you'd never enjoy duck soup or roasted pheasant again, I am certain you'd find a way to do away with your delicate sensibilities," Lady Georgina retorted with a chuckle.

"Perhaps I will adjust well to eating solely from my family's gardens."

"And perhaps you will find you enjoy walking on all fours and nibbling at grass," Adeline added at his side.

Lady Melton sucked in a breath and glared at Adeline as the young woman, Lady Josie, appeared to shrink into herself as her shoulders caved and she returned her stare to the ground, her hands clutched at her chest.

"My apologies, Josie, I did not mean…"

"There is no need, Adeline," the woman mumbled. "I know you think I should be more daring; though I am uncertain that trait lies within me."

"My words were still uncalled for," Adeline said. "And I apologize."

Lady Josie's gaze snapped from the ground to Adeline, narrowing as if securitizing the sincerity behind her apology.

Glancing about, Jasper was confused to see Lady Melton and Lady Georgina doing the same. Certainly, Adeline hadn't meant to be harsh and unkind to her friend. She'd never appeared such while at the Abbey.

"Ah, well, with the party fast approaching, I believe I was invited to see you all ply your skills at archery," Jasper said, breaking the uncomfortable silence. Adeline turned to him with a thankful smile. "I am much looking forward to your displays of marksmen—er, markswomanship."

Finally, the peculiar cloud that had settled over them lifted when Lady Melton laughed at his word choice, Lady Georgina following suit as they collected their bows.

"We line up here," Lady Melton said over her shoulder as Lady Georgina and Josie took their places and set their stances.

"Theo corrects and guides us as we practice," Adeline offered as they stood a few paces away from the others while they prepared their arrows. "She is accomplished at calculations, wind speed, and angles."

Lady Melton adjusted Lady Josie's positioning, having her shift one foot so the toe of her boot faced the target on a straight line.

"Odd, but I've never considered my stance when shooting," Jasper mused.

"You will find it increases the accuracy of your shot by twenty-seven percent." He glanced at her, her brow furrowed. "Or at least that is what Theo always says."

"On most occasions, I am hurried to release my arrow before the stag or pheasant catches my scent and flees."

"Shhhh," Adeline whispered, leaning close enough for him to catch the scent of vanilla that clung to her. "Take in this moment."

The pair released their bow strings in unison and hit their targets in the exact same spot.

"That was a spectacular feat!" Jasper applauded, receiving smiles from the women and a wave from Lady Georgina.

"My turn." Adeline took her place before her target and removed her bow from her shoulder. She looked as captivating now, in Regent's Park, as she had during their turkey hunt at Faversham, though her hair was not wildly cascading down her back, but instead pinned mostly atop her head in what Jasper could only assume was the proper style for London ladies. He could nearly picture her in true trousers with her skirts tucked as they were, her trim waist leading to toned legs with delicate ankles.

Lady Melton joined her with her own bow and quiver at the ready, and Jasper pulled himself from his scandalous musings.

Jasper watched as the women breathed deeply, exhaled, and then took another, far more shallow breath—and then loosed their arrows.

When both hit—and stuck—dead center of their targets, Jasper exhaled, not realizing he'd been holding his breath in anticipation of Adeline's shot.

The women embraced at their victory.

"Marvelous," Jasper called once more, applauding their talent.

The women were supremely talented with their

bows and would likely best any man who dared challenge them.

Pride surged through him, though it was not his pride to feel.

"Good morn, ladies!" a man called from behind them. "I see you have attracted a crowd."

Jasper turned to see a smartly dressed man striding toward them, lanky but not overly tall, and dressed in garb finer than Jasper's. He was certainly born to an elevated class, and the man knew it. His hair was combed with precision, and his boots shone in the morning sun.

He did not stop when he arrived but went straight to Lady Georgina, wrapping her in a tight embrace before setting his lips against hers. "I have missed you, my lady bug. Must you be away from me all these hours? If I were a less confident man, I would doubt your love and devotion to me."

Lady Josie's cheeks flamed red at the intimate nature of their conversation.

"Oh, Felton, if I were not so in love with you, I might declare that you are smothering me with your neediness," Lady Georgina countered.

"You wound me, as always, my lady." The man sighed dramatically.

"Is it not better for words to wound your heart than my arrow, my dear Mr. Crauford?"

Jasper watched the couple with envy. What exactly he coveted about their relationship, he was uncertain. Perhaps it was simply having another person to be close with in all regards: mentally, physically, and emotionally.

Finally, Lady Georgina pulled from the man's embrace and turned toward Jasper.

"Lord Ailesbury, may I present my preening, indigent, lovingly committed husband, Mr. Felton Crauford." Lady Georgina swept her arms up and down in front of her husband as if showing off a prized statue.

"Felton, this is Lord Ailesbury, a friend of Adeline's from Kent."

"I do hope you did not fall prey to their womanly charms and accept a challenge of skill," Mr. Felton Crauford said. "Because, I assure you, they will best you…and take their purse prize without a second thought."

Jasper instantly liked the man—his warm smile and wit were likely a fine match for Lady Georgina's daring tongue.

"It is a blessing my bow remains in the country, or I'd likely have been swindled out of anything not entailed to my Earldom," Jasper countered with a chuckle. He hadn't felt so light and unburdened in years, and it all revolved around Adeline. "A pleasure to make your acquaintance, Mr. Crauford."

"And you, my lord." Crauford pulled his wife close to his side. "Will you be joining in the celebration tonight?" He cringed and glanced at Adeline.

Lady Georgina patted his chest. "Do not fret, Felton, Adeline has already discovered the details of her party. You have ruined no surprise."

The man exhaled. "I am relieved it is not I who let the cat out of the bag."

"I will be attending," Jasper said.

"Very good." Felton placed a quick kiss to Lady Georgina's forehead. "While I would relish another chance to best Lady Melton with a bow, I must be getting my wife home to prepare for our evening."

"Are you certain it is not you who needs time to ready themselves?" Adeline teased, her eyes lighting with merriment once more.

"I can neither confirm nor deny your question," Felton responded with a wink.

"It is time we all return and prepare ourselves," Lady Melton said. Two footmen stepped from the shadows of a tree and began collecting the targets.

Ailesbury had as yet not noticed the footmen keeping watch over the women, but it satisfied him greatly to know Lord Melton did not leave Adeline—and her friends—unprotected. "It was lovely seeing you again, Lord Ailesbury. My husband and I look forward to gaining an increased acquaintance this evening. I hope you will see Adeline home safely?"

A sheen of sweat broke out on Jasper's forehead despite the cool morning breeze still playing over the grassy area. *See Adeline home safely?*

As he stood mute and confused, a footman returned and collected Adeline's and Lady Melton's archery gear and then disappeared again.

"We shall see everyone this evening," Lady Georgina called with a wave before turning and departing with Crauford.

"Come, Josie." Lady Melton slipped her arm through Lady Josie's, and they followed the footmen from the clearing. "Good day, Adeline."

Jasper kept his stare trained on the retreating women, certain they would turn at any moment and laugh at their jest. They could not be serious about leaving Adeline in his care without a proper chaperone, especially after the fuss her brother had made about their time in the country.

The sinking sensation that he'd been duped by none other than Lady Melton froze Jasper where he stood.

CHAPTER 19

ADELINE SHIVERED IN the morning chill, noticing the brisk temperature for the first time since Jasper's arrival. She remained quiet as Jasper unbuttoned and removed his coat, settling it around her shoulders with care. The new clothes suited him well, and anyone would be hard-pressed to believe this was his first time in their fair city. He walked with the confidence of a man who knew his place in life, who had no question about his worth and could give a damn what others thought of him. It was the thing that had drawn her to him during their first meeting when he stuck his rain-soaked head into her carriage and gave her a simple ultimatum: find refuge at Faversham Abbey, or remain stranded alongside the road.

"Thank you, my lord." She pulled her skirts from her waistband and tugged the coat tighter around her shoulders. "This is very kind of you."

He brushed his dark hair back, and she noted he'd had it trimmed since their arrival in London. She could not say whether she preferred the shorter, more fashionable style or his locks hanging over his collar.

Adeline allowed her stare to wander from his hair to his face and down to his neck, his scars only slightly visible above his collar. In her opinion, the burn marks did more to enhance his appeal rather than deter from it. Odd that no man in society had gained her notice beyond a single dance—or refreshment—at a ball, yet Jasper, despite his stern demeanor, caused her to think through her every remark and take extra care with her appearance.

The ache of her head from the pins placed with precision to hold her curls high atop her crown was evidence enough of this. If Theo had noted the extra time she'd spent preparing for this usual archery practice, she hadn't mentioned it.

However, leaving Adeline in Jasper's care was enough to solidify in Adeline's mind that Theo was meddling…which was highly suspect as Theo was not usually one to notice connections between individuals, especially from simple glances or witty remarks.

"My carriage is across the park to the east at Albany Street," he said as if apologizing. "Is the walk too far?"

He glanced down at her feet, and Adeline was happy she'd selected her well-worn half boots that morning.

"I think a stroll through the park sounds lovely, Lord Ailesbury." Adeline made no attempt to hide her grin. Since their return the previous day, she'd thought they would never again enjoy a moment of privacy without her brother hovering close by with a watchful eye. It had been something she'd taken for granted while at the Abbey. London afforded no seclusion, but that found behind the closed doors of a married couple's bedchamber. Even at her family's townhouse, there were her siblings and servants always about. And Jasper and she would never know the privacy of a bedchamber.

A walk through Regent's Park long before the fashionable members of society ventured forth from their homes was the most solitude they could hope for in London.

Adeline was shocked Theo had departed without leaving so much as a chaperone to accompany them. When Alistair learned of it, she would likely receive a sharp reprimand from her husband.

They'd all accept such a fate to help one another, though, Adeline included. Had she not assisted Theo and Georgie in their scam to compete in their first tourney and thus faced her brother's wrath?

She and Jasper fell into a companionable silence as they followed the path toward the more populated section of the park. The sun rose ever higher, and soon, Adeline could feel nothing but Jasper's warmth. Though he knew nearly nothing of London, she felt protected and safe by his side, much as she'd been when they first met.

"The park is lovely, so serene for an area surrounded by such a bustling city." He kept his steps short and unhurried, matching Adeline's measured pace. It appeared he was in no rush to return to his coach and deliver her home. "If I were to close my eyes and listen, I could swear I was back on Faversham land."

"Amazing, is it not?" Adeline turned her face skyward, allowing the breeze to caress her skin but confident Jasper's coat would keep the chill at bay. "One would not believe the marvels to be seen within London if they did not see them with his or her own eyes."

"I can now understand your love of London," he replied.

Adeline felt his stare on her, and heat blossomed at her core. Something about the man—his strength, his resilience, his kind heart—had Adeline doubting her own character. He was a far better person than she. He'd shown that at the plant, helping the villagers rescue one of their own even though none of them would lift a finger to help him if he were in need. In fact, as soon as the crisis was resolved, they'd dispensed without so much as a thank you or a nod to Jasper for his bravery.

It had been insulting and hurtful to Adeline, and she couldn't imagine the pain it caused Jasper.

"Tell me, Miss Adeline, I hope your brother was not overly vexed with you after my departure." He pulled her a bit closer as he said the word *vexed*. "It might have been better for all if I'd dropped you in the drive and not complicated your arrival with my presence."

But then he would not still be in London and attending her celebration.

"I fear my brother would be vexed if the sun dared to set a moment early. He'd also, more than likely, find a way to blame me for a summer storm. His contrary nature is something one gets used to." Adeline hadn't the need to explain her complicated relationship with Alistair before. Certainly, she loved her brother—and he her—yet, they were uniquely different people. "Alistair and I have been at war since birth. He's the eldest sibling, and with our father sick more often than not before his death, my brother took his duties as patriarch of the family very seriously. Continues to do so. Heaven help us all if I were in command."

"I would never doubt his love for you, and all your siblings," Jasper sighed. "And I know much about responsibilities and the burden of taking on so much at a young age."

The sorrow rolling off his shoulders much like the mists off the Scottish marshlands at dawn had Adeline regretting the choice of topics; however, she did not want Jasper to think less of Alistair. Despite their quickness to anger with one another, they were loyal to a fault.

"Yes, you and Alistair have much in common," Adeline agreed by way of steering the conversation to safer ground. "I think you do for your people what

Alistair does for us. Though you are not always rewarded for your efforts."

Why did pointing out the similarities between Jasper's and Alistair's situations have Adeline questioning her exacting treatment of her brother? The family did not call Alistair a beast behind his back, nor did they make light of his hardships.

Adeline must remember that Alistair was not Jasper.

Though she had much to do with Alistair's current burdens. Namely, her. She cringed, remembering the hateful words she'd spoke in the study the day before. She might as well have called Alistair a beast.

Blessedly, their path led them to the main area of the park where people had started arriving for their daily constitution: men and woman on horseback, groups of ladies strolling with parasols raised, and open-air carriages moving at a snail's pace to allow their occupants the opportunity to socialize and be seen by those present. The hour was still early, but a growing number of Londoners were not averse to braving the chilly, late-morning air for a few hours outdoors.

Lifting her arm, Adeline waved to Lady Cecilia and her mother, who rode by on horseback. Their townhouse bordered the park to the south, and they commonly stopped to watch Adeline and her friends at their morning practice.

The women nodded in her direction but did not slow their mounts to visit.

"I envy your social ease, Miss Adeline," Jasper said at her side. "I have lived in solitude for so many years, I sometimes forget how to speak with even my servants."

"It is quite simple, really. You see, when I feel myself getting nervous around someone, I think what dreadful secrets they keep—some serious, many funny, but always enough to make certain my unease recedes."

"Interesting. Do elaborate."

Adeline glanced at two men walking, their heads lowered in deep conversation. "Take that pair for example," she said, nodding in the men's direction. "One could be a duke and the other a marquis with powerful French relations. But to me, I think, does the man on the left still employ his nursemaid from when he was a babe? And the man on the right, does he have an overwhelming fear of horses?"

Jasper chuckled, and Adeline's stomach fluttered. The sound was deep and masculine, but at the same time soothing. "And what of the woman stepping down from that carriage?"

Adeline turned in the direction Jasper nodded to see a matronly woman alighting from a carriage in pursuit of two young boys, a stern frown on her face and a satchel slung over her shoulder. "Oh, I suspect the woman's name is something like,"—Adeline paused, tapping her chin in thought—"Myrtle, because for some reason, her mother knew she would be as tall as a tree and lithe in frame. Those children she is chasing belong to her sister, who is traveling through Italy on the arm of a wealthy count. Your turn."

They renewed their walk, and Adeline feared he would not continue with their game, but finally, he nodded to an elderly man, making his way down a rutted path, careful to use his cane for stability.

"That man there. He is hurrying to the house of his mother, who is wedding her fourth husband."

"His mother?" Adeline barked with laughter. "The man is dreadfully old himself, his mother would be ancient!"

"Giving her ample time to outlive three husbands and take a fourth."

Adeline scanned the growing crowd for another lady or gentleman who might have an interesting story. Instead of spotting yet another stranger, her gaze settled on the Duchess of Balfour, Georgie's stepmother. The woman, while awfully unkind to Georgie during her childhood, had never cast a stone in Adeline's direction.

She waved to the woman, escorted by a pair of ladies Adeline was not acquainted with, and she and Jasper moved in their direction.

"That is Georgie's evil stepmother," Adeline whispered before they were close enough for the women to overhear. "She produced an heir last year and has been in most agreeable spirits since."

Jasper made no comment as they arrived to greet the trio of women, each dressed in their finest walking gowns with hats to match. Adeline did not favor grandiose headwear perched atop her head that could tumble to the ground with the slightest movement.

"Good day, Duchess," Adeline greeted with a curtsey. "Lovely to see you. I fear you only missed Georgie by a few minutes."

The woman sniffed, her chin rising several inches until she stared down her nose at Adeline. "I see Felton still allows Georgina to run about London like a hoyden. Pity."

The pair of ladies flanking the duchess nodded in agreement, their heads bobbing up and down like a couple of chickens scratching for their next meal.

The duchess glanced in Jasper's direction, her glare returning to Adeline quickly as if the sight of the earl at Adeline's side had burned her eyes. "We must be off. Good day, Miss Adeline."

"Before you go, allow me to intro—"

The women pivoted in unison and hurried off in the direction they'd come, cutting Adeline's introduction short.

"You would think a duchess would be in possession of better manners," Adeline huffed.

Jasper did not respond, only placed her gloved hand in the crook of his elbow and started off once more, following the trio of women at a far more sedate pace.

"Wait until Georgie hears how impolite her stepmother was." Certainly, the woman had never been overly cordial with Adeline but never had she given her the cut direct.

Glancing sideways, Adeline tried to determine if Jasper noticed, but his gaze was trained straight ahead, his usual smile in place. If his back were a bit rigid or his steps stiffer than normal, Adeline suspected it was due to this being his first time encountering the lords and ladies of the *ton* in their natural habitat—London.

"Miss Adeline! Miss Adeline!" a young woman called, rushing toward Adeline and Jasper, leaving her chaperone hurrying in her wake. "What a wonderful surprise. I received an invitation—"

The woman stopped short, her sable stole falling over her shoulder.

Adeline searched her memory, but could only vaguely remember the girl she'd met on one other occasion.

"My apologies, I must be going..." The woman turned and fled.

"Good heavens, I have no notion what has gotten into everyone today." Adeline turned to Jasper as he pulled his collar higher, attempting to cover his scars. "I have never met so many—"

"Do not allow them to bring you to anger."

"I am not angry..." However, that was a lie, evident from the flush of her skin and the speed of her heart as it raced. "It is only that I do not understand."

"I have had over a decade of such encounters—the jeers, the stares, and the obvious avoidance by people I once saw as friends." He cleared his throat when his voice cracked on the last word. "It is not you they wish to avoid, but me. I can assure you, I am quite used to this."

"Well, I most certainly am not," she retorted. "I

will speak with Georgie and her father about the duchess's impolite behavior, and I will make certain the dark-haired woman is not allowed through our door this evening."

Jasper chuckled, raising the hairs on the back of Adeline's neck. "No matter what you do, you cannot change their actions, only how you respond to them."

"It is not fair—"

"Life is never fair, Miss Adeline," he said, pulling her close once more. Certainly too close for their walk in the park. "Besides, it rarely matters what you do or say, people will view you through their own distorted eyes."

Adeline settled into their slow pace once more, careful to keep her gaze focused straight ahead and not making eye contact with anyone.

"You are wise, Lord Ailesbury."

"There were many life lessons learned before I was taught to disregard the unpleasantness of others."

"Who taught you?"

"My aunt and uncle." He sighed. "After my parents passed, they came to Faversham to care for me, as I said. And their task was made no easier by the villagers."

It was exactly what she'd been waiting for him to say, something to give her some insight into his past. She remained quiet, silently begging him to continue. She longed to know what had transpired between him and the villagers, and how he'd kept from falling into a pattern of cruel behavior.

"My aunt sheltered me from the hurt, the judgment, and the prying eyes of everyone who sought to harm the parentless boy who survived the Faversham fire. She hired tutors to see to my education at Faversham, my uncle instructed me on the proper running of an estate, and most of all, the pair gave me the love I desperately needed to recover from the devastation of losing my family." He paused. When she glanced over at him, he swiped at his eyes with his free hand. "They created a safe haven for me at Faversham Abbey, though the cruel world lay only a short walk away in the village."

"I heard them call you the Beast of Faversham." She hadn't meant to speak the words, hadn't wanted to so much as think them, yet they pushed past her lips on a breathless sigh. "Even after you saved Grovedale."

"Yes, well, there were others lost in the fire, servants who came from the village," he said. "Eight people died that night, including my parents. Eight people I was too weak to save. And a handful of families lost someone they loved."

"And they still take their anger out on you." It wasn't a question for Adeline had witnessed the villagers' disdain for Jasper firsthand.

"Yes, and they have every right to."

"But you were just a boy."

"That does not matter," he retorted, his tone deepening to one of harshness. "They were my family's people. Their families had served my family for generations. And they lost people they loved, just as I did."

"That should have brought you all closer in your grief."

"No, they needed someone to blame, someone to cast in the shadows to help them through their grief."

"And that was you." Another statement without a hint of a question.

"It was easier to cast aspersion on a marred, damaged boy than live a lifetime never understanding the hows and whys of the situation. If my accepting the fault gave them a measure of comfort and the ability to move forward, it has all been worth it."

"But you continue to allow them to blame you." How had their conversation taken such a dark turn? "Clearly, no one has moved forward."

"That is not true," he countered, pulling to a stop to face her. "My close servants have forgiven me."

She should argue that no forgiveness should have been needed.

"And your scars…do they pain you still?" Adeline kept her focus away from Jasper. If her questions made him uncomfortable, she did not seek to make it worse. "I mean, I do not know their extent, but I can only assume your recovery was a long, arduous time."

He chuckled lightly, but she was uncertain if it was to distract her from her line of questioning or if he found a jest in her words. "They have not hurt in many years and cover only my cheek, neck, arm, and part of my side to my hip. Yes, it was painful, but nothing as grave as that which my servants suffered at the loss of their loved ones."

How could he think to compare the two? And how had his people been so blinded as not to see the man beneath the scars? Adeline had no doubt that Jasper had hurt just as fervently—if not more—than those who called Faversham home.

"When I purchased the gunpowder plant after the government abandoned the factory when the war ended, I promised paying positions to any man, woman, or growing boy who sought employment. I've worked hard to make amends and bring the people of Faversham back together through prosperous growth in our small town." His voice cracked once more. "And I nearly lost everything I gained when that wall collapsed on Grovedale. If he—or anyone else—had been seriously injured, my connection to Faversham would have been permanently severed."

"But that did not happen."

He began to walk once more. "No, it did not."

"However, they still call you the Beast of Faversham."

"It is a title I am used to, Miss Adeline." He patted

her hand where it sat nestled at his elbow. "My aunt preached kindness and compassion in all manner of situations, even when it is necessary to look past unfair treatment of myself."

"You are superior to me, my lord," Adeline commented.

"I have had over ten years of practice, Miss Adeline," he said with a chuckle—not the deep, lighthearted laughter from earlier, but a dark, gravelly sound that had Adeline wondering what other pain he suppressed. "But now, it is time I return you to your brother and ready myself for my first London ball."

Adeline was shocked to realize they'd arrived at his waiting coach. George, the Ailesbury driver, held the door wide and waited for them to enter. She didn't want to move, didn't want to break the private moment they currently shared. There were so many questions still unanswered.

However, when Jasper turned his strained smile on her and held his hand out to assist her up into the waiting conveyance, Adeline knew, rather than suspected, that their conversation was over and Jasper would not be sharing any more about his past...at least for the time being.

CHAPTER 20

ADELINE STARED INTO the looking glass as Poppy slipped the final button through its intended hole and dipped her head to her mistress before departing the room. The door had not so much as latched closed before her friends leapt from their various seats around her bedchambers to stand beside her.

Each woman had selected a gown befitting their individual style. Georgie's was a low-cut, daring dark red with a glittering jeweled waistband. Josie wore a peach concoction better suited to a girl fresh from the schoolroom than a woman of her age. And, Theo, as always, had chosen a conservative, high-necked, full-skirted, light green dress that enhanced the sheen of her dark hair.

Adeline's gown was a shimmering blue with a moss green overskirt and cream lace embellishments, and she had a tight pearl choker around her throat. Against her mother's wishes, Adeline had had her hair curled and left it to hang free over her shoulders and down her back. She cared not a whit women her age preferred their hair arranged high atop their crowns and beaded through with lengths of ribbon or pearls.

Her entire ensemble would not have been something she'd chosen only a month before. Not even a week before.

"You are stunning, Adeline," Theo gushed.

"The coloring matches your complexion superbly," Josie sighed, clutching her hands to her chest as she looked ready to swoon.

"And quite reserved for you," Georgie added.

The gown was nothing like she would have longed for in the past. Normally, she would have selected a dress far more similar to Georgie's with its daring neckline and bold hue, perhaps in a deep blue with sapphires at her neck, ears, and wrist.

"The dress is perfect." Josie glanced down at her own gown, her pale complexion matching the peach colored material that was likely altered from a morning gown design to fit the night's festivities. It was no secret that the woman's family barely had the funds to even remain in London; however, Georgie—with Adeline's help—made certain their friend never went without. "I envy your talent for commissioning gowns, Adeline."

Adeline smiled at her friend in the looking glass. "This night would not be possible if it weren't for all of you."

It was hard to believe the trio had gone to such lengths to make sure Adeline's birthday celebration was a success. Even now, the strings of the small orchestra carried up the stairs from the ballroom below and echoed through the halls to be heard in Adeline's chambers.

Guests were likely arriving in droves.

All for her…

But she only thought of one man—longed to see one lord, and desired only his eyes on her.

"Do you think Lord Ailesbury will come tonight?" Adeline hadn't meant to put voice to her concerns. Hadn't intended to bring up the man's name at all, especially before three women who knew her as keenly as she knew herself.

"Did he not say he was coming when he delivered you home this afternoon?" Theo asked, reaching forward to adjust the shoulder of Adeline's gown.

"Yes, but—"

"Then he will be here," Georgie replied, matter-of-factly.

"How can you be so certain?" She'd had to stop herself from sending a missive around to his townhouse earlier, verifying his attendance at the ball.

"While I have only just met the man, my deductive reasoning says he is a lord of his word: polite, well-mannered, and gentlemanly at every turn." Theo nodded as if her *deductive reasoning* were all the proof Adeline needed to gain confidence in her words. "Lord Ailesbury accepted Alistair's invitation and also spoke to you about attending. He will be here, I am certain of it."

Adeline wished she held even a fraction of Theo's confidence, but after their turn in the park, she was not at all certain Jasper relished an entire evening on display before the *ton*.

"He is a fierce lord," Josie said. "I barely found my tongue when around him."

"…the man is dashingly handsome, despite his, errr, damage," Georgie added.

It was the first time her friends had mentioned Jasper's scars, and Adeline fought back the need to bite out a harsh retort. She must remember that these women were her friends and would never say anything to disparage Jasper.

"What do you think of the man?" Theo's intense stare met Adeline's in the mirror, and she looked away quickly, forcing her interest to the lace at her waist. "Come now, you must have some fondness for the man if you accepted his offer to escort you back to London and invited him to our practice this morning."

If she made eye contact with any of the woman in the room, they would see the true fondness that had grown between her and Jasper—or at least the attraction she had for him.

"You are likely hesitant to speak of him or have him attend you in public." Georgie shrugged and turned to collect her dance card from the table next to Adeline's bed.

"Whatever do you mean by that?" Adeline snapped.

"Only that his physical scars are not what most women find themselves drawn to."

"I do not notice his scars." Her voice held a force she hadn't intended, belying everything she'd said. Taking a calming breath, she faced Georgie. "Jasper, Lord Ailesbury, is far more than his scars. I have gotten to know the man behind them—very well."

Georgie only huffed and focused her attention on tying the ribbons of her dance card around her narrow wrist.

"I have witnessed his kind heart firsthand," Adeline stumbled over her words in her rush to defend Jasper— to the only group of people she'd never thought she'd need defend him to. "He saved a man from certain death at his plant in Faversham. And he was humble about it. A child thanked him and he…he…" Adeline hadn't known the exact words that passed between the pair before her mother collected her, but he'd been kind to the child. She was certain of that.

"Do you know his intention with you?" Theo asked, still at her side.

"Yes, Adeline, do you think he will offer a proper courtship? Mayhap speak with your brother about offering for your hand?" Josie lowered herself to sit on Adeline's neatly arranged bed. "Imagine being betrothed to Lord Ailesbury!"

"Nothing has been promised nor mentioned beyond him escorting me back to London and accepting my brother's invitation." Adeline sighed, surprised to discover she wanted his intentions to reach farther—last longer—than the mere few days they'd had together. "He has been a gentleman since the moment we met. He is kind to his servants and is an admirable listener. He has much dedication to his people and the land surrounding his family home in Kent."

"No mention of handsomeness, title, wealth, or landholdings…"

"A man is more than the title and wealth he possesses," Adeline threw back at Georgie.

The woman held up her arms, palms out, a smirk settling on her lips. "Oh, we understand that, evident by my marriage to Felton and Theo's marriage to Alistair; however, you've never taken an interest in any lord beyond what could be yours in the marriage contract."

"That is vulgarly offensive." Indignation flared, and her pulse thrashed in her head, distorting any conversation happening around her. "Besides, I have not shown attention to any man since coming out in society."

Neither Josie nor Theo would meet her glare as they moved about her chambers, collecting their belongings. Georgie rested her hands on her hips, her smug grin remaining in place.

Adeline wanted to yell, throw her hands wide, and stomp her slipper-clad foot. But she suspected her irritation would only incite their further scrutiny regarding the connection between her and Jasper. She did not want any attention focused on the pair of them, especially during the ball to come, as Adeline hoped to find a few moments of privacy with Jasper before he returned to Faversham Abbey—and disappeared from her life.

Thankfully, Poppy tapped lightly on the door, rescuing Adeline from any further inquisition. "Lady Melton, Miss Adeline, m'lord be request'n your presence and assistance with greet'n the guests."

"We will be right out." Theo straightened her gown and checked her hair in the mirror, each woman following suit. "Shall we, ladies?"

CHAPTER 21

JASPER TOOK A single—albeit small—step forward.

Any progress is progress, he reminded himself.

And after waiting in the long line of carriages outside the Melton townhouse to be deposited in the drive, the receiving line was not nearly as daunting in its length. As far as he'd noticed, he was the only gentleman to arrive unattended, without a woman on his arm or friends at his side. Jasper recognized he lived a modest lifestyle in Kent; however, he could not comprehend how any one person—or even family— was acquainted with so many people.

Undoubtedly, every member of society had been invited…and arrived at the same moment to celebrate Adeline's birthday.

How had he completely missed her station in the *ton?*

Every man of marriageable age who was not already wedded or betrothed stood in line before and after him, with likely much more already in the ballroom.

Jasper pulled at the sleeve of his finely pressed shirt and adjusted his cravat. Bloody hell but he appeared the strutting peacock, a confirmed London dandy, in the coat and trousers he'd been given, with the iridescent, pale blue neckcloth tied precariously about his neck. The thing should be black, not a blue that seemed to change color with the lighting. The hue was one he'd never seen before and certainly not something he would ever don again—nor the rest of his garb. It was all rather wasteful, though Jasper was loath to admit his change of heart after ordering a completely new wardrobe from Lord Melton's tailor.

The funds would have been better spent on restoring the east wing of the Abbey or adding a new warehouse at the plant.

He moved forward once more, this time three paces.

Jasper noticed a familiar face not far off, the butler who'd greeted Adeline the previous day…and he had a tray of tall flutes.

When Jasper nodded in the man's direction, he hurried over and inclined his head. "Lord Ailesbury. Lord and Lady Melton are happy to have you present for Miss Adeline's celebration. Refreshment?"

"Thank you," Jasper said, relieving the man of a glass. "I thought this was to be a small gathering."

"Oh, yes, my lord." The butler's head bobbed up and down. "Only two hundred invitations were hand-delivered to the most deserving households in London and the bordering countryside." He paused as if remembering something. "You, Lord Ailesbury, made two hundred and one."

From the servant's widened eyes, Jasper suspected his complexion had turned a rare shade of green. Two hundred invitations, multiplied by several family members in each household…that must be…

"Five hundred and fifty-three, errr, fifty-four, guests," the butler said, supplying the number Jasper was too dumbfounded to compute on his own.

"And that is a *small* number?"

"Certainly, my lord." The butler nodded as the

group of men behind him each took a flute from his tray. "Lady Melton found it necessary to eliminate over one hundred and fifty guests."

"And Lord and Lady Melton are familiar with all these people?" Jasper had never felt so insignificant in his entire existence. The villagers rarely allowed him to forget that they were keeping watch over him. "That is rather difficult to believe, or perhaps I am simply unfamiliar with town ways."

"You will grow accustomed to the extravagant nature of London, my lord." With a reassuring smile, the butler moved down the line and nodded as guests took refreshments from his tray.

Whatever did the man mean by his comment that Jasper would grow accustomed to London?

He was counting down the hours until he was on his way back to Faversham Abbey and away from the senseless, absurd, and excessive ways of town life. He breathed deeply, picturing the simple life he led in Kent: his estate, his business, and his people, regardless if they denied him as their provider and beneficiary or not.

Taking another step forward, Jasper glanced over the shoulder of the woman in front of him to see that he was nearly to the ballroom doors, though he was still unable to gain sight of Lord and Lady Melton where they greeted guests. Every once in a while, the deep chords of Melton's voice carried out of the grand ballroom.

Jasper must have gotten a fraction too close, for the woman turned around, her eyes narrowing before widening—in surprised alarm?—as a smile settled on her lips. She took in his height and seemed to appreciate his neckcloth before her stare halted at his cheek and his burns traveling lower into his shirt. The woman's welcoming smile turned to a frown, and she pivoted back around, taking a step closer to her escort for the evening.

Swinging his gaze back to the door behind him, Jasper noted the young woman who'd sought Adeline's attention in the park before turning sharply and quickly scurrying away.

He smiled and nodded when he caught her eye. Despite his civility, the lady turned toward the couple she stood with—from the matching hair color and stature, her parents—and laughed as if she'd been part of their conversation the entire time.

The cut direct—or indirect, as it were.

His stomach clenched, and his breath froze in his chest as disbelief and disappointment coursed through him. Why had he thought London would be any different than Kent?

And bloody hell, why did it bother him? The villagers avoided him as if he carried the plague. It appeared those in the *ton* could spot a pariah as well as any country dweller.

Pivoting forward once more, Jasper took several steps and entered the ballroom.

Another servant stepped forward, relieving him of his flute.

He need only make it through the next hour or so, wish Adeline the best, greet her family and friends, and finally take his leave…from the ball and London altogether.

It should not be overly difficult.

Jasper had seen difficult, witnessed it firsthand, *lived* with it nearly his entire life.

A crowded London ballroom filled to bursting with the haughty *beau monde* was not enough to send him cowering and scurrying home, his proverbial tail between his legs.

"Lord Ailesbury," Lady Melton called as he arrived at the front of the line. "We are pleased you came."

Jasper bowed to his host and hostess. "Good evening Lady Melton, Lord Melton. I am honored to be present to celebrate Miss Adeline's birthday."

His attention remained on Lady Melton, not daring to glance farther down the line. Would Adeline be waiting to greet him, or had she already taken to the dance floor? Even the thought of her in another man's arms had his cravat closing off his airway.

Next, he greeted a tall, stately woman with hair the same hue as Adeline's but lacking the shine and luster of the younger woman's curls.

"Lord Ailesbury." His name was exhaled on a raspy sigh. "I was beginning to wonder if you'd become lost on the London streets."

Jasper swung his stare farther down the line, past two young men and a girl who looked fresh from the schoolroom, until he spotted Adeline.

It took everything in his power not to push the couple in front of him out of the way to get to her, to take her proffered gloved hand and press his lips to the delicate spot at her wrist. If he closed his eyes, he could envision her as she'd been at Faversham: hair wild and loose from their breakneck ride across the meadow, her skin damp from the rain, and her eyes…alive from the thrill of it all.

This Adeline, the one standing several feet away, was nearly unrecognizable.

Her hair was loose and artfully arranged over her shoulder and down her back, but nothing else was the woman he'd come to love—love?—while in the country. This woman was everything a lady of the *ton* should be: poised, dignified, reserved, and shining in all her splendor.

For a moment, Jasper wondered how she hid the woman she truly was under all these grandiose adornments, but then the thought struck him, nearly knocking him back a step. Perhaps this was the true Adeline, and the woman he'd come to know in the country was merely the mask she wore to fool him.

He would not believe it, *could* not believe it.

There was no doubt in Jasper's mind that Adeline belonged here. Not in this ballroom per se, but here in London, surrounded by the streaming light from the overhead chandeliers, dining in grand homes, dancing long into the night, attending the latest performance at Covent Garden, and, at the end of the night, returning to her home with a lord who loved her, cherished her, and gave his every waking thought to her happiness and well-being. Adeline would be the center of attention at every social gathering for years to come, and damn it all if Jasper would be the man to distract from her beauty, her wit, and her charm.

At the park—and in the receiving line—he'd garnered attention he didn't want. With Adeline at his side, even for just this one night, would others look past his scars to the worthy woman on his arm?

The couple blocking his path to Adeline blessedly moved off and into the ballroom, clearing Jasper's way to stand before Adeline.

His breath hitched at the sight of her, and a peculiar flutter assaulted his stomach.

The woman was dressed in a gown matching the exact hue of his neckcloth, and damn it if it did not shimmer in the light from above.

Jasper dared a glance over his shoulder, and Lady Melton's innocent grin told him everything he needed to know.

His new tailor had been compromised. His loyalty purchased by a meddling viscountess.

It should irritate Jasper; however, confusion was the emotion that filled him. Why would Lady Melton seek to make it appear as if Adeline and he were a matched pair?

His shoulders stiffened, and the smile drained from his face. Would Adeline be angry? She could not think he had aught to do with the coincidence of their matching garb.

The gentleman behind Jasper cleared his throat, properly indicating that he was slowing down the line.

He need greet Adeline, and then he could escape to a quiet corner of the ballroom to think through the predicament he'd been forced into.

"Miss Adeline, it is lovely to see you again and a very merry birthday to you." He took her offered hand and bowed over it, not trusting himself to bring his lips to her gloved fingers. "Thank you for the invitation."

There. He'd met social requirements and could now sulk off, perhaps hide himself behind one of the potted ferns lining the fabric-draped walls.

"You look dashing this evening, my lord." Her deep, sultry voice held him captive. "I must say, the ladies will be falling all over themselves for an introduction to the darkly handsome and captivating Lord Ailesbury. I can only imagine what they'd wager for one dance."

"It is only you, Miss Adeline, I wish to dance with this eve," he countered. Where in the bloody hell had that come from? Certainly, he'd been thinking it, but to say it out loud was highly improper. "What I mean to say, Miss Adeline, is I do hope you will save a place on your dance card for me."

She held her wrist high, rotating the card to give Jasper a better view. "I have saved every spot for you, my lord." Her brow rose in question. She was obviously enjoying their scandalous banter—and his unease. "In fact, as it is my special evening, I will take you up on one of those dances now."

Without another word, she stepped from the line and set her hand in the crook of his elbow. He covered it with his own palm as if they had walked thusly a million times before.

A wave of her hand, and the musicians struck a new chord before settling into a rhythmic melody Jasper had heard his aunt hum from time to time.

A waltz, deemed indecent and scandalous only a few years prior, was now favored in many London ballrooms, or so he'd read in the *London Daily Gazette* his solicitor sent him every few weeks.

As they entered the dance floor, other pairs moved to join them, as Jasper pulled Adeline into his embrace and stared into her hazel eyes.

She was the beauty to his beast.

The elegant, refined maiden to his dastardly, dark scoundrel.

And he wanted all of her, though the reality of it was he might only have this one dance.

"You look ravishing, Miss Adeline," Jasper leaned in close to whisper. A shiver coursed through her entire body, so strong he felt it. "I must say, you are certainly the belle of the ball."

Her face flushed a deep scarlet, and Jasper chuckled lightly, pushing from his mind everything but that precise moment.

"I do believe my tailor and your modiste must have a fondness for one another."

"Would you blame them if they did?" she asked, her enchanting smile returning as they increased their steps in time with the music. "Besides, I must admit, I was hesitant to don such a gown; however, I can see the color was selected because it suited you, my lord."

"And what will others think about our coordinated attire?"

"Should we concern ourselves with what others think?" she countered.

"I am only thinking of you, Adeline." He could not stop himself from uttering her given name, though it was the height of impropriety, especially surrounded by a roomful of people who would likely—and savagely—take hold of the morsel of gossip and spread it far and wide. "There are many worthy men in attendance this night, come to celebrate your special day. It would be greedy of me to keep you all to myself or cause gossip where none is warranted."

A spark of disappointment flared in her eyes, but she covered it quickly by affecting yet another inviting upturn of her lips. "A little gossip never killed anyone. You should know that, Jasper."

They twirled around the floor. Jasper was utterly lost in the moment with her, so enthralled he nearly collided with another couple as the music halted all too soon.

It was time he returned her to her family—and her line of suitors.

To his chagrin, she steered him away from her brother and mother where they'd completed their duties as the host family and were now conversing amongst one another.

"You are an accomplished dancer, Lord Ailesbury."

"For nothing but a country squire?" He kept a respectable distance between them as he followed her lead around the fringes of the dance floor. "I will admit, I have not often danced with anyone besides my Aunt Alice and my housekeeper."

"Well, your aunt certainly taught you well."

A man stepped into their path, a tentative smile transforming his serious demeanor as he grew closer. Jasper had the urge to growl and walk straight through the man, continuing his conversation with Adeline; however, she slowed her pace to greet her guest.

"Good evening, Lord Cartwright." Jealousy spiked when Adeline turned her bright smile on the man. "It is lovely to see you once again. May I introduce Lord Ailesbury from Kent?"

"A pleasure, I am certain," Cartwright mumbled, sounding anything but pleasured to meet him. "I only wanted to give my well wishes for your birthday, Adeline. I must needs leave quickly."

"I do understand, Lord Cartwright," Adeline said, accepting the stiff embrace the man offered. "Your situation is certainly one to be cautious of."

Jasper was uncertain what irritated him more: the man's use of her given name, Adeline's knowledge of his *situation*, or that Cartwright's arms were presently touching her back.

"Lord Cartwright—Simon—is Theodora's elder brother," Adeline offered, doing nothing to dampen the jealousy at the man's familiar relationship with her. "Simon, you will be quite interested in Lord Aliesbury's endeavors in Faversham." She turned an appreciative look in Jasper's direction, settling his ire. "He bought the gunpowder plant after the war ended and employs a large number of the villagers."

Cartwright's brow rose. "I know very little about weapons of war, but I would be very interested in visiting your plant."

"I am currently renovating an area of the building that collapsed during the recent storms, but when they are finished, I'd be happy to show you how things work." Why, oh why, had he offered to escort Cartwright on a tour of Home Works? He knew exactly why. This man meant something to Adeline...and he was determined to find out what. "A wall recently gave way and injured one of my workers."

"A wall, you say?" When Jasper nodded at Cartwright's question, the man tapped his chin and closed his eyes, his brows moving up and down before his lids snapped open once more. "It would be my pleasure to work through the calculations and coordinate the measurements and weight requirements to better determine what would constitute a sound, load-bearing wall, as well as the appropriate thickness of the supporting beams to withstand future storms."

Jasper stared at the man in wonder, partly because he was unaccustomed to such kindness from strangers, but more accurately because he could not fully understand the assistance Cartwright offered.

"It was certainly a pleasure, Lord Ailesbury, but my dear wife is waving frantically at me, and my situation may have suddenly escalated from cautious to dire."

Jasper followed Adeline's stare to see a tall, dark-haired woman, heavy with child, leaning against the refreshment table—one hand waving while the other cradled her swollen midsection.

"It appears Theo is to be an aunt for the third time," Adeline said. "I think it best you hurry and return her home, Simon."

"Olivia waited fourteen hours to arrive, and Samuel came after twelve. Using simple calculations, I have ten hours until this babe graces us with its presence."

"I do not think it works that way, my lord," Jasper said, eyeing Cartwright's wife, who, while in the late stages, made no show of needing to be whisked away to her birthing suite.

Adeline laughed, pushing Simon in his wife's direction. "Do see to Jude. The evening is young, and I find myself in need of fresh air, and a stroll on the terrace before Lord Ailesbury and I seek the dance floor once more."

If the man found it shocking Adeline had promised Jasper another dance, he did not show any signs of it. "Very well, I will take my leave, but please, there is little reason to upset Theo with news of Jude's less than perfect health. This night means much to her."

"Your secret shall not pass my lips. But do keep watch over her, Simon."

"I endeavor to do exactly that." With a quick embrace for Adeline and a bow to Jasper, Cartwright moved through the crowd to his wife's side.

"A peculiar man," Jasper mused.

"You have no idea how peculiar, my lord." She slipped her arm into his once more and turned her bright eyes on him. "Now, the Melton gardens, while small, are beautiful under the moon's glow."

CHAPTER 22

THE CHILLY NIGHT air, as they stepped through the open doors onto the terrace, was a balm to Adeline's overheated face, neck, and arms. It had nothing to do with the ballroom being warmer than usual and everything to do with Jasper. His hand on her lower back, pulling her ever tighter to him as they danced. His stare on her as they conversed with Theo's brother.

Every inch of her blazed with unbidden heat, and, at some point, that heat had changed to a deep-seated need. A desirous longing that she'd never experienced before.

One dance with Jasper was not enough.

An entire day would not be sufficient to keep her satisfied, her mind full of memories after Jasper returned to Faversham.

This night was their goodbye.

She'd known from the moment they left Kent Jasper would deposit her in London and his duty to her would be fulfilled. She should be content with the additional time she'd been allowed to spend with him; though it only seemed to make her want him more.

It had taken but a brief moment to realize the shiver running down her body, the flutter in her stomach, the tightening in her chest was due to one thing.

One complex, all-consuming emotion.

Love.

It went far beyond mere infatuation.

It would not be dampened or diluted by giving in to a lustful tryst. Or satisfied by a harmless walk in the park or ices at Samson's.

No, this sensation coursing through her, driving her every move, pushing her to claim Jasper as hers would not be easily ignored or assuaged.

His presence in London had made it clear why Adeline hadn't met a man who captured her notice beyond a mere glance. No man of her acquaintance held a candle to Jasper. None were as loyal, devoted, capable, courageous, and confident as the man who presently walked at her side. He stood—tall and proud—though she knew his every instinct told him he didn't belong in London and among society; that his place was in Kent, hiding the burns that had nearly taken his life.

Yet, Adeline was confident in one thing: society would benefit by knowing Jasper. He would make London a better place, if only for her. The *ton* could learn much from a man who gave up finding his own happiness to serve those who'd dedicated generations to his family.

Adeline released his arm and walked to the railing separating them from the gardens below. Though she heard nothing, she knew he followed. She sensed him behind her as she placed her hands on the railing. The cold soaked through her thin gloves, sending a shiver down her back. The chilly evening air would not drive her back inside, however.

No.

The terrace was deserted, it being too early in the evening for others to seek the outdoors yet.

It was only she and Jasper and the strings of a light melody drifting out from the ballroom at their backs.

"Adeline," he whispered close to her ear. The single word was enough to banish any doubt she had about how he felt about her. "I do hope you are enjoying your celebration."

She glanced up at the clear, night sky. The moon overhead shone down on the gardens, creating shadows and darkening alcoves of privacy. Even the stars twinkled brighter than she'd ever noticed before. "Now that you are here, I am enjoying myself immensely, my lord."

"I am certain it is not my presence that makes a difference," he countered.

"You are correct." She turned to find he was scant inches from her. "It is you who makes all the difference...to me," she added, making certain there was no question as to her meaning.

Adeline held his stare, losing herself in his moss green depths. It was much like entering the woods at Faversham, the hue of his eyes matching the foliage as if the surrounding countryside had laid claim to him—and would soon demand his return.

Tentatively, she set her fingers on his cheek, allowing them to caress lower until they met his damaged skin. She could feel the warmth of him through her glove, more powerful than the cold of the railing from a moment before.

It was Jasper who broke their connection first, his eyes closing as her touch slid lower to his neck. She longed to remove his cravat, unbutton his shirt, and explore further what he kept hidden.

His scars did not reveal weakness, not in the least.

They *proved* his strength.

He'd lost his parents and cherished servants in that fire.

The people who should have been there to catch him had only labeled him a beast.

Adeline would not allow that to continue. Never

would she allow another to force Jasper into the shadows; a forgotten man and something to be feared.

"I do not fear you, Jasper," she confessed in a whisper. "Since the moment we met, I have become a different person, a *better* woman. I am far more patient and do not see the worst in every person upon first inspection. I owe that to you."

"It is not only you who has noted a change within themselves," he confided, his remaining closed. Could he not look at her when he spoke? "I have lived many years alone, and now I wonder what I have gained from any of it."

Adeline could not let him stand before her with his emotions so bare. "It is because of you I can think of understanding a situation as opposed to judging others for their choices before I know their reasoning."

His eyes sprang open, and he searched her expression as if he thought to find she was misleading him in some way. He pulled away from her, his exhale labored, and her hand fell to her side.

But she could not allow him the distance, and so she followed him.

"Adeline…I—"

She gave him no opportunity to speak, to offer an excuse to flee or put more distance between them—either physically or emotionally. If this were to be the last night they had together, she would not let it pass without giving him some hope for his future, even if that future did not include her.

Jasper needed to know he was loved, that his years of caring for others had come full circle.

Standing on her tiptoes, Adeline pressed her lips to his. At first, neither of them moved, and Adeline lost herself in the warmth of his mouth.

She knew when he gave in, threw caution to the wind, and stepped closer to her.

Adeline did not question it nor give Jasper time to

change his mind as she moved her lips against his and pressed her body close until they touched from chest to hips.

There was no line crossed, no warning given, no change in tempo, but suddenly, it was Jasper who commanded, led, tempted her further. His hands settled on her waist, lifting slightly, and her toes barely felt the ground beneath her. They were so close, she felt his heartbeat against her bosom as he claimed her lips, setting the pace as his tongue darted across her lower lip.

She'd never kissed a man before, had never met a male worthy of a stolen embrace, but her body knew what to do as she parted her lips and allowed his tongue to explore. Every instinct told her they'd done this a million times before: pressed their bodies close, sealed their lips. And she could not let him go. Adeline's hands clutched at his shoulders, kneading them as his mouth moved with hers.

This connection between them was more than the sum of them together.

He was everything, and without him, she would be reduced to nothing.

Less than nothing.

His need for her was evident in the hard length pressed to her midsection, obvious even through their many layers of clothes.

Did Jasper know she wanted this, too—likely far more than even he?

Heat coursed through her, pooling at her core as if it waited for something, but what, Adeline was uncertain.

Suddenly, something pulled her away from Jasper, their bodies stumbling apart, and her hands ripped from his shoulders.

But no, it wasn't something *pulling* them apart, it was Jasper *pushing* her away.

Adeline found his stare in the darkened evening, and she searched for her answer, but his gaze was hooded as he hid from her and returned to the man he'd been for over a decade.

Jasper had not only kept himself physically hidden from others, but he'd also kept himself sequestered emotionally.

Did he not realize she would never harm him? Did he have no understanding of how he affected her?

She reached out toward him, her stare begging him to return to her, but he only took another step back. The light escaping the ballroom at his back cast a menacing shadow over her. His eyes were wild and frantic as his hands clenched into fists at his sides.

He appeared the beast his people claimed him to be.

But Adeline knew the truth of the matter…

Jasper was her beast.

And she would have him as hers, no matter the consequences or hardships to come.

CHAPTER 23

EVERY MUSCLE IN Jasper's body tensed as light, melodic female laughter sounded at his back, followed by the deep voice of a man questioning what the commotion was on the terrace—the cultured London drawl so different from his people in Kent. His best chance for saving Adeline's reputation was to keep whoever sought to invade their private moment behind him and out of view of Adeline, or more accurately, keep Adeline hidden from the gawking crowd.

His drive was to pivot toward the interlopers and demand they retrace their steps into the ballroom, forget anything they'd seen, and never breathe a word to anyone.

However, that would draw far more attention as the sight of a beast was difficult to forget in the country, and likely all but impossible when seen in a London ballroom.

Jasper took a calming breath, his exhale visible in the dropping temperatures.

Adeline shook before him, and he resisted the urge to go to her, to wrap her in his embrace once more and banish any chill that threatened her.

He hadn't wanted to embarrass her, especially on her birthday. But this—being caught in his embrace on the terrace—would lead to far more than mere embarrassment. It could ruin her and her family. Make her name synonymous with *compromised* and *unmarriageable*.

Had she heard the rumbling of discourse behind him?

Her eyes widened, and she attempted to side-step him, but he moved effortlessly to keep her blocked from view.

She'd heard the laughter, too. The hissed questions about what was happening on the terrace. The start of gossip long before the guilty parties were even so much as identified.

Yet, no shock or terror showed on her face. Her legs did not tremble from the scandal that would soon follow if she were discovered as the compromised party.

"Perhaps it is time I depart," he mumbled loud enough for her to hear, but soft enough so it did not travel to the people pushing out of the ballroom.

Her back stiffened, and her chin lifted in defiance. The same as it had when he'd forbidden her from accompanying him on his hunting excursion. The same as it had when he'd discovered she followed him into the storm and made her way to the plant despite the danger. "You will do no such thing."

"Miss Adeline?" a male voice called over his shoulder. "It is you. But who is this man with you, and what abomination has marred his neck?"

Several females gasped at the man's word—*abomination*.

Yet, Adeline appeared unaffected by their cruel reactions. Her shoulders straightened as if a decision had been made.

His chin dropped, nearly touching his chest as he suppressed the urge to pull his collar high, to hide his injuries from view. Despite his efforts, he suspected the light from the ballroom cast a knowing glow on his most visible scars.

It was too late to save her from the gossip that would come.

He had failed her, and all because he wanted something that was never meant to be his.

Keeping her stare locked on his, she stepped forward, a serene smile upon her lips, and slipped her fingers into the crook of his arm before turning to face the growing crowd behind them.

She straightened her shoulders, pressing tightly to his side as she stared down her nose at her *guests*. An odd term as they were looking on as if they were vultures circling before the kill.

A matronly woman fanned her face as if she'd stumbled upon a licentious display of flesh in the midst of a bawdy house, while a group of young women tittered amongst themselves, sending veiled glances in his direction. But it was the men who incited Jasper's rage. They'd been gentlemen when they stepped through the doors of the Melton townhouse, but now, they appeared as wolves. Their lewd glares raked up and down Adeline as if she were their prey. Not a prize, but a target easily caught.

Blessedly, Lady Melton, with Lady Josie and Lady Georgina in tow, arrived on the terrace threshold and called for attention as they attempted to usher everyone back inside.

"Ladies and gentlemen, the card room is now open." Lady Melton clapped her hands. "With only six tables, you will want to hurry if you favor a seat. And my dear husband, in honor of Miss Adeline's birthday, has brought round several coveted bottles of fine French cognac besides."

The men were the first to turn away, the lure of competition, money, and fine spirits enough to focus their sights elsewhere. However, Jasper did not doubt they'd keep in mind the compromising situation Adeline had been discovered in.

A growl threatened to escape him at the thought of another man thinking they could speak to Adeline about such a delicate subject—or coerce her in any way.

Jasper would not allow it, though he might well be helpless to stop them.

Within moments, he would be cast from the Melton house by Adeline's brother, or worse yet, challenged over the woman's honor.

He would not harm Lord Melton, but he would never back down and allow Adeline's reputation to be questioned either.

She was the woman he would have selected as his wife, had that future still been available to him.

"I think this next dance is promised to you, Lord Ailesbury," Adeline announced for all to hear as she pushed past the remaining guests and into the ballroom. She nodded to the musicians upon the dais, and they stopped their current song and began anew.

Jasper noted Lord Melton watching them as they stepped onto the dance floor, but that did not stop him from swinging Adeline into his arms. If she wanted to dance, he would dance.

Whatever she commanded, Jasper would do.

He was incapable of doing otherwise.

They began swaying to the smooth strings of the violinist, and before long, they twirled and swirled about the dance floor. Jasper could not take his eyes off her upturned face. Her smile alone was enough to hold him prisoner, to banish from his mind the coming consequences of their first and only kiss. Did she suspect the power she possessed over him?

A twinkle in her hazel eyes changed their normally olive hue to that of honey.

There was no hesitation on his part as he sank into their depths, relished the thought of living for eternity under her watchful gaze.

There were others on the floor, dancing so close Jasper feared they might collide and Adeline would be injured. Raising his stare from hers, he noted Lady Georgina and her husband, Lady Josie and a man who looked much like a younger version of Adeline's eldest brother, and, finally, Lord and Lady Melton. Widening his stare, Jasper was shocked to see Lord Cartwright and his wife, moving at a far more sedate pace, also on the floor, and another woman, who was clearly Lady Cartwright…though not large with child.

They were protecting Adeline, and in turn, shielding him.

Did they think him incapable of caring for Adeline and himself?

Jasper had long been the man everyone relied on for their needs. He'd never been one to count on others for something he could do himself.

These people, they offered him a gift, yet it felt more like a decree.

Jasper turned his attention back to Adeline as the music swelled, and they moved effortlessly across the polished dance floor as if they'd paired one another on a thousand other occasions and in hundreds of similar ballrooms.

Too soon, the music came to an end, and so did their dance.

The musicians set their instruments aside and stepped off the dais as couples, each in turn, fled the dance floor. Young debutantes were returned to their chaperones, men disappeared into the card room, lords escorted their companions to the refreshment table, and a few disappeared onto the terrace.

All while Jasper stood frozen on the dance floor, Adeline at his side.

He need return her to her brother or Lady Melton.

He need depart with haste.

He need pray that scandal and gossip would not

take root and destroy Adeline and her family.

Jasper would never forgive himself if he were the cause of more families suffering. As the only surviving Ailesbury, the loss of his servants in the stable fire had been his fault. It had been his fault children had been raised without their father and mother present. It had been his fault that even now his people could not look him the eyes, could not trust him to care for them, could not look past his scars and see the man he'd worked hard to become since the tragedy at Faversham.

"It is time I return you to Lord Melton," he sighed, not having the heart to meet her gaze. "You are the guest of honor, and I cannot monopolize your time any longer."

Without another word, Jasper tucked her gloved hand in his elbow and started for her brother.

"Lord Melton." Jasper's voice shook slightly, and he cleared his throat before continuing. "Thank you for the kind invitation." He turned to Adeline next, focusing on her lips as opposed to her eyes, glistening with moisture. "Miss Adeline, it has been a pleasure. I do hope your celebration is all you hoped for. It is time I take my leave and return to my home in Faversham."

Melton's eyes narrowed on Jasper as he bowed curtly and turned to depart before Adeline—or her brother—could offer any objection.

Giving Adeline one last look over his shoulder, he hoped she understood he didn't want to leave her. If it had been up to him, he would have stayed, gossip be damned.

His footsteps were solid, if not confident, as he made his way to the double doors and the foyer beyond. He need only make it outside into the fresh air and out of sight of the *ton*. Then, and only then, could he allow himself time to dwell on his night.

Placing his hand on the doorframe, Jasper glanced over his shoulder once more, but Adeline was already out of her brother's grasp and headed deeper into the ballroom. Jasper had no right to stop her or dissuade her from enjoying her ball. Nor did he possess the means to care for her in any way she'd see as satisfactory.

"My lord," Jasper glanced back toward the foyer, the Melton butler having appeared at his side. "May I be of assistance?"

"My carriage, please."

"Right away, Lord Ailesbury," the butler bowed. "Do wait here, and I will summon you when your conveyance is ready."

Jasper nodded, knowing there was nothing more he could do but depart into the cold night in search of George and his carriage. Instead, he moved into the shadows outside the ballroom and stared into the celebration.

An outsider.

An outcast.

An interloper.

These were not terms to be applied to those of the *ton* who'd discovered them on the terrace, but to Jasper's own standing among the *beau monde*.

He was the one who did not belong. He was the one to forever watch from the shadows.

It was better this way. His scars would be kept hidden, and Jasper could hold tight to his guilt.

Scanning the crowd one last time, Jasper could no longer pick out Adeline from the throng of people in the ballroom.

It was better this way.

She would forget him in time, and he would hold tight to the memory of her in his arms. Perhaps then, and only then, he could allow a bit of the guilt that had plagued him for over a decade to loosen its hold on him.

CHAPTER 24

ADELINE HAD QUITE SIMPLY had enough.

Enough of Jasper's thinking he knew best—for her and for himself.

Enough of her brother's superior attitude.

Enough of the *ton*'s petty, judgmental arrogance aimed at anyone they questioned as being one of them.

Enough of her friend's overbearing protection.

They thought she hadn't noticed the way they *saved* her from certain ruination on the terrace or came to shield her and Jasper on the dance floor as they closed in and swirled near Adeline and Jasper.

She was not a child, nor ignorant of the ways of society.

She'd known the repercussions she faced if she and Jasper were discovered on the terrace together, pulled close in an intimate embrace.

And she did not care a whit.

Pushing her way through the milling crowd of haughty, insufferable matrons and leering lords, Adeline arrived at the dais as the musicians began to once again take their places.

These people may think to intimidate Jasper, but Adeline had been a part of their ranks for far too long to cower in a corner, accept a fate she did not want, and allow Lord Ailesbury to walk out of her life.

She would not allow *them* to do that to her.

And if her brother and Theo stood in her way, then they would earn the right to be cast in with *them* and become a confirmed enemy of Adeline's.

At nearly twenty-one, Adeline was free to seek her own home, her own way in life, her own future—free of her brother...and her friends, if it came to that. Which, Adeline desperately hoped it would not. Without Theo, Josie, and Georgie at her side, Adeline would have little idea who she was. Odd that this was the same for her and Jasper.

In his arms, she felt protected, safe, and loved.

The moment he'd fled the ballroom, she'd been cast into doubt, left angry and confused.

But no longer.

Adeline nodded to a waiting footman who hurried to her side and assisted her onto the dais, where her scowl was enough to send the musicians fleeing for safety.

Moving to stand in the middle of the dais, she faced the crowd of people she'd once considered her friends, her kin, her community. These were people whose homes she'd visited, whose lives had been inexplicitly intertwined with her own. They were her brother's friends, her mother's companions, her friends' parents. They were the people Adeline should want surrounding her on the momentous occasion of her twenty-first birthday. Yet, she found herself desiring only one man: Jasper. It was his opinion that held weight for her. It was his feelings she wanted to soothe. It was his heart she prayed was not damaged by *these* people.

This—her fury, her sorrow, her doubt—had naught to do with her or her own standing in society.

If she were labeled a ruined woman, so be it. As long as Jasper's name remained above reproach, and he was spared the scandal.

In a way, Adeline was more equipped to handle the ramifications of their terrace tryst. She was capable in a way Jasper was not, no matter how many hours, days, *years*, he spent gaining the strength to one day make amends for the fire at Faversham Abbey. And Adeline did not doubt he blamed himself for everything.

A hush descended on the crowd as one by one, couple by couple, group by group, the *ton* noticed her presence on the dais.

Every pair of eyes turned in her direction.

As Adeline looked to where Jasper had fled, his tall stature now out of sight.

That did nothing to lessen her irritation. Nothing to banish her need for vengeance in *his* honor.

Friendship…loyalty…and honor above all.

It was the Lady Archer's Creed, written when she and her friends were mere girls at Miss Emmeline's School. Yet, the relevance of the words hadn't diminished, hadn't paled, and hadn't lost their meaning in any way.

In fact, the creed meant far more in that moment than ever before.

Jasper was her friend, and Adeline owed him loyalty, among many other things.

He'd saved her life before they even knew one another. He'd offered her shelter without a moment's hesitation. He'd honored her. Even attempted to shield her from view on the terrace.

He was a fool if he thought she'd been unaware of what he was doing.

In return, Adeline would honor him, even if he were not around to hear her, and she never saw him again.

It was more than her mind that pushed her, it was her heart.

She allowed her glare to survey the crowd standing

below the dais, waiting for her to speak. Though she was above them, she did not look down on them—so why did she have the overwhelming sense that many who looked on thought less of her? Judged her for actions they knew nothing about? Cast stones in her direction without any understanding?

Her chest seized. Adeline had once been the same. Done the same. At one time, she'd judged others with no regard for their feelings, their troubles, and the wounds that belonged solely to them. The time she'd made disparaging remarks about a debutante's putrid-colored gown, or the occasion where she'd been asked to dance by a mere merchant's son, and she scoffed at his offer. Even when she'd wastefully commissioned several gowns for her first Season without thought to Alistair's other financial obligations—Adelaide and Arabella's tutors, Alfred's medications for his harsh breathing, and their father's enormous physician's bills.

Who was Adeline to stand before this crowd and condemn them for their actions?

She was little different than anyone in attendance.

Yet, since meeting Jasper, she was well aware of her shortcomings.

Knew them well and was attempting to change…for him.

"Esteemed guests," Adeline called across the hushed ballroom. The only noise disturbing the growing unease was the rustle of a gown, the clearing of a throat, and the murmured question of an elderly matron wondering what in the damned hell was keeping the musicians from playing. "It is with great shame that I stand before you today."

The hissed whispers surged as gossip likely spread about the scene witnessed on the terrace. Though, they would learn soon enough, it was not shame for herself or Jasper she felt...

"You have all been invited into my brother's home

as esteemed guests of Lord and Lady Melton, as well as the Ladies Georgina and Josephine. However, you have all cast this house in hues of midnight blue and scalding red—shame." She made a point to look around the crowd, making eye contact with as many men and women as she could. "Lord Ailesbury graciously accepted my brother's invitation to attend my birthday celebration, a time of joyous festivities, and instead of welcoming him into our home, and our society, you have all turned your nose up at him, leered at his scars—wounds that were beyond his control—and now, he has departed." She paused when her voice cracked, her gaze settling on Theo, Josie, and Georgie as they made their way to the dais. If they thought to hush her, they were sadly overestimating their power. Adeline would have her say, and then she would leave…her own party and her home. "Lord Ailesbury—Jasper—is my friend. He is kind where most are not. He is caring where most are critical. He rescued me from a storm, offered me refuge, and escorted me safely back to London when my carriage proved unusable. He is a man above all others—a kindred soul, a male most honorable, and a gentleman unlike any I have met before. I knew well his aversion to society, yet he was willing to put aside his concerns and discomfort…for me."

Without realizing it, her words had dropped in volume, and the gathered lords and ladies strained forward to hear her every utterance. If it was because they were actually listening or were only seeking more fodder for the gossip mills, Adeline was uncertain.

Adeline picked her brother out of the crowd, standing close to the dais's edge. She could not read his expression, but the likelihood of punishment for her brazen display was assured.

"Adeline?" Theo held her hand out from where she stood below the dais. However, Adeline was not ready to descend, she had not yet had her say.

Shaking her head, Adeline refocused on the ballroom at large. "You all should be grateful for the opportunity to make Lord Ailesbury's acquaintance. A finer, more noble man does not exist in all of England. But truly," she said on a laugh, "none of you are worthy of his friendship. I included."

She sensed the tears coming, knew a complete breakdown was imminent as her head swam and her legs trembled beneath her.

An instant later, her friends were at her side, helping her down from the dais as her guests stared on in absolute shock—many in disgust, and a few smirking. If her time on the terrace hadn't ruined her, her tirade before the entire *ton* had.

Adeline glanced between her friends as her eyes welled with tears. "I love him so," she breathed, her steps faltering, causing Theo and Georgie to hold her weight. "I cannot bear this cruelty toward him. He deserves so much more than this."

"I know," Josie soothed from somewhere out of Adeline's sight but likely trailing them as they moved toward the side door which led into the foyer.

They exited through a single door, nearly hidden from view by cascading fabric, and emerged in the hallway bordering the entryway. It was the only route that would not have them making their way through the crowd on the dance floor.

Adeline's indignation flared once more, and she pulled from Theo's grasp and rounded on her trio of friends as Alistair followed them through the door, pulling it soundlessly closed behind him.

"Have you come to speak ill of Jasper, as well, dear brother?" she demanded, her heart nearly hammering through her chest. "Do you think him less of a man, or unworthy of respect, due to his scars?"

She knew her eyes held the fire of a thousand suns

when Alistair took a step back, his previously narrowed glare widening in surprise at the venom in her tone.

Adeline's glare swung from her brother to Theo and back.

When no one said anything, Adeline blinked several times to clear her sight, blurred from her tears.

However, the swell of tears returned when she noted the pitying looks on everyone's faces.

Adeline deflated in that moment, her fury subsiding as quickly as it had been sparked.

She'd stood before a crowded ballroom and all but declared her love for Jasper.

And, yes, she knew with every breath she took that she loved him.

Would love him until her dying day.

Her chest ached so deeply at the thought of losing him—a man she'd known for such a short time, but who had affected her in ways she'd never dreamed possible. She could not envision a day in which she did not see him, speak with him, ride uninhibited across a meadow at his side, stand in the rain as he cared for his people, and live a life secluded at the Abbey if that meant they could be together.

"Theo...Alistair...I love him." She shook her head back and forth, begging them not to question her words, to take her feelings for what they were. "I know you might not understand, but, I fear I cannot help where my heart takes root."

A hiccup escaped her, and she clamped her mouth shut, determined not to fall apart until she'd found the safety of her room—a room that would not be hers for long when Alistair cast her out for bringing disgrace upon their entire family.

But Adeline would be fine, she would find her way, even without her friends and her family.

If Jasper could survive the loss of his parents—and later, his aunt and uncle—not to mention the harsh cruelty of those who blamed him for their family's deaths, then Adeline could muster the courage to live a life on her own terms, free of society, and satisfied in her own right.

Would she not be content—if not happier—to live a life unburdened by social responsibilities, unrestricted by the rules and guidelines for what made a proper lady? She would be permitted to help others, live in a way that allowed her to be kind to all, and compassionate to other's plights.

It was the way of things at Faversham Abbey.

CHAPTER 25

THEO…ALISTAIR…I love him.

Adeline might have said more, but Jasper heard none of it as he stood in the foyer down the hall from where Lord and Lady Melton, along with Adeline's other friends, stared at the woman; a mixture of shock, apprehension, and pride on their faces.

All of those emotions were coursing through Jasper in that moment, as well, along with at least one more he was able to identify: love. Jasper could not remember feeling such for anyone other than his aunt and uncle. Certainly, he'd loved his parents, but he'd been a mere child, taking for granted he'd been blessed with a caring family, an adequate home, and fine things. In time, Jasper had come to respect and care for his servants and a few men who allowed him close at the plant.

But love? True, unconditional love…for a woman?

There was no mistaking that was the type of love Adeline spoke of. No woman, especially a lady born and bred to be above reproach, would jeopardize her status in a society she cherished if she did not wholeheartedly love another. And she'd stood before all of London, her family's closest friends, and all but proclaimed her love…for him.

Jasper watched as Adeline threw her arms wide, her

back to him. Lady Melton was the first to spot him over Adeline's shoulder.

"My heart is solidly telling me Jasper is the only man for me." Her shoulders shook with her words, as if she kept her sobs inside but had no control over her body. "He is fair and kind to his servants and staff at the plant, he has a shrewd business sense, he is empathetic to the plight and misfortune of others, he is trusting and selfless"—she ticked off the list on her fingers—"and he is, above all else, loyal and compassionate."

She stumbled on the last words, and Jasper longed to go to her, wrap his arms around her, and tell her everything would be fine. He desired nothing more than to put a stop to her ramblings. He was not the man she described with such passion. He strived each and every day to fit those characteristics, but attaining them had been difficult and, more often than not, out of his reach.

Jasper started in her direction, but her shoulders tensed and her chin lifted.

"Honestly, dear brother, I cannot imagine that I deserve a man such as Jasper, or that he would ever think to take me to wife." She whimpered when no one made any move to respond to her. "I am his complete opposite in nearly every way. I have a vanity that runs far too deep, I am critical of others, I am petty and selfish, I demand things I have not earned, I cause so much trouble for you and Theo, and I am overly harsh with Josie. I do not deserve his loyalty…or yours, my flaws are so great."

Jasper could not, *would* not, believe any of those things to be true or that they represented who Adeline was. This was not the woman he'd gotten to know in Faversham. That woman had been confident to a fault. She'd been undaunted by the storm, hadn't hesitated to assist him in providing food for his people, and she rode across the meadow to the plant to make certain Jasper was not injured, and Emily's husband was rescued.

He'd retreated into himself after the fire. Yet, Adeline's own father had died the previous year, and she'd stepped forward to take her younger siblings all the way to Canterbury. She hadn't hidden in her room and wallowed in her grief.

Adeline had met Jasper head-on and refused to balk or back down from him. And neither had she turned away from him due to his scars and the villagers' ramblings proclaiming the beast.

It had only been she who'd taken the time to recognize that his beastly appearance had not rotted his insides.

"Besides," Adeline began again, her voice strong once more. "I will be twenty-one in less than a fortnight. I will not need your approval or blessing to live my life any way I see fit. I will wed any damned man I choose, or I will never marry at all. But it will be my choice, my decision, and my cross to bear if I muck everything up."

Lady Georgina let loose a loud snort of laughter while Lady Melton fell into a light, feminine giggle. Lady Josie appeared ready to faint on the spot as her eyes settled on Jasper as he walked slowly down the hall. He was uncertain when his legs began to move, but move they did—toward Adeline.

Jasper hadn't the nerve to meet Lord Melton's stare, yet he could visualize the viscount's narrowed glare.

He only kept his attention on Adeline's back. Ten more paces and he'd be to her.

Someone must have alerted her to his presence because her chin lowered and she pivoted to face him.

Her cheeks were streaked with tears as they continued to roll down her face and off her chin, turning her light blue gown to a darker hue from the moisture.

"...not that I am to wed Lord Ailesbury, or that

we've even spoken of mutual affection," she stammered, her eyes locking on his as all color drained from her face, leaving her skin pale—almost green.

"And what if I desire to speak of marriage?" Jasper's brow rose in question.

"Then I would think this is a subject better discussed in private." Lord Melton stepped forward, gesturing back toward the foyer. "If you will follow me, Lord Ailesbury, we can discuss this in my study."

"I will have Adeline present," he said without thinking. He could offend Melton as women were not usually present during business negotiations, and Jasper was not fool enough to think this was anything but a business and a negotiation—even if it was a matter of the heart for him.

"Oh, have you not met my sister?" Lord Melton asked, his smirk hard to hide. "She would beat down the door—or climb down the hearth flue—if I did not allow her in. It is safer for all involved if we invite her straight away. Besides, this is her future as much as yours, Ailesbury. I do hope you've thought this through."

"There is naught to think through, my lord, though I appreciate your warning."

Jasper glanced in Adeline's direction. She'd remained quiet during Melton's and his back and forth; however, her eyes swelled with a fresh round of tears, and they spilled over her lids and down her cheeks.

Without thinking, Jasper took the final steps to her, brought his palms to the sides of her face, and brushed the tears away. If they'd been alone, he would have placed a kiss to each cheek where the moisture had left matching trails.

If they wed, he silently vowed she would never have need to shed another tear—unless it was in joy.

That was one promise he could make her.

CHAPTER 26

ADELINE STARED INTO Jasper's green eyes, the warmth of his hands framing her face and his body near hers was all it took to banish her tears.

Jasper was here. He hadn't fled the ball.

As she'd pleaded with Alistair, she'd feared that Jasper was gone forever. That thought hadn't deterred her from confessing her love for the man or any consequences that followed, though. She'd been prepared to suffer them in silence, resolved to her fate, and all because she'd found the strength to speak her true feelings. If Alistair cast her from their family home, so be it. If her friends turned their backs on her, she would live. If society shunned her, Adeline would only be better for it.

She loved the man standing before her—his hurt, his sorrow, his loyalty, his compassion, his heart. She loved and cherished every inch of him.

And the way he looked at her now—his reserved smile, the yearning in his eyes, his labored breaths—told Adeline he felt the same soul-deep love for her.

Adeline's entire body flushed with heat as time seemed to slow to a standstill, only to find her heart jumping back into action as it raced in her chest.

This love—*their* love—was more than a fluttering

of the stomach or a weakening of the knees.

"Jasper, I—" she started.

"Adeline, my study…now!" Her brother's tone left no room for argument. "Come. This is a family matter and not one suitable for the entire ballroom."

Adeline glanced over Jasper's shoulder and, sure enough, guests had started to mill about outside the main ballroom door, attempting to hear their conversation.

She had no choice but to follow Alistair.

To her surprise, Jasper grasped her arm, while Josie and Georgie fell into ranks on either side of them.

Adeline wanted to scream that she didn't need their protection, she was confident in everything she'd said and every emotion coursing through her. For once in her life, she needn't hide behind petty retorts and snide comments.

The only thing that could harm her now was if Jasper turned her away.

Much like a funeral precession, they all trampled down the hall, past the onlookers in the foyer and into Alistair's study, the door solidly thudding closed behind them. Adeline was certain that Donovan would station himself directly outside to keep the guests from attempting to move close and hear what transpired behind the closed doors.

The quiet of the room only intensified Adeline's knowledge of Jasper's presence.

His hulking frame stood by her side, while Josie and Georgie took seats on the lounge closest to the hearth. Alistair immediately sought the safety—and separation—the seat behind his desk provided, and Theo sank into her usual chair. The same seat she'd resided in the first time Adeline had brought Jasper to meet the pair.

Had that been only the previous day?

It felt as if years, no, *decades* had passed since her

return to London. A city she'd always felt she belonged in, but which was now as foreign to her as Egypt or Greece would be.

When everyone remained silent, Adeline realized they waited for her to speak.

This was her life, after all. Her future…and Jasper's.

She needed to say her piece to Jasper. She owed him that much.

In slow motion, she turned to him, knowing her words would impact the rest of her life. She would either wed this great man before her or be relegated to a life of solitude, devoid of everything she'd once held dear.

But love, or the prospect of love, was worth it, even if she was alone in the end.

So, at that moment, surrounded and protected by the people who cared about her the most, Adeline was determined to be honest and open with Jasper. If he did not return her immense affection and love, at least her friends and family—hopefully—would be there to catch her.

"Jasper," –she paused, taking a deep breath to clear her mind and allow her heart to speak—"since meeting you, I've chosen to be a better me. At the plant, when the wall collapsed, you blamed yourself, but I knew you did everything in your power to help your people."

His eyes watered, and she noted his shoulders caving in on themselves, yet he kept his gaze solidly on hers.

"I have found what I wanted—the future I envisioned for myself—is no longer important to me. What you need and want, specifically a thriving Faversham and Home Works with happy, healthy people, is paramount to securing my own happiness. I know your future does not lie in London but in Kent, and I've discovered my destiny resides there, too." She stilled, searching his eyes, determining if he understood what she was implying. "With you, Jasper. By your side, day and night. Good and bad. During favorable years, and through the harsh winter nights."

"You would give up all this—?" He raised his hands, encompassing the well-appointed room surrounding them, and Adeline sensed he also meant her friends and family. "You would leave all this for a life in the country, surrounded by villagers who do not accept me and a home steadily decaying around us?"

"My home will be where you are, wherever you determine that to be," she replied, bringing her hands to his neck and allowing her fingers to graze the area of his scars. His eyes drifted closed at her intimate touch. "My heart never left Faversham Abbey, despite our return to London. Your people love, they understand all you've done to make amends for those who were lost, and your house, the Abbey, is perfect."

"Certainly, you will return to London from time to time, or allow us to visit Faversham," Josie inquired quietly, reminding Adeline that she and Jasper were not alone in the room.

"We shall return often, and you are all welcome at the Abbey," Jasper said, lifting his head to stare at the group surrounding them. "I will have rooms prepared for every Melton sibling if that is what it takes."

"I do not believe there is anything further to discuss," Alistair said, coming back around his desk to stand before Jasper.

Nothing further to discuss? Was her brother discrediting all that had transpired? Would he call Donovan and a footman to throw Jasper out?

Her heart stopped in her chest as Alistair stared at Jasper.

Surprisingly, Jasper's gaze hardened as he met her brother's scrutiny.

Adeline glanced at Theo, then Josie, and finally,

Georgie. None of the trio jumped to her defense or cried at the injustice about to take place. In fact, they all smiled...well, Georgie's expression was best named a smirk.

Could it be that her friends, the women she'd grown to love in her youth, found Alistair's disapproval of Jasper warranted?

No, it could not be...

She would not allow it to be so.

Swiftly, Alistair wrapped Jasper in a tight embrace. "It would be a pleasure to call you brother, Lord Ailesbury. Jasper."

Adeline's eyes welled with tears once more, blurring her vision but in a good way.

"It will be an honor to join our families, Lord Melton. Although, I must admit, I am the lone survivor of the Ailesbury clan."

Alistair stepped back and clasped Jasper's shoulder with a chuckle. "It is lucky for you that I have siblings aplenty, and I am not averse to sharing them. Which do you prefer, male or female? The males are quite sneaky, though the females come with an entirely different set of difficulties."

"I appreciate the offer, and I plan to call in the promise as soon as the Abbey is renovated to Adeline's tastes." Jasper grew silent as everyone around them laughed at Alistair's jest.

She felt helpless as she noted his eyes darken, and the space between them grow, though neither of them moved.

"I fear there is one last thing that needs to be discussed. No, there is no discussion on this topic, it only needs to be stated."

Her heart stopped once more, her entire body turning cold as Jasper pivoted to face her, taking her small, shaking hands in his large, warm grasp.

"Miss Adeline Price." He coughed to clear his

throat as his gravelly voice pushed on. "You were the outer light to my inner demons, but now I recognize your inner light is enough to overshadow my outer beast. You think yourself not worthy, but it is I who will spend eternity pondering the hows and whys surrounding our joining. You have an inner light that will brighten the darkest storms—and those storms will come. They will be fierce. They will be all-consuming. However, with you by my side, your light will guide us through the worst tempests life throws at us. Adeline, your affection is more than simply returned, it is multiplied a thousand times over and cast far and wide in every direction. I love you, and you would honor me if you will have me as your husband."

"Truly?" Adeline's breathless whisper echoed around the room.

He nodded, pulling her against him and settling his lips against hers.

It was more perfect than any answer he could have given.

This kiss was far different than the one they'd shared on the terrace. This kiss was more than a spoken promise, more than a verbalized assurance of their future together, and far more than anything Adeline deserved.

This kiss was a silent vow from Jasper to her—an unspoken pledge that he would care for, cherish, and love her forever.

Her brother was correct, no further words needed to be uttered.

As she wrapped her arms around his neck, their lips never releasing one another, Adeline vaguely heard her friends—and then Theo and Alistair—depart the room, pulling the door closed behind them.

No doubt Donovan remained to continue making certain no one disturbed her and Jasper.

Yet, in that moment, Adeline didn't care if the

entire ballroom invaded the room to see the love and happiness surrounding her—all made possible because the Beast of Faversham had given her his heart.

EPILOGUE

Faversham, England
August, 1827

ADELINE TOOK IN the majestic view of Faversham Abbey, seeing it for the first time through the eyes of her family and friends as their carriage rambled down the long drive. After much research and discussion with Jasper, she now knew the place had once been a monastery with its tall, picturesque towers protruding at precisely measured intervals. Every doorway was graced by columns and concentric aches. The narrow windows made the structure appear much like a medieval castle, readied to defend its occupants against invasion.

Likely similar to the way Jasper must be feeling with the entire Melton family descending on him, with Georgie and Felton, and Josie, in tow. Arabella and Ainsley would be the last to arrive on the morrow when Alistair and Theo set off at first light to collect them from Miss Emmeline's School.

And the following day…she and Jasper would be forever wed in a late-morning ceremony, followed by a feast for all. Every villager, servant, and plant worker had been delivered an invitation, personally written by Adeline, their soon-to-be countess.

While it had been a shock to Jasper, Adeline hadn't been surprised in the slightest that each and every invitation was met with a confirmation.

Every door would be thrown wide to welcome all and sundry to the Abbey.

Adeline's heart warmed at the thought of all of Faversham coming together to bless Jasper's marriage.

"Are you ready to see your betrothed once more?" Josie asked.

Adeline stared at the woman across from her, taking in her subtle beauty: the way her dark hair highlighted her pale skin, and her reserved interest that most took for a weakness, though Adeline knew firsthand was one of her greatest strengths. Soon, very soon, she prayed Josie would find the happiness that she, Georgie, and Theo had been blessed with. Until that day came, she could always depend on her friends.

"It has been nearly a month since Jasper came to London last, and I've missed him tremendously." Adeline paused, smiling to herself. "Distance does make the heart grow fonder, I can assure you."

"Well, let us hope all of us housed in one building does not diminish your fondness," Georgie laughed as she stared out her window toward the Abbey. "Lord Ailesbury is out front and prepared to greet his betrothed."

"He is what?" Adeline leaned out her window, joyous to see that Jasper, indeed, stood in the drive, awaiting her arrival.

"And I must say, this carriage ride has me missing my dear Felton ever so much."

"He resides in the carriage behind us, Georgie," Josie retorted.

"And we stopped for a meal with them in Rochester only a few hours ago," Theo added.

"Be that as it may, Felton finds it hard to be separated from his love," Georgie said with another laugh.

Adeline settled back in the plush squabs of the carriage interior as they traveled ever closer to her heart. Yes, distance was difficult, far harder than Adeline had ever imagined it would be. But she was at the Abbey now, and never would she depart again without Jasper by her side.

At times, it was still nearly impossible to believe that she'd found love and everyone who mattered to her had come together to see her wed. Even now, two carriages followed the one she and her friends traveled in. Her brothers, Abel and Alistair, along with Felton were tucked safely in Felton's traveling coach. Thanks to Jasper's generosity, Alfred, Adelaide, Amelia, Adrian, and her maid, Poppy were ensconced in the newly repaired Melton coach.

And they were all making the journey for her.

It had felt close to a century since Adeline had been at the Abbey, but at the same time, only moments.

Her carriage rolled to a stop, and Maxwell pulled the door wide and set down the steps for the women to disembark, but Adeline needed no assistance down, only the strong, muscled arms that appeared in the open doorway.

One moment, Adeline was sitting in the carriage; and the next, she was wrapped securely in Jasper's arms, where she belonged, as he swung her around and around, placing kisses on her forehead and cheeks before setting her on the ground.

"I am home—"

"You are home—"

They both spoke at the same time, laughing all the while.

Looking up into Jasper's shining eyes, Adeline knew that it wasn't so much the Abbey that brought her the overwhelming sense of *home*, but the man standing before her.

And Jasper's words from several months before were never truer than in the moment of their reunion, knowing they would never need be parted again. There would be dark, tumultuous storms and shining, happy days to come in their future, but they would face them together, as one.

"I love you—"

"I love you—"

This time, their laughter was joined by that of her dearest friends as Adeline threw herself into Jasper's arms once more. For the last time, because she never planned to leave them after this moment.

AUTHOR'S NOTES

Thank you for reading *Adeline*
(Lady Archer's Creed, Book 3).

If you enjoyed *Adeline*
be sure to write a brief review at any retailer.

I'd love to hear from you!

You can contact me at:
Christina@christinamcknight.com

Or write me at:
P.O. Box 1017
Patterson, CA 95363

www.ChristinaMcKnight.com
Check out my website for giveaways, book reviews, and
information on my upcoming projects,
or connect with me through social media at:

Twitter: @CMcKnightWriter
Facebook: www.facebook.com/christinamcknightwriter
Goodreads: www.goodreads.com/ChristinaMcKnight

Sign up for my newsletter here:
http://eepurl.com/VP1rP

**For more information about
the Lady Archer's Creed series, turn the page!**

LADY ARCHER'S CREED SERIES

A love of archery brings four young girls together to form The Lady Archer's Creed. Through their mutual love of the sport, they solidify an unbreakable bond, and each woman has a unique quality that adds to their dynamic friendship:

Theodora, Lady Archer's Creed Series (Book One)
Lady Theodora with her sharp mind and love of academics becomes the perfect archery coach. Despite being the last to join their group, and the obvious outcast, she will risk her future for her friends.

Georgina, Lady Archer's Creed Series (Book Two)
Lady Georgina makes the perfect financier. The forgotten daughter of a wealthy duke, she seeks to belong to something—or someone—by any means necessary.

Adeline, Lady Archer's Creed Series (Book Three)
Miss Adeline is a natural leader. Having grown up in a large and often spirited family, she now allows no one to place her in the shadows.

Josephine, Lady Archer's Creed Series (Book Four)
Lady Josephine, having a sweet and impressionable nature, strives to please everyone—and keep their bond intact, even after they return to London for the Season.

Adeline, Georgie, Theo, and Josie live each day by the Lady Archer's Creed, which they developed during their school days at Miss Emmeline's School of Education and Decorum for Ladies of Outstanding Quality. "Friendship, loyalty, and honor above all" is their mantra. Now, as they face the challenges that come with adulthood, the creed is more important than ever.

Theodora
Book 1
Now available

Friendship...
Lady Theodora Montgomery departed Miss Emmeline's
School of Education and Decorum for Ladies of
Outstanding Quality to attend her first London
Season—her three dearest friends by her side. With her
sharp wit and skill on the archery field, Theo is far more
interested in winning a large purse prize than securing a
husband. But when she is unmasked on the tourney
grounds, her face exposed to all, she fears her identity
and days spent gallivanting around London will cause
not only her undoing, but the downfall of her friends as
well.

Loyalty...
Mr. Alistair Price, heir to the elderly Viscount Melton,
arrived in London with his eight younger siblings in
tow. He is charged with keeping his family name above
reproach until the Season starts and his sister, Miss
Adeline Price, is presented to society—though that
proves far more difficult than Alistair ever expected
when he discovers his rebellious sister climbing down
the side of their townhouse and scurrying off to
Whitechapel for an archery tournament. His focus
remains on saving his family from the certain ruin and
disgrace Adeline's actions invited—until Alistair catches
sight of another female archer, her arrow connecting
with far more than the center of her target.

And honor above all...
With Theodora's future—and that of her friends—in
jeopardy, will she agree to a marriage devoid of
affection, or risk everything for the man who won her
hear

Canterbury, England
April 1819

LADY THEODORA MONTGOMERY sat stock-still before the massive table that served as the headmistress's desk and waited for the woman to put down her pencil and greet her. She'd been shown into the inner sanctuary of the headmistress over ten minutes prior by a young woman—Miss Dires—who'd explained that she'd taught history at Miss Emmeline's School of Education and Decorum for Ladies of Outstanding Quality for going on ten years. The woman didn't appear more than a handful of summers older than Theo.

When she'd taken her seat, and Miss Emmeline hadn't so much as looked up to greet her, Theodora decided it was in her best interests to wait patiently until the woman acknowledged her presence. To keep occupied, Theo took in the room around her—it was far more masculine than the office should be since the school proudly boasted an all-female staff with only one male groundskeeper who took no active role in the daily life of Miss Emmeline's pupils.

The problem Theo currently wrestled with was keeping her eyes open and her posture straight. She'd spent nearly two days in a carriage to reach her new boarding school from her brother's London townhouse. She was dirty, exhausted, and wanted nothing more than to be shown to her bed, where she'd gladly obtain a full night's rest. If she had the opportunity to wipe the dirt and grime from her skin, that would be wholly welcome, as well.

"Your application states that you prefer to be addressed as 'Theo' or 'Lady Theo,' is that correct, Lady Theodora?" Miss Emmeline looked up for the first time, setting her pencil aside, and Theo was delighted to see a bit of mischief in the lady's eyes, even though her tone was severe. When Theo nodded, the older woman continued. "Here at Miss Emmeline's School of Education and Decorum for Ladies of Outstanding Quality, we pride ourselves on allowing our young ladies to discover who they are, and providing the time and resources to help them become the women they want to be."

It was in the printed brochure Cart had presented to her nearly three months prior. The name for the school was outlandishly pompous. She and her sibling had had quite the chuckle at it, but they'd quickly settled on Miss Emmeline's school because the mission statement matched Cart's hope for his only sister's future endeavors and education. Their mother, Dowager Countess Cartwright—Anastasia Montgomery—had reluctantly agreed to part with her younger child at the insistence Theo write her immediately if the school did not suit her needs.

What her mother actually meant was that she felt it improper for her daughter to be well-studied, her belief that educated women had no place in polite society was the foundation she used to justify her own lack of learning.

She was thankful that her brother, Simon—the current Lord Cartwright, and Theo's legal guardian—better known to his friends as Cart, was not of the same dated mindset.

"Lodging," the headmistress said. "My school houses four girls to each room. This allows a sense of camaraderie between students and enables each girl to seek help in a subject they are not well-versed in. Do you take issue with sharing a room?"

Theo didn't know how to answer the question. She'd spent most of her life with only her mother and servants for company until her brother had returned from Eton. However, he was much older than she. She'd always possessed her own room, her own space— even though she'd secretly longed for a sibling closer to her in years; a sister to share her dream with, to accompany her on adventures about her family gardens, or just to act as a companion to laugh with during the long, dark nights.

"A shared room is preferred, Headmistress," Theo answered.

"Do call me Emmeline or Miss Emmeline, dear." The woman's tone was still stark, but Theo suspected she tried to put her new pupil at ease. "Now, to decide on whom you shall room with it is necessary to discover your talents."

A sense of dread washed over Theo as the woman smiled for the first time, her lips pulling back to reveal tea-stained, crooked teeth.

"And how shall we find my talents?" Theo gulped after asking, a clammy moisture overtaking her clasped palms.

"Oh, I have devised a fine method for ascertaining the strengths and weaknesses of each of my girls," the headmistress said in a whisper as if they were plotting a grand scheme together. "I dare say, I would have made an excellent teacher in the applied sciences."

Theo felt encouraged that Miss Emmeline knew what the applied sciences were. It hinted that her days would not be filled with learning social etiquette and needlepoint and utterly neglecting all other subjects: arithmetic, geography, science, and history.

Theo's exhaustion receded as the woman continued. "Each girl is asked to present in three different departments of learning: academics, art and music, and a physical sport. Based on their choices for each—and how well they do at their chosen talent—I select which room each pupil is assigned to." Theo had to admit, it was an interesting method to determine sleeping arrangements. "It is also necessary for each student to learn something from her roommates during their stay at my school."

It was sound methodology, and Theo could not deduce a flaw in the headmistress's plan, though she was extremely tired and her mind had been sluggish since her arrival at the school.

"Are you ready?" Miss Emmeline asked as she stood.

"I am to present now?" Theo squeaked. She thought to have a day—or at least a night—to ponder her known talents before being presented to the other students. Even a decent meal would be appreciated. "Is it not nearly time for the evening repast?"

"You will need a bed in a few short hours, correct?"

"Yes, but..." Theo quickly stood, running her

hands down the front of her wrinkled traveling gown. It would be the height of embarrassment to be seen by the entire school in such a filthy dress. They would think her nothing more than a country miss. Not that Theo had ever labored over long regarding the opinions of others, but her time at Miss Emmeline's was important to her.

"You are correct, all of the girls will be gathering shortly for our evening meal." The headmistress touched her coal-stained hands to her upswept, mousey brown hair before running them down the front of her dark grey dress—leaving behind a trail of black streaks. "Wait here while I ready the girls in the music room for your first talent. I will send Miss Dires to collect you when all are seated." The fear must have shown clearly on Theo's face for the headmistress hurriedly added, "Do not fret. Every girl is called upon on her first day here."

Nothing about her reassurance made Theo feel…reassured, but at least it completely dispelled her fatigue as anxiousness set in. Her heart beat at an erratic rate.

The moments passed, feeling like hours as Theo awaited Miss Dires. She progressed from exhaustion to anxiousness to outright dread. She scanned the headmistress's desk for a blank piece of paper. How long would a note, begging her mother to rescue her, take to arrive in London? Certainly longer than Theo had before she was called to the music room.

Dashing her final hope of avoiding the coming discomfiture, Miss Dires returned and motioned for Theo to follow, her smile kind. Upon closer inspection, Theo noted the woman's slight limp as she walked— maybe she was older than she appeared.

The music room was off the main hallway—the only hallway Theo had seen since her arrival—and boasted high ceilings with several chandeliers for light. Large, long cracks in the walls could be seen from the doorway. The door she entered was at the front of the room, and belatedly Theo realized that while she'd been taking in the architecture and disrepair of the space, the other girls had been given the opportunity to inspect her.

Theo thought it best to keep focused on the task at hand and not the many eyes assessing her.

On the raised dais was a piano, a harpsichord, harp-lute, dital harp, a flute, table of bells, and a guitar—all positioned far enough apart to enable the entire audience an unobscured view of Theo.

Theo hadn't applied herself to any musical instruments, outside of the occasional lesson at the piano. She'd studied many varieties of harps at the museum where Cart was an assistant curator, but she'd never touched one. Wind instruments were not in her repertoire, as her brother had never allowed her to even so much as hold the Greek panpipe—purportedly crafted by Hermes himself—that resided in his collection. As soon as Theo had a moment to herself, she planned to write a strongly worded letter to Cart, denouncing his actions at not allowing her a turn with the panpipe. Certainly, it was a severe detriment to her learning career. Since wind instruments were out, she took in the bells and guitar—both beyond her realm of knowledge, as well. There was no hope—not a single instrument did Theo feel competent in performing with.

"Students of Miss Emmeline's School of Education and Decorum for Ladies of Outstanding Quality, please welcome Lady Theodora Montgomery—though she prefers Lady Theo or just plain Theo." The words rolled off the headmistress's tongue as if she said them daily, and no tongue twisting was necessary to say the name five times. "Lady Theo will first apply her hand to a musical talent—either the piano, harp, guitar, bells, or vocals."

Theo's singing voice was dreadful—far too high to be anything but a screech.

"Next, she will present her academic talent," the headmistress continued. "Lastly, her physical sport, which we will all adjourn to the outdoors for. When everything is complete, we will return to the dining hall for our nightly meal."

A loud cheer with reserved clapping filled the room; however, Theo wasn't sure if they applauded her or their promised meal. The only thing she was willing to celebrate at the moment was a warm bed—it did not even need to be comfortable, only cozy…and quiet.

Though she doubted with all these students Miss Emmeline's was ever a quiet place.

Theo surveyed the many instruments before her. There was truly no choice to be made—it was the piano, or flee the room in disgrace.

With a weak smile to the gathered crowd, Theo sat behind the piano and set her fingers to the ivory keys as she'd been taught. The keys were smooth under her touch from years of use. Her nails were chipped from toting her luggage from the carriage, and her hands were pale and clammy. It was odd these were her thoughts as she sat before roughly forty girls her age while they awaited her piano solo.

Theo was most comfortable reading about adventure and tense situations from the comfort of a soft chair, snuggled under a warm blanket with a fire roaring nearby—or in the garden under a large shade tree with the sun beaming. To actually be an active participate in such a situation was entirely different than reading about it in a book. The sensation of her blood humming through her veins in anticipation, her labored breathing caused by her nerves, and the sheen of perspiration was something no writer could accurately describe with the written word. She tucked the theory into the back of her mind, planning to write her brother about it as soon as she'd had some rest. It made for an interesting observation, certainly, something they could discuss during her Christmastide holiday.

The thought of home and her family brought Theo a bit of comfort. She was here, in Canterbury, and they were in London. Her brother was sacrificing much to afford the tuition at Miss Emmeline's School, and Theo knew she could not disappoint him or her mother by begging off and crying to return home.

With a calming breath, her fingers began to move across the keys in a melody she'd only played a half-dozen times, though the memory of the music sheet with the notes was clear in her mind. All she need do is concentrate on visualizing the sheet music and block out the rustling of clothes, the various whispered comments between girls, the echo of a book being dropped onto the hard floor, and the congested cough coming from the back of the room.

The tones floated about, bouncing off the bare, cracked walls and high ceiling, slower than the composer had intended, but in line with Theo's musical ability. She'd rather play at her leisure with accuracy than speed through the intended music and risk missing a key change. It was a soft melody, increasing in tempo as the song progressed. She pictured the final line of notes as her fingers found their rhythm and sped up, pushing gently on the smooth keys.

Only a few strokes left, and it would be over; she'd be able to move on to something a bit more familiar to her.

A door slammed somewhere in the room, and Theo's hands slipped across the keys in fright at the sudden noise, the song ending on a sharp note and not the quieter culmination intended for the piece.

Laughter broke out, and several instructors could be heard shushing the girls.

Theo kept her eyes on the piano, and her head lowered, afraid to face the merriment currently taking over the room at her less than stellar performance.

"Wonderful rendition, Lady Theodora," the headmistress said, returning to the stage. "And now, it is time for presentation of your academic talent."

Theo hadn't thought past her time in the musical round. Certainly, she had many talents revolving around academia, and selecting one should not be overly difficult, but any knowledge she possessed had fled with the other student's laughter in the face of her last failure.

Standing from the piano, Theo made a show of returning the bench to rest slightly under the keys. It gave her a moment to think.

"Many of our girls focus on history for their talent—Lady Josephine is skilled at reciting every British monarch going back five hundred years. Miss Alexandria has memorized every great battle in recorded history. Others find great interest in the sciences or literature, expounding on formulas or reciting lengthy poems." The room became still and silent as Miss Emmeline spoke, even Theo found herself holding her breath. "I will give you a moment to prepare. Remember to speak loudly and clearly so all can hear."

There was no mention of her missed final key— nor words of encouragement for success in the next round, and Theo sensed the headmistress was not one to coddle her students.

Theo raised her gaze to the crowd, noting the various clusters of girls. Many whispered behind their hands or paid her no mind at all. She spotted one pupil drawing in a notebook. Theo brought her hand to her long braids. Most of the girls favored a more mature look with their hair loose around their shoulders or upswept in elegant fashion rivaling many of the women Theo had seen shopping on Bond Street or promenading in Hyde Park.

The headmistress cleared her throat.

"May I return to your office and retrieve something?" Theo asked.

"Of course, Lady Theodora."

Theo cringed at the use of her full name; even her mother had acquiesced to calling her Theo when in private. More giggling could be heard circling the room as she fled the same way she'd entered. She found her way back to the office and snatched her book of maps, holding it close to her chest as she returned to the main room.

Theo knew the talent she planned to show was highly obscure, but with such a short time to decide and no time to prepare—and the haze that had settled over her due to her exhaustion—this was the best she could do.

The headmistress clapped, calling everyone back to their seats, and Theo returned to her place at the head of the room.

"What have you chosen as your academic talent, Lady Theo?" Miss Dires asked from her seat between two groups of girls close to the front of the room.

The woman's encouraging smile pushed Theo to speak. "I have a great passion for maps." Again, the other students moved about restlessly, losing interest in Theo's presentation, but she continued. "One of my talents is spotting mistakes within books—namely, volumes filled with maps."

A few *Oohs* and *Ahhs* could be heard around the room, though they were said with a certain mocking intent.

For the second time since her arrival, Theo deliberated writing to her mother and begging Lady Cartwright to come collect her; stating she'd been horribly wrong in her decision to seek an education outside the tutors available for hire in London.

Even now, Theo could be ensconced in her family's library, debating the merits of the scientific principles with Cart and his wife, Judith. Or playing with Olivia and Samuel, her niece and nephew. Instead, she was far from home, surrounded by a roomful of strangers who had no interest in her or her talents.

Theo opened her book to a marked page and held it high for all to see. "For example, here, on page seventeen, the illustrator mislabeled two cities in France, and utterly forgot to add the Sicilian Island off the coast of Italy."

Miss Dires, bless her kind soul, motioned for Theo to approach her so she could have a closer look at the text. Next, Theo moved down the front row of girls, showing them the erroneous errors.

"In this book alone, I've found forty-two such inaccuracies."

"And what exactly do you do with this knowledge?" Miss Emmeline asked from the stage.

Theo smiled at a blonde girl in the front row as she inspected the page before she returned to the headmistress's side. "Nothing at this time, but my future plan is to work with mapmakers to increase their accuracy in not only their labeling, but also land proportion versus oceans. I would also like to consult on a new method of tracking elevations on printed maps."

"Very commendable of you." Miss Emmeline nodded, her first sign of approval since Theo's arrival. "We all wish you the best in your endeavors."

Theo allowed a small grin to settle on her lips, then closed her book and tucked it under her arm. Her presentation had gone far quicker than she'd expected— and had not been as embarrassing as her piano performance—though she suspected her talent in academics was no more fascinating to the gathered girls than her song choice.

"Next, we shall all venture outside." Everyone stood as if they'd been waiting for the chance to escape the indoors. "Lady Theo, please inform me if you'll need to change into a riding habit."

Dread infused Theo. She'd never in all her days ridden a horse, nor did she own a riding habit. Her mother had spoken of the need to acquire the skill, but the large beasts frightened Theo. Even when she journeyed to the stables, she steered clear of their stalls, preferring to sit in the straw and cuddle the ever present kittens. "No, Miss Emmeline."

"Very well." The headmistress waved her arm in the direction of the double doors—pushed wide to reveal a grassy area with several stations, each housing equipment for various outdoor activities, most Theo didn't recognize. She followed the rest of the girls outside, the sun beginning to set on the far horizon. The headmistress stopped beside her and spoke once more. "We also have a lake not far away if your talent lies in rowing."

"Rowing?" Theo gulped. No amount of studying books had prepared her for all of this. "No, certainly not."

The other teachers, along with the students, hurried to an area set up for spectators and watched with anticipation as Theo walked between the five stations. Two held gear she could not identify or align with a known sporting activity. Another was set up with shuttlecock, a game she'd seen played at several garden parties she'd accompanied her mother to, but Theo had never bothered to learn the rules. Moving along, the next station held a row of guns—she didn't even bother with pausing to inspect them. The final area had a row of pegs with archery bows hanging in perfect order from a half-wall obviously erected for the sporting area. Several yards away, a line of hay-stuffed targets with red and white circles painted on them stood, each dotted with holes from use.

Theo and Cart had studied force and trajectory just months before as *Silliman's Journal* had dedicated an entire volume to the principles behind the study. They'd spent days dropping different items from the roof of their London home—much to their mother's dismay— and skimming rocks across the ponds in many of London's parks. They'd calculated the force and angle necessary to accurately throw a pebble across the water as opposed to the power needed to do the same with a much larger rock.

Surely their discoveries could be applied to the use of an archery bow and arrow.

Theo eyed the various sizes of bows hanging from the pegs as she calculated in her head the distance to the target and the length of the weapons. Though her thoughts were muddled, she should fair far better at archery than at the piano—and if not, an unpredictable flying arrow would captivate her audience more than her skills at error detection.

"You can use my bow," a dark-haired girl stepped up beside her and retrieved one from its peg.

"Thank you," Theo said with a tentative smile.

"I am Josie—err, Lady Josephine." The girl returned Theo's smile. She was one of the students who preferred to allow her hair freedom from its pins; her long, brown tresses—almost the exact color of Theo's—hanging loosely about her shoulders.

"I am Theo." She immediately regretted her words as the headmistress had introduced her before the entire gathering in the music room. "Thank you, again."

"Good luck," Josie called before hurrying back to the spectator area—or maybe it was the safest spot to watch when arrows were being shot.

Theo would need more than luck to hit the target, or even come close. Testing the weight of the bow in her hands, she moved to the square directly in front of the closest target and took an arrow from the quiver propped up by a wooden stand. The projectile's tip was not pointed but flat, reducing the chances of injury if a perilous shot resulted in a stray arrow. The shaft was made of a flexible wood with feathers connected to the end. She combed through her collective memories in search of a diagram she'd seen that featured an archer in a readied stance for a shot.

It was necessary to place her feet at shoulder width and slightly angled from the target. Placing the split end of the arrow against the string, Theo positioned her hands as best she could, sure to keep a firm hold on the arrow while adjusting her fingers.

The position felt highly uncomfortable and unstable, but was a mirror image of the illustration she'd seen.

Not a sound could be heard as she pulled the string back approximately fourteen inches to create the force and trajectory necessary to at least have the arrow fly as far as the target, though if it penetrated the circle was anyone's guess.

Theo's arm shook from the strength needed to continue holding the bow high, string pulled back with the arrow aligned and ready to shoot.

One final calculation and adjustment and Theo was satisfied with her angle.

She released the string and sent her arrow flying—straight toward the target.

Theo closed her eyes, she couldn't bear to see if the arrow landed in the lawn before the target or soared past it entirely. It had been the best attempt she could muster, having never handled the equipment before.

A loud gasp erupted from the spectator's area, and Theo kept her eyes tightly shut. Had she hit an unintended target? Had the shot gone wild after leaving her bow? Would she be made to leave the field in disgrace?

Maybe she'd have no need to write her mother, but be loaded into a carriage this very night and sent back to London.

Applause sounded behind her with several calls of "fine shot" and "she's a natural archer."

Theo opened her eyes to see her arrow protruding from the exact center of the target. She heard someone say, "It seems you have competition, Adeline."

Turning back to face the crowd, two blonde-haired girls stood next to Josie. One girl's arms were crossed, and a frown marred her delicate face. The other smirked. The displeased girl must be Adeline—and she did *not* look happy.

The group broke, and Josie, along with another girl, rushed to Theo's side, offering their congratulations on a perfect shot. Even Adeline, the most accomplished archer at Miss Emmeline's hadn't executed a shot as flawless, Josie crooned, only to gain another nasty look from the girl.

The urge to confide that she had never picked up a bow before today was strong, but Adeline had finally decided to put her sullen manners aside and approach the group.

"This is Georgie and Adeline," Josie introduced the two girls. "It is clear that Headmistress will assign you to our room."

"It is lovely to meet you all," Theo said when Josie took back her bow and returned it to its peg on the half-wall.

"Come," Georgie said, her voice far deeper than Theo would have imagined for a girl so tiny. "It is mealtime, and if we do not arrive soon, all the candied desserts will be gone."

"She does not look the sort to enjoy sweets," Adeline snapped. "But, nonetheless, Georgina is correct. If we don't hurry, there will be no table left except the one next to Headmistress's...and I do not wish to have her lecture me again on my mealtime manners."

"If you hadn't exchanged her sugar for salt, she would not keep such a close eye on you," Georgie laughed.

"That was some time ago," Adeline muttered. "For a woman of her advanced age, she certainly has a stellar memory."

Josie returned and slipped her arm through Theo's, pulling her after Georgie and Adeline as they advanced back through the double doors of the school. "That was a fine shot, Lady Theo. I know we will be bosom friends, all four of us."

Theo allowed her new friend to lead her to the

dining hall—all the way chanting silently to herself that she would enjoy her time at Miss Emmeline's School of Education and Decorum for Ladies of Outstanding Quality—it was either that or return to London and a future under her mother's thumb and careful watch. Even at the young age of twelve, Theo knew she was not destined to live the tedious life of a sheltered London debutante.

Available in print, audiobook, and e-book now!

ABOUT THE AUTHOR

USA TODAY Bestselling Author Christina McKnight writes emotional and intricate Regency Romance with strong women and maverick heroes.

Her books combine romance and mystery, exploring themes of redemption and forgiveness. When she's not writing, Christina enjoys trying new coffeehouses, visiting wine bars, traveling the world, and watching television.

Email: Christina@ChristinaMcKnight.com
Follow her on Twitter: @CMcKnightWriter
Keep up to date on her releases:
www.christinamcknight.com
Like Christina's FB Author page:
ChristinaMcKnightWriter